Whitey and the Rustlers

An Errand to Town

Ko-mo-ki of the Cliffs

Magic Lariat

Angus and the Ducks

Old Log House

The Picnic Basket

Log Cabin Theatre

The Hunter Who Was Saved by Eagles

Dressing Up

O Sailor, Come Ashore

Pirate Wind

Ferry Boats

Rabbits

Out of the Antarctic

The Duel

A Pop Corn Song

Freight Boats

The Willow Whistle

Tom's Little Dog

Through Golden Windows

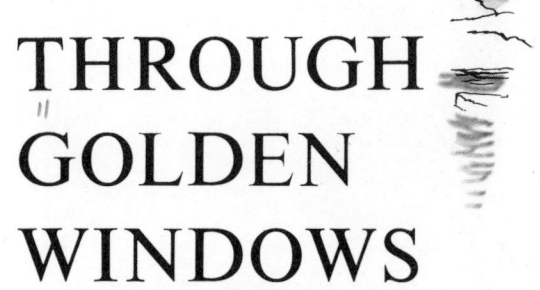

THROUGH GOLDEN WINDOWS

Edited by

Nora Beust, M.A.

Phyllis Fenner, B.A., B.L.S.

Bernice E. Leary, PH.D.

Mary Katharine Reely, B.A.

Dora V. Smith, PH.D.

Editor-in-Chief
Jeanne Hale, B.A.

Assistant Editor
Muriel Johnstone, B.A.

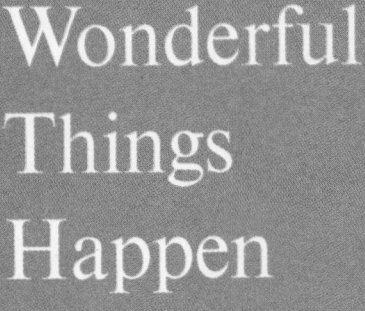

Wonderful Things Happen

E. M. HALE AND COMPANY

PUBLISHERS · EAU CLAIRE, WISCONSIN

Acknowledgments
and Copyright Notice

ABINGDON PRESS, — "Off to Adventure," from *Cowboy Boots* by Shannon Garst, Copyright, 1946, by Doris Shannon Garst. Reprinted by permission of Abingdon Press.

ADAMS, VEOTTA McKINLEY, — *Captain Joe and the Eskimo* by Veotta McKinley Adams, Copyright, 1943, by Veotta McKinley Adams. Reprinted by permission of Veotta McKinley Adams.

AMERICAN BOOK COMPANY, — *The Camel Who Took a Walk* by Jack Tworkov, Copyright, 1951, by Jack Tworkov. Reprinted by permission of American Book Company.

APPLETON-CENTURY-CROFTS, INC., — "A Pop Corn Song" by Nancy Byrd Turner, from St. Nicholas Magazine. Reprinted by permission of Appleton-Century-Crofts, Inc.

BARUCH, DOROTHY W., — "Rabbits," from *I Like Animals* by Dorothy W. Baruch, Copyright, 1933, by Dorothy W. Baruch. Reprinted by permission of Dorothy W. Baruch.

CHASE, EDITH H. NEWLIN, — "The New Baby Calf," from *Very Young Verses* by Edith H. Newlin, Copyright, 1945, by Edith H. Newlin. Reprinted by permission of Edith H. Newlin Chase.

CHUTE, MARCHETTE, — "Dressing Up," from *Rhymes About Ourselves* by Marchette Chute, Copyright, 1932, by The Macmillan Company. Reprinted by permission of Marchette Chute.

DOUBLEDAY & COMPANY, INC., — "The Picnic Basket," with two illustrations, from *The Poppy Seed Cakes* by Margery Clark, illustrated by Maud and Miska Petersham, Copyright, 1924, by Doubleday & Company, Inc.; "Rikki-tikki-tavi," from *The Jungle Book* by Rudyard Kipling, reprinted by permission of Mrs. George Bambridge and Doubleday & Company, Inc.; "Angus and the Ducks," with four illustrations, from *Angus and the Ducks,* written and illustrated by Marjorie Flack, Copyright, 1930, by Doubleday & Company, Inc.; "Little Lost Lamb," with three illustrations, from *Little Lost Lamb* by Golden MacDonald, illustrated by Leonard Weisgard, Copyright, 1945, by Doubleday & Company, Inc. Four illustrations from *Hester and Timothy, Pioneers* by Ruth L. Holberg, illustrated by Richard A. Holberg, Copyright, 1937 by Ruth and Richard Holberg. Reprinted by permission of Doubleday & Company, Inc.

DRESBACH, GLENN WARD, — "Magic Lariat" by Glenn Ward Dresbach, from Child Life Magazine. Reprinted by permission of Glenn Ward Dresbach.

E. P. DUTTON & CO., INC., — Seven illustrations by Roger Duvoisin, from *The Camel Who Took a Walk* by Jack Tworkov, Copyright, 1951, by Jack Tworkov; "Daniel Boone," from *I Sing the Pioneer* by Arthur Guiterman, Copyright, 1926, by E. P. Dutton & Co., Inc., renewal, 1954, by Mrs. Vida Linda Guiterman. Reprinted by permission of E. P. Dutton & Co., Inc.

EYRE, KATHERINE WIGMORE, — "Lottie's Valentine," from *Lottie's Valentine* by Katherine Wigmore Eyre, Copyright, 1941, by Katherine Wigmore Eyre. Reprinted by permission of Katherine Wigmore Eyre.

GROSSET & DUNLAP, INC., — One illustration by Meg Wohlberg, from *The Illustrated Treasury of Children's Literature,* edited by Margaret E. Martignoni, vi

McINTOSH & OTIS, INC., — "Pirate Wind," from *Top o' the Morning* by Mary Jane Carr, Copyright, 1941, by Mary Jane Carr. Reprinted by permission of McIntosh & Otis, Inc.

HAROLD OBER ASSOCIATES, — "Hester and Timothy, Pioneers," from *Hester and Timothy, Pioneers* by Ruth L. Holberg, Copyright, 1937, by Ruth and Richard Holberg. Reprinted by permission of Harold Ober Associates.

OXFORD UNIVERSITY PRESS, — "A Bell for Ursli," with three illustrations, from *A Bell for Ursli* by Selina Chönz, illustrated by Alois Carigiet, Copyright, 1950, by Oxford University Press; "Picken Goes in Search of Gold," with four illustrations, from *Picken's Great Adventure* by Norman Davis, illustrated by Winslade, Copyright, 1949, by Oxford University Press; "Little Tim and the Brave Sea Captain," with six illustrations, from *Little Tim and the Brave Sea Captain,* written and illustrated by Edward Ardizzone, Copyright, 1936, by Oxford University Press. One illustration by Tasha Tudor, from *A Child's Garden of Verses* by Robert Louis Stevenson, Copyright, 1947, by Oxford University Press; two illustrations by Nils Hogner, from *Barnyard Family* by Dorothy Childs Hogner, Copyright, 1948, by Oxford University Press. Reprinted by permission of Oxford University Press.

PEDERSON, ARTHUR S., — "Roads," from *The Pointed People* by Rachel Field, Copyright, 1924, 1930, by The Macmillan Company. Reprinted by permission of Arthur S. Pederson.

RANDOM HOUSE, INC., — "My Father's Dragon," with six illustrations, from *My Father's Dragon* by Ruth Stiles Gannett, illustrated by Ruth Chrisman Gannett, Copyright, 1948, by Random House, Inc. Reprinted by permission of Random House, Inc.

RINEHART & COMPANY, INC., — "Magic," with four illustrations, from *Kintu,* written and illustrated by Elizabeth Enright, Copyright, 1935, by Elizabeth Enright Gillham. Reprinted by permission of Rinehart & Company, Inc.

RUCKEL, MARION PLEW, — "Silver Ships" by Mildred Plew Meigs, from *Child Life Magazine.* Reprinted by permission of Marion Plew Ruckel.

WILLIAM R. SCOTT, INC., — Five illustrations by Barney Tobey, from *Captain Joe and the Eskimo* by Veotta McKinley Adams, Copyright, 1943, by Veotta McKinley Adams. Reprinted by permission of William R. Scott, Inc.

CHARLES SCRIBNER'S SONS, — "Elephant-Town" by Marion Edey, from *Open the Door* by Marion Edey and Dorothy Grider, Copyright, 1949, by Marion Edey and Dorothy Grider. Reprinted by permission of Charles Scribner's Sons.

SHIDELER, MURIEL SCHULZ, — "Hayride" by Muriel Schulz, from *Stories Magazine.* Reprinted by permission of Muriel Schulz Shideler.

THE SOCIETY OF AUTHORS, Literary Representative of the Estate of the late Walter de la Mare, — Canadian permission to reprint "Tom's Little Dog," from *Bells and Grass* by Walter de la Mare.

THOMPSON, DOROTHY BROWN, — "Maps" by Dorothy Brown Thompson, from *Target Magazine.* Reprinted by permission of Dorothy Brown Thompson.

THE VIKING PRESS, INC., — "A Field Mouse Visits School," with eight illustrations, from *The Taming of Giants* by Patricia Gordon, illustrated by Garry MacKenzie, Copyright, 1950, by Patricia Gordon and Garry MacKenzie; "Tom's Little Dog," with one illustration, from *Bells and Grass* by Walter de la Mare, illustrated by Dorothy P. Lathrop, Copyright, 1941, by Walter de la Mare. Reprinted by permission of The Viking Press, Inc.

A. P. WATT & SON, THE MACMILLAN COMPANY OF CANADA, LTD., AND MRS. GEORGE BAMBRIDGE, — Canadian permission to reprint "Rikki-tikki-tavi," from *The Jungle Book* by Rudyard Kipling.

A. P. WATT & SON, ALFRED NOYES, AND WM. BLACKWOOD & SONS, LTD., — Canadian permission to reprint "A Song of Sherwood," from *Collected Poems of Alfred Noyes.*

WIESE, KURT, — Four illustrations by Kurt Wiese, from *The Jungle Book* by Rudyard Kipling, published by Doubleday & Company, Inc. Reprinted by permission of Kurt Wiese.

THE JOHN C. WINSTON COMPANY, — "One Day with Tuktu," with five illustrations, from *One Day with Tuktu,* written and illustrated by Armstrong Sperry, Copyright, 1935, by The John C. Winston Company. Reprinted by permission of The John C. Winston Company.

Great pains have been taken to obtain permission from the owners of copyright material. Any errors are unintentional and will gladly be corrected in future printings if notice is sent to E. M. Hale and Company.

Through Golden Windows

IN A reading world filled with children's books the addition of one more anthology or set of anthologies leads naturally to the question "Why?" We, who compiled *Through Golden Windows,* first asked ourselves that question almost ten years ago. We are still asking it. Always we arrive at the same answer. "The books are needed."

The power of books has long been recognized. And never more than today when material things are assuming increasing importance, and even the simple act of opening a door is fast getting out of human hands; when global and continental distances are shrinking from weeks and days to hours and minutes, and nearness at home means crowded living, crowded schools and playgrounds, crowded streets and highways; when family ties are weakening and children suffer from want of close, two-parent affection and guidance.

What can books give to a child who is growing up in today's curiously complicated world? Many things, we believe, although the evidence is not altogether conclusive. Facts and information, of course, about almost everything; understanding of himself and others; confidence and security; fun and laughter; friends and friendships; escape from reality at times, and again the courage to face reality—all these are possible results if the right book is used with the right child in the right way.

But suppose the right book is not available? Crowded living means limited space for books, at home and at school. Or suppose parents and teachers do not know the right book? Many, by their own admission, do not know children's books well. Must the child's values in reading be left to chance, while he struggles with his everyday problems, or grows up without feeling the full rapture of a good book?

Through Golden Windows grew out of a fear, on the one hand, that children's needs are not being met well enough through books; and out of a faith, on the other hand, that carefully compiled anthologies, easily accessible, would help teachers and parents do a better job of guiding children's reading.

Such books, we believe, should give children experience—here, there and everywhere. It should give them variety—sober fact and gay fantasy, practical prose and picture-filled poetry, lives of the great and the everyday intimacy of home folks, history of the past and history in the making, high adventure and the small thrills of daily living. It should show them some of the wonders of the earth and sky and the great achievements of great men. It should assure them the safe moorings of home and country, of family and friends. It should give them confidence in themselves and in others, and in a world that, for all its problems, is a wonderful world to grow up in.

To be most useful, each book should be not too large and not too small, not too easy and not too difficult, but "just right" for the child in pre-school and primary grades or in middle and upper grades. Based on children's interests and reading preferences, it should have not too much nor too little of any one type of material, but a balanced content that would invite all readers.

Through Golden Windows, therefore, was made with an eye on the child and his needs and interests at different stages of development. Bound in ten volumes, each book is attractive to look at, comfortable to hold, interesting to read, and easy to talk about.

Taken together, these books represent five large areas of interest: fun and humor, adventure, children everywhere, the story of America, and science. For each area there are two volumes, one for children of pre-school and primary age, and the other for intermediate grade readers. Hence, as a child grows in reading power, he may move from *Mostly Magic* to *Fun and Fantasy,* and satisfy his need for fun in both. Again, for adventure he may enjoy *Wonderful Things Happen* until he is ready for *Adventures Here and There.* His broadening interest in people finds satisfaction first in *Good Times Together* and later in *Children Everywhere.* Similarly, *Stories of Early America* eventually gives way to *American Backgrounds* and *Wide, Wonderful World* to *Man and His World.*

Within each volume, the selections are loosely tied together into related units, in order that a child may pursue an interest in Pets or Pioneers or Plants, for example, without searching for "more." The obvious overlapping of units and of volumes is not without purpose or benefit. Were it possible to organize reading materials into airtight, dark little compartments, *Through Golden Windows* would defeat its purpose to help "the whole child" to live and grow. On the other hand, a free, less exacting organization allows him to find the same inter-relationships and similarities among his reading experiences as exist in his daily life.

Through Golden Windows, then, aims first to satisfy the child, meet his everyday needs and help him find early the absorbing joy of reading. It aims, also, to acquaint teachers with much of the best in children's books. Used as basic reading in a college course in children's literature, *Through Golden Windows* will help to overcome the limitations imposed by a barren reading childhood and give teachers and parents that first security they need to guide children's reading. Beyond such a course lies a whole world of books that teachers will continue to explore, year after year.

It aims, finally, to help parents by providing a basic home library for their children. Here are stories as old as "Once upon a time" and as new as the children themselves. Here are stories and poems to read aloud and to read to one's self in a quiet corner, "to-go-to-sleep-by" and "to-get-up-with," to laugh at and to learn from, to sing and to act, and sometimes to read for no other reason than the fun of doing something together as a family.

It is to children, teachers, and parents everywhere that these books are affectionately dedicated, in the hope that through the pages they may see, as "through golden windows," the rewarding vista of life itself.

BERNICE E. LEARY

X

Wonderful Things
Happen

BETWEEN the covers of this book wonderful things happen. You will find with Harry Behn, a poet of today who enjoys adventure:

> *It's not very far to the edge of town*
> *Where the trees look up and hills look down,*
> *We go there almost every day*
> *To climb and swing and paddle and play.*
>
> *It's not very far to the edge of town,*
> *Just up one little hill and down,*
> *And through one gate, and over two stiles—*
> *But coming home it's miles and miles.*

You will travel to distant Switzerland where you meet Ursli, in pictures and story, who goes alone to find a great bell in a cottage high in the mountains to carry at the Spring Festival. ,

Or you can read how Terry kept his head and saved his sister with the swimming steers, one summer day during the haying season in New England, in a story written by Elizabeth Coatsworth. She is another modern author who lets you have the fun and excitement of being someone else.

Armstrong Sperry takes you to the frozen North Land to spend *"One Day with Tuktu,"* and Rudyard Kipling to India to be thrilled by a fight between a cobra and a mongoose.

The Willow Whistle, by Cornelia Meigs, a Newbery prize-winning author, takes you back to pioneers and Indians and buffalo of the great plain. Eric uses his head and after a dangerous adventure finds his friend and playmate.

Some other adventures you will enjoy are those of *Little Tim and the Brave Sea Captain, Captain Joe and the Eskimo* and *Robin Hood and Allen-a-Dale;* and look for *Whitey and the Rustlers* in which a young cowboy traps the thieves who have been stealing cattle in Lone Tree County.

NORA BEUST

Contents

xiv

Wonderful
Things
Happen

ALL through the summer in the Engadine Mountains of Switzerland the cattle feed in the mountain meadows, carrying bells round their necks. The calves have little bells and the cows have big ones. When they come into their sheds for the winter the bells are taken off. In March when winter is over, the Spring Festival comes, and the bells are rung in the village to celebrate the end of the cold, dark days. All the boys march in procession through the street, each one carrying the biggest bell he can, and they ring their bells to drive the winter away and welcome back the sunny spring. And the village people smile, and fill the bells with cakes and nuts and apples. But only the big boys can carry the big bells; the little boys come at the tail of the procession carrying little calf-bells. This is the story of Ursli, and of the adventure he has when the Spring Festival comes round and he decides that he is old enough to have a big bell for the first time.

A Bell for Ursli

BY SELINA CHÖNZ

Illustrated by Alois Carigiet

High in the mountains, far and blue,
There lives a small boy just like you.
See the wee village, poor but neat?
His is the last house in the street.

2

The house is old and snug and small,
With pictures painted on the wall.
Look closer. Do you see those two
Standing there dressed in red and blue?
A man and wife, with one small son.
His name is Ursli. See him run!

Yes, here our mountain boy you see,
Quite like a man, you must agree.
Upon his head a pointed hat.
(The mountain, too, is shaped like that.)
It's made of soft wool from the sheep
That now in Ursli's stable sleep.
For Ursli's mother spins, weaves, stitches,
And knits his shirt and hat and breeches.
His father has the boots to make,
And toils all day for Ursli's sake.

But Ursli helps his father, too,
As much as any man would do,
Waters the cows and brings them hay,
Cleans out the stalls by break of day.
When mother calls him to the house
Ursli comes scurrying like a mouse
To bring the yoke with water pails,
Or help to cook. He never fails
To milk his friend the goat, and see
The milk froth white as white can be.

3

When he's done everything he's able
In house and yard, in shed and stable,
He rushes out with cheerful noise
To play with all the village boys.
Today he tells them he must borrow
A bell that he can ring tomorrow
In the Procession of the Bells.
See how with pride young Ursli swells!
He thinks he'll get one large and loud,
And help the big boys lead the crowd.
At Uncle Gian's farmhouse, all
The boys for bells have come to call.

Good uncle quickly brings them out,
And everyone begins to shout:
"The big one's mine!" "I want the best!"
Ursli is pushed behind the rest.
And when at last the front he gains
The tiniest tinkle-bell remains.
Now he sheds sad and bitter tears,
He'll be a laughing stock, he fears,
The boys already laugh and boo:
"Tinkle-bell Ursli, look at you!
When the Procession marches past,
Tinkle-bell Ursli, you'll be last!"

The boys go off. They all despise him.
Poor Ursli's bell quite horrifies him.
He'd hoped to march in front this year,
Not with the small boys in the rear.
In front the fine young men march proudly,
Swinging their bells and singing loudly.
They lead the way, with clang and yell,
Past every stable, every well.
In every house they march about
Ringing to drive the winter out,
And then with all their might they sing
To welcome back the happy spring.
Then everybody's glad and thrilled,
With nuts and cakes the bells are filled.
But outside, in the crisp, cold snow,
The little boys must wait, you know;
With little calf-bells back they come,
And bring their empty pockets home.
Ursli no calf intends to be.
Tinkle-bell Ursli? No, not he!
He's ready to do anything,
But all ideas have taken wing.
He thinks and thinks, then gives a hop—
Their summer hut on the mountain top!
There on a nail there used to hang
As big a bell as ever rang!

As quick as thought he's on his way,
No fears would make our Ursli stay.

He braves dark forests, footpaths steep,
The narrow bridge, the chasm deep.

But soon his burst of joy is done.
As he climbs higher, near the sun,
The snow is melting. In he sinks
Above his knees. Poor Ursli thinks
He's going to cry. But who will hear?
No crying will bring mother near.
Perhaps the great bell, after all,
No longer hangs upon the wall—
"If it's not there," he thinks in sorrow,
"Whatever should I do tomorrow?"

But forward go his steps again,
And now, the hut grows near and plain,
Glowing beneath the sunset light
As Ursli sees it come in sight.
The hard climb's done, he's here at last.
But now he finds the door shut fast,
Nor will his shaking move the thing.
The key is kept on Father's ring!
Still, there's the window. Ursli's thin.
He can just manage to squeeze in.

The nail's still there. And on it, yes,
The great bell hangs, as we can guess.
"Tinkle-bell Ursli!" See him grin.
"Oh, how they'll stare when I walk in!"

He's scrambled on the bed,
    and stretched
High up the wall—
    and down it's fetched.
Heavy and round,
    how fine to see!
A belt of flowered
    embroidery
To hang it from,
    with clasp of gold.
And how it rings!
    So clear and bold!

By now he's hungry
    as can be,
He looks all round,
    what can he see?
Ah! Hanging up
    above the dishes,
A loaf, the very thing
    he wishes.

Then he sits down. It's grand to eat.
But he's tired out, from head to feet,
And since he's free from every care
Slumber comes softly, light as air.
The bed of straw's a cosy nest.
In deep, sound sleep can Ursli rest.

Now in the valley, far below,
To house and stable homeward go
Tired men and beasts, to dream at ease.
But underneath the mountain trees
Small fox and chamois, deer and hare,
Out in the snow must coldly fare.

There in the moonlight they can trace
Child footprints on the earth's white face.
And up the snow track softly creeping
They reach the hut and Ursli sleeping.
Fox pricks his ears, and says to deer:
"What can that boy be doing here?"

Mother is waiting. Darkness reigns.
Small stars shine through the window panes.
She looks all round in street and square
To see if Ursli's hiding there,
While Father by the stove sits down
And asks quite crossly for his son.
But though at every house they call,
No one has seen the boy at all.
Now everybody seeks all over,
But still no Ursli they discover.
In vain the lantern lights the gloom,
Its beams do not bring Ursli home.

His anxious parents, worn and sad,
Go home again without their lad.
They sit and watch the pine-logs burn,
And still their boy does not return.
Poor mother weeps. The clock ticks on.
Alas, where has young Ursli gone?
Father can't settle anyhow;
He starts to carve his son a cow.
The village sleeps, but wide awake
They sit and wait for day to break.

Now swiftly flies the deep, dark night.
The mountain sees the sun's first light.
And as the sunny morning breaks
Young Ursli rubs his eyes and wakes.
He must at once be on his way—
Whatever will his parents say?
He takes the bell. Quick, see him go
Running across the firm, hard snow,
For overnight it froze again
On mountain, pasture, wood and plain.
The animals flee far and wide
So swift is Ursli's homeward stride.

A twinkling, and, as you can see,
Before his own carved door stands he.
Three times he bangs the knocker down,
And footsteps to the door have flown.

Quick at the latch his mother tugs,
Her darling son she sees and hugs,
While Ursli climbs her skirt and clings,
Arms and bell round her neck he flings.

The Bell Procession's
     on its way,
And who is that
     in front? Hurray!
It's little Ursli,
     ding, dong, dell,
Who has by far
     the biggest bell.
And everyone
     is full of joy
To see once more
     that little boy.

To dinner now
    the three sit down,
Vanished is every
    care and frown,
And Ursli, his
    adventure past,
Tells all that happened,
    first to last,
And how he has
    escaped from shame.
Father's too overjoyed
    to blame.
Mother brings chestnuts,
    piping hot,
With cream poured over—
    such a lot!
And while they watch him
    happily,
Young Ursli eats
    enough for three.

ABOUT ten minutes to four, in that darkest time before the dawn, the first whistle of the *Wild West* train sounded down the valley. The whistle of a show train is like no other train whistle in the world. Just what the difference is, it would be hard to say, but there is something more shrill, more wild and strange about the whistle of the show train. There is a hint of the calliope in it, something of the hooting of the clowns and the trumpeting of the elephants and the yahooing of the cowboys. Ardeth turned over in bed and flung her arms out over the covers, but it was hard to wake up.

The whistle sounded again and again, coming nearer up the valley among the western hills. Ardeth stirred restlessly, and then a shower of pebbles struck her window and brought her wide awake. She sat up in bed in a fright.

"Hey, Wienerwursts!" a guarded voice called from below the window.

Breakfast with Buffalo Bill

BY
CAROL RYRIE BRINK

Illustrated by
Wladislaw Finne

Ardeth sprang out of bed and ran to the window. Below her on the lawn were the shadowy forms of Martin and Henry Dawlish.

"Hurry up!" hissed Martin. "It's nearly in. We'll miss the fun."

"Don't go without me," begged Ardeth.

She flung on her clothes any which way, shivering with excitement. Every summer as long as she could remember she had gone to see the circus or the *Wild West Show* and the parade, dressed in her best starched pink chambray, all washed and curled, and holding onto Jenny's large, perspiring hand. But she had never thought of seeing a show *un-load* before she knew the minister's boys.

Ardeth didn't stop to wash her face or do her teeth or hair, but, when she had put on her clothes, she climbed out of the window and went down the morning-glory trellis. This was one of the chief conveniences of Ardeth's room—the morning-glory trellis came right up to her window like a little ladder.

In a moment she was hurrying down the dark street between Martin and Henry. The street seemed all unfamiliar at this time of day, and Ardeth felt a cold lump of excitement at the pit of her stomach. The whistle of the *Wild West* train shrieked twice from the other side of town.

"It's in!" said Martin. "It's in!"

Yes, there stood the engine, panting and puffing, beside the railway station. The swaying light of lanterns fell on dark, hurrying figures, on crates and carts, on the name of the town printed in large white letters on the side of the station—*Warsaw Junction*. Men were shouting and pushing hand trucks or adjusting gangplanks to car doors. There was a smell of horses and animals and unknown things; there were unexpected noises: a dull roaring, shrill neighing, and the sharp hiss of escaping steam.

Ardeth felt suddenly that she must hold onto someone or something or she would be swept away and lost forever. But Martin and Henry were not much for holding hands, and the best she could do was the tail of Martin's jacket.

15

"Jimminy Christmas!" said Martin. "It's all right. We got here in time to see it all."

"In time to see it all!" echoed Henry fervently. "Where's Buffalo Bill, Martin? I want to see Buffalo Bill."

"Well, hold your horses, Henry. He'll be along," said Martin.

"We shook hands with Buffalo Bill last year in Montana in our last pastorate," said Henry.

Ardeth had heard this several times before, but it always thrilled her. "Do you think he'll remember you?" she asked.

"I'll bet he will," said Henry confidently.

Now the big work horses were being unloaded and they were set to work, pulling the heavy, creaking wagons full of poles and canvas to the meadow beyond the station where circuses and shows always pitched their tents.

Martin and Henry ran here and there trying to see

everything. It was bad enough trying to see everything that went on in the three rings of the show during the performance, but this was even worse. Things were being unloaded from all the cars, wagons were being assembled, cowboys and Indians were driving oxen and leading rearing, neighing ponies. Over in the meadow Indian tepees were being pitched in the midst of the field, the enormous show tent was going up to the accompaniment of shouts and cries, grunts and swearing.

"Goodness, such awful language!" said Ardeth.

"They're all good Bible words," said Martin, "only they put them in the wrong places."

"Where's Buffalo Bill?" asked Henry of everyone he met. The answer was usually: "Out of the way, kid. Gangway! You're going to get hit." But finally someone said: "Colonel Cody will be in on the next train, kid. Look out for your head now, here comes another pole."

In all of her starched-chambray and neatly curled life, Ardeth had never been so excited and pleased. The sky grew rosy pink over the meadow with its jumbled masses of canvas. The second train came in with a hooting whistle and was shunted onto a side track for unloading. Cowboys and Indians streamed out of it and began unloading more spotted ponies and bronchos and cages of buffalo and bear. Yes, and there was the famous Deadwood coach, but no Buffalo Bill.

The rosy pink grew yellow and then white, and presently it was broad day; but if she was hungry Ardeth didn't know it, and she had entirely forgotten for the moment that such people as Jenny and her father existed.

"Where's Buffalo Bill?" Henry was still plaintively asking.

"Oh, dry up. We'll find him," said Martin kindly.

17

"Let's go and see them have their breakfasts now."

"Breakfasts?" asked Ardeth. "Do they eat?"

"Sure. You can't move shows and do trick riding, and shooting, and broncho busting without food, you know," said Martin patiently.

The first tent to be completely set up was the dining tent. Stoves were already installed and smoking pungently on the morning air, and a smell of frying ham, bacon, buckwheat cakes, and coffee went forth invitingly across the meadow. The Dawlish boys' noses were excellent guides in the matter of food. In a few moments the three stood in a row by the open flap of the tent watching the cooks in their greasy white caps and aprons making the show's breakfast. To Ardeth's surprise and delight, she saw that they fried their ham and flipped their pancakes right on the tops of the stoves without the bother of frying pan or "skillet." The *Wild West* people came in as they found time and sat down to long wooden tables without tablecloths. It was like a picnic every day. There was a girl there in divided skirt and cowboy hat who might have been Annie Oakley, the sure-fire shot, herself; and there were Indians, too, eating ham and eggs as peacefully as white men. Just opposite the children sat a cowboy with a purple shirt and a ten-gallon hat, and he was reading a

18

paper-covered book with a red and blue and green picture on the front of horsemen holding up a train. The book was called *The Life and Death of Jesse James, the Outlaw*.

Martin sniffed the air appreciatively.

"I sure would like some breakfast," he said regretfully, "but I can't spare the time to go home and get it."

"Oh, no," said Ardeth. "Let's not go home!"

Just then Henry, whose eyes had been roving in search of just one person, let out a whoop of delight and began to run.

"Buffalo Bill!" he yelled.

Across the trampled meadow from the main tent cantered a white horse carrying a very erect rider with a white imperial and long white hair which fluttered in the wind beneath his wide-brimmed hat. Colonel William Cody, the Indian fighter, the buffalo killer, the scout, and now in his latter years the showman and idol of small boys the country over, was riding in to get his breakfast.

"It's him!" said Martin. "It sure is!"

Henry ran on like one possessed, his arms spread wide, shouting: "Buffalo Bill, you 'member me? I shook hands with you last year in Mon—"

The horse was coming faster than Henry realized, and, frightened by a blowing paper, it swerved suddenly toward him and knocked him over. He rolled over and over on the dusty grass, and lay still. Ardeth screamed and Martin began to run. The old scout reined in his horse and cantered back. A little crowd began to gather. For a moment Henry lay quiet, his face white against the trampled dog fennel and clover. Buffalo Bill sprang off his horse and bent over him.

"Henry!" called Martin. "Henry! Henry!"

Then Henry sat up, shaking his head as if to rid himself of the fog that clouded his vision.

"—last year in Montana in our last pastorate," he finished.

"Well, now, young feller, you kind of ran amuck, didn't you?" said Colonel Cody.

"He was so glad to see you," explained Martin, coming up with Ardeth. "Are you all right, Henry?"

"Sure," said Henry, still a little dazed and gazing around at the gathering crowd to see what was bringing them.

"His head's pretty tough," said Martin to Buffalo Bill. "Once he got it caught in a cider press, but nothing happened. Mama says he's got the Dawlish skull—you can't crack it."

"He'd make a good Indian fighter," said the old scout.

"You bet I would!" said Henry, beginning to take an interest in the conversation.

"Can you stand up?" asked the Colonel. "You don't hurt anywhere, eh? No bones broken?" Henry stood up and dusted himself off.

"I reckon I'm all here," he said.

"What's all this about your last pastorate?"

"Me and Martin shook your hand then. Do you remember?"

"Well, I'm an old man, now, Bud. My memory's not what it used to be."

"I told you he wouldn't remember," said Martin sadly.

"Oh, gee!" said Henry. "I had on my new straw hat, too."

"Well, no wonder!" said the Colonel reproachfully.

20

"How was I to know you without your hat? I've shook thousands of boys' hands since last summer. Had your breakfasts?"

"No, sir, and we've been up since four."

"Come along, then, we'll see what we can do for that."

Ardeth had an awful pang of fear. This was a man's affair and they were going off without her! She gave a little involuntary gasp of disappointment, and Martin turned around and remembered her.

"This is Ardeth," he said politely. "We call her Wienerwursts because of her hair. She's never had the pleasure of shaking your hand."

"Petticoats, eh?" said the Colonel.

"She's all right," said Henry loyally. "She has a pony and she knows how to ride it."

"That's different then. Shake hands, my girl."

Ardeth felt her hand being gripped hard by the very hand which had slain so many buffaloes. In a daze of delight, she followed along to the dining tent.

Buffalo Bill ranged them along one of the wooden benches and banged on the bare wooden table for attention.

"Ham and eggs!" he shouted. "For Buffalo Bill and guests!"

The cooks ran about with a new burst of speed. "Coming up, Colonel! Pronto!" they cried.

Outside the tent a group of less fortunate townsboys formed a silent semicircle to watch Ardeth and the new minister's boys eating breakfast with Buffalo Bill.

In a few moments they were all talking like old friends, and Martin and Henry were telling Colonel Cody how they meant to be Indian fighters, too, as soon as they could get a horse, but how horses never seemed to go along with the Presbyterian manse in any pastorate they'd ever occupied; and Ardeth was describing her pony so that even she herself was surprised to discover how much more he sounded like a fleet Indian hunter than a fat Shetland pony who never trotted if he could in any way avoid it. As for the food, ham and eggs and buckwheat cakes had never tasted better. The plates might be thick and greasy, and the service not of the best or cleanest, but this was the meal of a lifetime!

Adventure   BY HARRY BEHN

IT'S not very far to the edge of town,
Where trees look up and hills look down,
We go there almost every day
To climb and swing and paddle and play.

It's not very far to the edge of town,
Just up one little hill and down,
And through one gate, and over two stiles—
But coming home it's miles and miles.

22

My Airplane
BY
JAMES S.
TIPPETT

I MADE an airplane.
I held it in my hand;
I carried it above my head.
It sailed across the land.

It sailed across the ocean.
It sailed around the world.
It looped the loop, it volplaned,
It twisted, and it curled.

I cannot say my airplane
Was quiet as a mouse
For it went zizz-zizz-zizzing
All through our house.

Hayride

BY MURIEL SCHULZ

Illustrated by Roger Duvoisin

THE very nicest way
To spend a summer day
Is jumping, jouncing,
Bumping, bouncing,
On a load of hay!

23

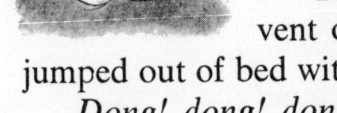

"*D*ONG! *dong! dong! Boom! boom! boom!* Get up! get up! get up!" sang the sunrise bells.

The day started early at the Convent of the Good Shepherd, and Lottie jumped out of bed with a rush.

Dong! dong! dong! Hurry! hurry! hurry! Don't be late! don't be late! don't be late!

Dong! dong! dong! Wipe your mouth! Brush up the crumbs! Fold your napkin! Say your prayers! Do your lessons! Sew, and knit, and scrub and sweep! *Dong! dong! dong!*

That was the way of it at the Convent of the Good Shepherd. But when the long busy day was nearly done, the bells in the tower sang a better song.

Dong! dong! dong! Time for play! Time to stretch your legs! Time to skip rope!

Lottie ran into the garden the minute that Sister Ursula dismissed the girls. It was cold. The pecan trees were bare and brown against the winter sky, and there were no flowers in the courtyard, but Lottie did not mind. She was glad to be free, glad to be out in the fresh air.

Lottie's Valentine

BY KATHERINE WIGMORE EYRE

Illustrated by Susanne Suba

There was a high wall all around the garden, with an iron gate to keep the world away, and she stood by it, pressing her face against the grille so that she could see down the road that led to New Orleans.

"Some day I'll get away from here," she murmured

24

wistfully, as she stared at the winding highway with its moss-hung oaks and giant magnolias.

"Some day I'll get past this gate, and then I'll see for myself what it's like outside. I won't stay here forever. I won't! I won't! Nobody can make me stay—!"

Suddenly her daydreaming was interrupted.

"Hello, Lottie! I was right! I knew I'd find you down here by the gate! I told the girls so, when they asked where you were. Why don't you come and play with us? Aren't you cold? Let's play tag! Let's skip rope, or something! What's the use just standing here staring down the road? Come on, Lottie! Come on and play!"

It was Thérèse speaking. Thérèse who slept in the same dormitory as Lottie—Thérèse who was ten years old. Lottie did not like her. How could one be friends with a tale bearer? How could one like a trouble maker —a horrid girl with a sharp tongue for teasing? And Thérèse really seemed to enjoy being a nuisance. She moved closer to Lottie and repeated her questions.

"Tell me Lottie, answer me, why do you stand here? Why do you come here every single day and stare down that road?"

"I don't know," Lottie answered slowly, "I don't know why, Thérèse. I don't know why I like to look out the gate so much—I just do, that's all! Some day I'll get away from here, and then the gate won't matter any more. There won't be high walls to keep me in any longer."

"Oh Lottie, how funny you are! You make me laugh! Get away from here? That's a good joke! Wait till I tell the girls! Why, you'll never get away, Lottie! Never, never! Every one knows that! You haven't any Mother

25

or Father. You haven't even a Tante Louise, as I have. You haven't a big sister, like Amélie, and a place to go on holidays. You haven't an uncle like Sophie's who takes her out on Sundays and fête days. You have no one. You were left here when you were a baby. And here you'll have to stay, Lottie, all the rest of your life. Silly Lottie. Silly billy Lottie! Always staring down the road and making up fine stories to fool yourself—!"

Lottie's heart burned with shame and rage. To be laughed at! To be unwanted! To have no one!

26

She turned on Thérèse furiously and shoved her with all her might.

Thérèse, unprepared for Lottie's angry push, and caught off her balance, fell into the middle of a rose bed. Down flat, ker-plunk, she went, with the thorns catching on her dress and scratching through her thick stockings.

"I'll get even with you, Lottie, for this! See if I don't! See if I don't! You'll be sorry, Miss Nobody!"

But Lottie did not wait to hear more. She turned and

27

ran. Anything to get away from that hateful Thérèse.

It was just by the fountain that she stumbled over a little bundle of feathers that lay on the flagstones. A pigeon—a poor hurt pigeon with drooping wings and bloody breast. Its beak was open, it was gasping for life.

Lottie picked it up and held it gently. Its ruffled feathers were gray blue, its feet red, and around one leg was a metal band stamped with numerals and letters so tiny that Lottie could not read what they said.

"Oh you poor thing! You poor little thing! Where did you come from? How did you happen to fall here, I wonder? Did a hawk pounce on you? Is that why you're so bloody and ruffled? Oh I hope you aren't going to die. You look dreadfully sick! And you're all cold and shivery. Oh dear, I wish I knew how to help you! Do you want a drink? Here, put your beak in the fountain, little bird, maybe that will make you feel better."

Lottie dipped the pigeon's beak in the water and it drank deeply. Then Lottie remembered a half roll in her pocket that was left over from lunch.

"Here—try these crumbs, pigeon. Try to swallow them when I put them in your beak. You'll feel lots better if you eat something. That's it! That's a good little bird!"

The pigeon swallowed a few crumbs. It tried to flutter its wings, but it was too weak to fly out of Lottie's hands.

"Don't try to get away," she said. "I won't hurt you,

you mustn't be afraid of me. I'll take care of you."

Lottie took the pigeon to her room. She hunted around in her wardrobe until she found a little cardboard box covered with pretty silver paper. It was a candy box that Sophie had given her, and Lottie treasured it highly. She took her scissors and cut some holes in the lid for air. She lined it with an old wool stocking, and laid the pigeon down gently.

"Now, isn't that nice? Isn't that cozy and warm, little bird? Don't you feel much better? Just lie still and rest, and I'll go get a bowl for water, and one for crumbs, too. Then you'll be all fixed. I'll be right back."

Lottie rushed down the back stairs to find Sister Ursula.

Sister Ursula was very kind. She rustled into the room and stooping by the little silver box, she picked up the pigeon and examined it closely. "Get me your

sponge, child. I'll wash the blood off the poor thing's breast. What a dreadful wound! A hawk must surely have pounced on it—somehow the pigeon got free from its claws, I imagine, and tried to fly to its home—but was so exhausted that it fell here in our garden. Look, Lottie. Look at this band around its leg. I don't know what the numerals and the letters stand for, but I do know that the band means the bird is a homing pigeon with a loft and an owner, somewhere. The kindest thing for you to do is to care for it now, and then let it fly away again just as soon as it grows strong. There, now I've washed it well—the wound is clean. Give me your towel, please Lottie, I will dry my hands. Take the pigeon and put it in the box again. You have made a nice little nest, and that is the best place for it. Keep it warm and well fed, and perhaps you will save its life, after all."

Sister Ursula stood up and smiled. "You are a good child, my dear, a real little Samaritan. Now I must go, and you must get ready for supper. The bells will ring any minute."

Dong! dong! dong! Supper time! Lentil time! Bread and molasses time! Hurry! hurry! hurry!

Lottie had to run. She kissed the pigeon and tucked it in under the warm wool stocking. She put the lid on the box, and then stood up with a little sigh.

"Never, never, never, have I been so happy," she thought gladly. "Never before in all my life!"

One day, weeks later, the pigeon looked up from her box and cocked her head to one side. She made soft bubbling cooing sounds in her smooth throat, and then she hopped out on to the floor and began to peck at the little bowl of peas that Lottie had left in the corner.

30

It was hard to believe that this was the same wounded bedraggled bird that she had found so many weeks before. Although the pigeon still limped a little bit, and had not attempted to fly again, her feathers were smooth and glossy, and her wings almost healed.

The halls were very quiet. All the girls were outside, and the whole convent grew still. The pigeon, more confident with every hop, began to explore the room. Under Lottie's bed, behind the washstand, pecking at the curtains, she wandered contentedly, her blue throat bursting with trills and cooing.

Suddenly, without so much as a creak of the hinges to betray it, the door of the bedroom opened a tiny crack. A little wider, a little wider—now there was room for

a child to slip through. It was Thérèse, sneaking in on tiptoe. Her cloak was wrapped around her, and underneath it, bulging through the heavy cloth, was a mysterious bump. A bump that wriggled and squirmed and made queer muffled noises.

Thérèse closed the door quietly behind her, and stooping down, took off her cloak. Out of it, struggling and scratching to be free, leapt the horrid gray skinny cat that prowled around the convent garbage pails, and haunted the storerooms looking for mice.

No sooner was the cat on the floor than Thérèse turned and ran. She shut the door behind her, trying hard to be quiet, but as her hand turned on the knob, she suddenly caught a glimpse of a nun coming up the front stairs. With a half suppressed squeak of fear and guilt, she let the door bang behind her, and fled down the hall. Sister Ursula, looking up from her breviary, caught only a glimpse of flying black legs and a gray cloak, as Thérèse tore down the back stairs at top speed. Sister Ursula frowned. Odd, one of the girls upstairs during play time. Very odd, indeed! Out of which door had she come?

The cat, free from Thérèse's strangle hold, sat back on its haunches and looked around with an exploring eye, and a questioning sniff. What was that in the corner? What was that soft blue feathery thing with its chuckling song, and its contented peck, peck? Fine sport for a tom cat!

Slowly, slowly, one step at a time, the cat padded forward slinking across the floor with arched back, and sly cruel eyes as yellow as topaz. Nearer, nearer, nearer.

The unsuspecting pigeon, her back toward the cat, pecked quietly away at the bowl of peas. Now she stopped, her crop full, and sidled, with her pathetic little limp, to the bath pan that Lottie had set near the window to catch the afternoon sun. Splash and flutter and preen! Her soft chuckles turned into a bubbling trill that filled the room with music.

Closer came the cat.

The tempting flutter of those blue wings as the pigeon preened herself was more than it could stand. With a wild jump, like the release of a spring, it shot forward.

The pigeon, cocking her head, and shaking the water from her feathers, saw the cat just in time. One split second before those frightful claws could grab her, she took flight. For the first time since Lottie had found her in the garden, she spread her wings, and fluttered out of the cat's reach. Up to the ceiling with weak uneven strokes, turning and swooping in wild fear as her wings beat against walls, reeling back from the glass window panes, bumping against the door, she somehow kept aloft. Able to fly, yes, but growing weaker with every flutter of her poor hurt wings.

The curtain rod saved her. Gasping and palpitating with terror, she found it at last, and clinging with all the strength of her red feet, she hung there, and took refuge from the horrible gray creature that stalked below. The cat was baffled. The curtains were short, and hung from the top sash. There was no way for it to grab them and climb to the rod. Baleful and frustrated, it fixed its unwinking glittering eyes on the pigeon and waited for the next maneuver. Swish, swish, swish, went its tail against the floor, and in one of its unsheathed claws it clutched a pitiful blue tail feather. And it was that way that Lottie found them when she ran in at supper time.

"Get out! Get out of this room, you horrid cat! Don't you dare come back, either! Shoo, get out, I tell you! Oh you mean, ugly cat, get out of here! Shoo, scat—!"

She snatched her hairbrush off the washstand and threw it with all her might. The cat yowled and spat as the heavy wooden brush hit it in the ribs. It hesitated for a moment, then dropped to its haunches again, and waited, ready to spring at the first flutter from the curtain rod. Lottie grabbed her Sunday shoes from the wardrobe. "Scat, I tell you! Get out of here! Get out, you awful cat! Leave my poor bird alone, do you hear? Hurry up! Scat!"

This time the cat gave up the chase. It slunk out of the room in a hurry, and Lottie, beside herself with fear for the pigeon, climbed on a chair and tried to

34

bring her down. Lottie held the little pigeon close and talked to her with gentle soothing words. She stroked her ruffled feathers, and she could see where one of them had been plucked out of the tail by the cat's ruthless jump.

She shuddered as she thought what might have happened.

"I've a good idea," she said, as she cuddled the pigeon close, and tried to calm her. "I've a fine idea. I'll ask Sister Ursula for a key to the door. Then I can lock you in whenever I have to leave you. That nasty old cat will be fooled if he tries any more tricks. Come along. I'll take you with me. We'll go right now, before supper, to ask for the key. I won't ever feel safe again unless I can lock you up good and tight, poor little bird."

She turned toward the door. As she opened it, she stopped to pick up a tiny object that lay on the threshold.

It was a tiny silver medal dangling from a frayed red cord. Lottie examined it curiously. A picture of a saint on one side, a Latin inscription on the other. It took her only a second to recognize it and to know to whom it belonged. Tante Louise had given it to Thérèse on her fête day, and Thérèse had worn it proudly, and boasted about it, so that every girl in the dormitory was familiar with it.

For a moment Lottie stood undecided. She stared at the medal, and turned it over in her hands while she tried to make up her mind. Her eyes turned to the pigeon with her heaving breast and missing tail feather. The temptation to run to Sister Ursula with the whole story was almost more than Lottie could bear.

"It would serve her right if I told on her! It would

serve her good and right, the mean old thing! Trying to get the cat to eat up my poor bird! But if I tell on her maybe all the other girls would call me a tattle tale tit—I guess I won't, after all. It would make an awful fuss, and get her into terrible trouble. Come along, little pigeon, we'll let her off this time. But she better not try any more tricks! Let's hurry and get that key! I'll feel a lot better when I know I can lock you up safely."

Lottie ran down the hall to Sister Ursula's room, with the pigeon clutched in her arms. She knocked on the door. The door opened, and Sister Ursula appeared with a surprised expression, as she looked at Lottie clutching the bedraggled ruffled pigeon.

"Please, Sister Ursula, may I have the key to my room? I know it's against the rules—but something awful just happened! At least, it didn't quite happen, but almost. Oh if you'd seen that nasty cat, Sister Ursula, you'd know why I want a key so much! I couldn't bear it if that cat got in again and ate up my poor pigeon."

Sister Ursula was amazed.

"A cat, Lottie? Why, that seems impossible, child. How could a cat get up in the dormitories, past Sister Agatha in the kitchen, and up the back stairs? Never, in all the years I've been here at the convent have I seen a cat in the dormitories."

"But it's true, Sister Ursula, there was a cat—a horrid skinny hungry one with big glarey eyes. Oh, it was awful!" Sister Ursula looked very grave. She was thinking hard. She was remembering the black legs and the gray cloak flying down the back stairs. And she remembered, too, a cubicle door slamming with a loud bang.

"Yes, Lottie, you may have a key—here, take this

36

one—but mind you are careful with it, and give it back to me when you are through with it. I agree with you —it would be dreadful to have that pretty bird of yours eaten up. But I still can't understand it, Lottie. Tell me, child, have you any idea how the cat could have got into your room?"

Lottie found it very hard to look Sister Ursula in the face. She grew red and embarrassed.

"I don't know, Sister Ursula," she said, twisting her skirt nervously, and looking down at the floor. "I don't know how it got upstairs. I guess it just did. I guess maybe it is an especially smart cat—and maybe it heard some one say that there was a pigeon in my room."

She shifted uneasily. Oh dear! It was terribly hard to keep secrets from those searching grave eyes of Sister Ursula.

"Well, I think maybe I'd better go now, don't you? It's almost supper time. Thank you lots for the key."

Sister Ursula nodded. There was a funny smile tugging at the corners of her mouth.

"Yes, Lottie, run along, and mind you take care of that key. I think you are right, child. It must have been an especially clever cat that paid your room a visit!"

Sister Ursula stood looking after Lottie as she ran down the hall.

"I am very glad that Lottie is not a tale bearer," she mused, "but I would give a great deal to know, just the same, who Mademoiselle Gray Cloak was."

Dong! dong! dong!

Supper time! Supper time! Supper time!

The girls filed into the dining room and took their

places at the table. Thérèse dodged around the room and sat down just as far away from Lottie as she could get. She could not eat. She had lost her appetite.

At last Sister Ursula stood up and led the way from the dining room. Thérèse bolted as fast as possible. She shoved past the littlest girls, and made a dive for the stairs to her room. But Lottie caught up with her in the hall.

"Here," she said simply. "Here's your medal, Thérèse. I guess you must have dropped it in my room. I knew you'd want to have it back."

38

She held out the medal, and Thérèse snatched it without a word. Her cheeks were as bright with shame and embarrassment as the scarlet cord.

Sister Ursula, watching the scene silently, came now and put her hand on Thérèse's shoulder.

Her eyes were cold, her mouth stern.

"Why don't you say thank you to Lottie?" she asked quietly. "Why don't you say thank you for your medal? It was good of Lottie to return it. Can't you talk? Have you no manners? Or is it possible, Thérèse, that a cat has got your tongue? I wonder!"

"*Dong! dong! dong! Boom! boom! boom!* Get up! get up! get up!*" sang the convent bells one fine morning. "Spring is here! Get up! get up!"

Lottie jumped out of bed before the bells had stopped their loud sweet jangling. The sun was shining and there was a soft balmy feeling in the air. It was fun to get dressed on such a morning. Winter was over. No more icy blasts coming in the windows. No more shivering and shaking as she pulled on her underclothes and wriggled into her uniform. The sun was delicious on her bare toes as she sat on the floor and turned her stockings right side out. She felt like dancing and singing. Surely it must be some special day. She got up and flipped the leaves of her calendar. Of course. It was a fête day. The Feast of St. Valentine.

Dong! dong! dong!

After breakfast and prayers and lessons, Sister Mary Josephine who was in charge of the school room, showed them how to make valentines. She gave them red paper, and scissors, and paste, and stickers with cupids on them, and doves, and flowers and mottoes.

39

"Valentines are messages of friendship and of love and of kindly thoughts," said Sister Mary Josephine. "If you make your valentines neatly, I will give them to the porter to post to your family and friends. Try hard to make them nicely. Don't put on too much paste. Cut the edges neatly. Do the very best you can to make them pretty."

Lottie cut carefully. What beautiful red paper! What lovely trimmings! The scissors were stiff, and hurt her hand where they pressed, and it was hard to make the edges even. She pasted doves and forget-me-nots on a red heart, and finished it around the edges with a lace paper frill. When it was all done, she admired it proudly, and held it up for everyone to see.

"Look, Sister Mary Josephine, is this all right? Do you think it's pretty? Do you like it?"

Sister Mary Josephine was on the other side of the room, and she did not hear what Lottie said. The girls turned around to stare at Lottie's valentine, and Thérèse, always on the watch for a chance to tease, could not bear to let this one pass by. Lottie always thought she was so smart! Lottie always had the girls on her side!

"Ha, ha," she whispered as shrilly as she dared, "ha, ha, Lottie, there you go being silly again! Wasting your time making valentines! Why do you bother? You haven't any one to send it to, no matter how pretty it is. You haven't any one to love. No one wants you for his valentine."

Lottie turned in her seat furiously. Thérèse was laughing, and the girls near by snickered. Lottie tried not to cry. She did not want any one to see tears in her eyes. She made an ugly face, instead. A bad one. She screwed up her mouth and wrinkled her forehead,

40

and then she stuck out her tongue. How unfortunate! How dreadful! Sister Mary Josephine turned around and looked sharply at Lottie. Sister Mary Josephine was deaf, but she had sharp eyes. She was quite sure that the long pink tongue had been meant for herself. She straightened up abruptly. She dropped the scissors with which she was cutting out hearts for one of the little girls. Her beads dangled and clacked against the desk, and the wings of her cap flapped indignantly.

"Lottie, Lottie, the very idea! I am surprised at you! Go to your room at once! Stay on your knees this afternoon and ask *le bon Dieu* to make you a good child, instead of a rude and silly one. Sticking out your tongue. Disgraceful, disgraceful."

There was a dreadful silence after that. The girls stared at Lottie and shuffled their feet nervously. Thérèse bent demurely over her desk, a sly smile of triumph on her face.

Lottie snatched up her beautiful valentine and marched out of the room without a word. Her eyes stung with tears and her face was crimson. When she reached her room she banged the door defiantly behind her, and lay on the bed and cried.

"What is the use," she sobbed bitterly, "what is the use? Nothing is fair, and everything always goes wrong. I hate this place! I want to go away! I want to go away!"

As she cried, the pigeon watched her from her perch on the washstand. Then she flew down and sat on Lottie's shoulder, cooing and chuckling sympathetically. The pigeon rolled her eyes comically and pecked at Lottie's hair and the tips of her ears. Lottie could not help laughing at these droll antics. She felt more cheerful and sat up, wiping her eyes and her nose on her petticoat.

"I don't care what that nasty Thérèse says," she confided to the pigeon, "she's stupid. She's not worth bothering about. And maybe if I try not to pay any attention to her she will get tired of teasing me. Let's not think about her any more. And as for you, you funny sweet little bird, I've got a surprise for you. A lovely one! I'm going to let you free.

"You look just like the dove on my valentine, did you know that? Only you are blue, of course, and the dove is snowy white. Look, I'll show you." She pulled the valentine out of her pocket. "There, see? Don't you think it's a beautiful valentine? Thérèse was right though. I hate her, but she was right. I have no one. In all the

42

world there is no one who wants me for his valentine. What a pity to waste this red heart! What a pity that there is no one in all the world who wants my message of friendship and of love!"

Lottie stared at the valentine. The pigeon cooed softly, and pecked at the lace paper frill. Suddenly, without any reason at all, a wild idea flashed into Lottie's head. She kept on staring at the valentine, fascinated. The white dove carried a letter in its beak. Lottie laughed out loud. What a wonderful idea! What a crazy idea! But what a perfect one!

She hunted around in her pocket and pulled out a stubby pencil. She smoothed the valentine on her knee, and wrote a message, very carefully, right in the middle of the red heart. She wrote in her best writing, "Please let me be your valentine. I am eight years old. I live at the Convent of the Good Shepherd. My name is Lottie."

When that was done, Lottie rummaged for a piece of string. She could not find any, so she took off a shoe, and pulled out the lacing. Then she rolled the valentine into a tiny wad and tied it to the pigeon's right leg. She tied it with hard knots. "There now, that can't come off. You can't lose my valentine now, dear pigeon. Wherever you go, wherever your home, my message will go along, too. And perhaps someone will find it and let me be his valentine. Surely, no one would mind, if he knew how I hate to waste this beautiful red heart."

Lottie picked up the pigeon and climbed on the iron balcony outside her window. She kissed her for the last time. "Good-bye, pigeon dear! Good-bye, good-bye! I wish I could keep you always. But I know you want to fly home. Good-bye, good-bye!"

Lottie tossed the bird in the air. The pigeon stretched her wings with a great rush of joyous strength, and swirled high above Lottie's head. Then, circling west, it flew off into the late afternoon sunshine.

Lottie watched her bird until she disappeared. Lottie went back to her room. She emptied the water bowl, threw away the dried peas. She put the cardboard box out of sight in her wardrobe. Then she looked around the room.

"Now I have nothing," she said. "Nothing at all of my own. Not even my beautiful red paper heart."

Whirr, whirr, caroo, caroo! Caroo, caroo, caroo! There it was again, soft and persistent. *Whirr, whirr!* The shadow of wings flashed over the skylight. Coo-Coo flew in the trap door like a swift blue arrow, and settled herself calmly on her perch. Yes, settled herself and

44

preened her feathers and pecked at the peas in her bowl as calmly and matter-of-factly as though she had been out of the pigeon loft for only a moment instead of the weeks and weeks that had passed since her disappearance.

Jules thought he was dreaming. He could not believe that it was Coo-Coo safely home again. What luck! What wonderful luck! He came out of his trance and grabbed the pigeon in both hands as though he were afraid she might take flight again at any moment.

"Papa Duval," he shouted at the top of his lungs, "Papa, come quickly! Coo-Coo is back! Coo-Coo is safe! Do you hear me? Come quickly, she's here in the loft, Papa—!"

Delphine, in the kitchen preparing supper, dropped her vegetable knife with a clatter. Down went the potatoes rolling all over the floor, and up the stairs went Mama, as fast as she could waddle. Right behind her came Michel. He had just passed through the courtyard gate when he heard Jules' wild shout. He could not wait for Delphine. He shoved past her and took the stairs at a bound. He ran into the loft and snatched Coo-Coo from Jules, and tears of joy spilled down his fat, red face. His moustache wiggled with emotion, and all the time he was crying, he was smiling from ear to ear.

"Coo-Coo, my little Coo-Coo, my blue beauty, where have you been all this time? What happened to you, my little queen? Shame on you, Coo-Coo, for making me worry so much! Why did you not fly home to me, eh? But I'm not going to scold you, little champion, no, no! I am too happy to waste breath on scoldings!"

Jules yanked Michel's coat sleeve excitedly.

"Look! What's that tied to her leg, Papa? What can it be?"

Papa Duval stared. What on earth was that clumsy lump? He pulled out his pen knife and hastily cut the knots in the black shoe string. He unfolded the wad of crumpled paper, and he and Delphine and Jules stared in amazement. A red heart. A wrinkled squashed-up valentine. Lottie's message of friendship and of love.

What did it mean? Where had Coo-Coo been all these weeks? Who was Lottie? Who was this odd child who sent valentines through the air tied to the leg of a pigeon? All these questions they asked in astonishment. What a mystery! What a complete and baffling mystery!

Mama Duval spoke first.

"One thing we know, at any rate," she said slowly, "the Convent of the Good Shepherd is out on the Bayou

Road. Everyone knows the place. The gardens with the pecan grove, and the high wall around it, the place where the nuns take poor children in, and homeless ones."

Michel nodded impatiently. "I know, yes, of course, I know where it is! It has been there for more years than I can count—but what has that got to do with us? How did she get hold of Coo-Coo in the first place, this Lottie child, and why does she send us a valentine, can you answer that one?"

No, they could not answer. They could only turn the red heart over in their hands and stare at the strange message. "Eight years old," said Mama Duval thoughtfully, "that is too little to have no other home but the convent. That is sad, poor little one. It is no life for a child. The nuns are kind. They are very good, but they cannot be mother and father to all the homeless little ones that come to their gate."

"All that is quite beside the point! The whole thing is that she must be thanked for sending Coo-Coo safely back to us. Yes, she must be thanked and rewarded. The very first day that we can leave the café we must go to the convent and see her. Do you hear me, Delphine? No one shall ever say that Michel Duval neglects his debts, or is lacking in gratitude."

Mama Duval nodded. "You are right, Michel. The very first chance we will go. It is easy to see that the child, whoever she is, has a good heart or else she would not have let Coo-Coo go free. It is all very strange, this affair, and it is too bad that Coo-Coo cannot speak and tell us what happened—but enough of this now. It is almost supper time. Get along, Jules, and you too, Michel!"

Jules ran to the stairs. Then he stopped suddenly. He turned around and tried to speak.

"Mama Duval—Papa—listen to me one little minute. Do not think me impertinent—but if that Lottie girl is lonely and if she has no one, if the convent is her only home, why do you not take her here for your own child? Why do you not ask her to come and live here at the *Bon Goût?* You could teach her to cook, Mama—she would be most useful. When you are old,

48

she could take your place. She could fetch Papa's slippers for him, she could read to him when his eyes are tired, she could laugh and make little jokes and keep things jolly around here. And if you took her in and loved her, that little Lottie, only eight years old, would not have to send any more valentines through the air tied to a pigeon's leg, I can tell you!"

Jules fled, after this remarkable speech. The door slammed behind him, and there was no sound in the loft except the sweet chuckle and coo of the pigeons.

Mama and Papa Duval could not say a word. They lifted their eyebrows and stared at one another in amazement.

Delphine told Jules the great news the next morning when he ran into the kitchen for his breakfast. She told him that she and Papa were leaving at once for a trip to the convent, and if all went well they would bring Lottie back with them to live at the *Café de Bon Goût*.

Michel wore his Sunday suit, and two gold coins jingled richly and importantly in his vest pocket. Delphine wore her best black silk and a fine bonnet trimmed with jet flowers. She clutched a bag of macaroons in her tightly gloved hands. Jules pranced madly on the curb and waved excitedly as they drove away.

Clop, clop, clop, went the horse's hoofs. Around the square, past the pawnbroker's three balls. Past the Rue de Dauphine. Past the old Negro flower woman with her woolly head tied up in a striped *tignon*, her basket, and her shrill cries of "Callas, callas, fresh vi'lets! Roses, roses!" Past the Opera House, past St. Peter's and past St. Anne's. Out the Bayou Road they drove, under palmettoes and magnolia trees, and mossy oaks, with Mama

Duval clinging to Papa Duval's hands all the way, and
with Papa Duval sitting on the edge of the seat looking
very solemn and nervous.

At last they reached the gate of the Convent of the
Good Shepherd. *Thump, thump, thump,* went their
hearts as they thought of the child Lottie who was waiting inside.

Delphine straightened her bonnet. Michel blew his
nose, and wound his great gold turnip of a watch.

The big gate swung open. Papa and Mama were received politely and ushered into the convent parlor.

Sister Ursula asked them their names, and inquired
what it was that they wanted. Michel cleared his throat

50

bravely, and plunged into the business at hand. What a curious story he had to tell! Sister Ursula listened attentively. She asked a great many questions. She made it quite clear that she liked Mama and Papa Duval, and that she approved of them. And in the end, when Michel stopped talking to catch his breath, she smiled and nodded, and said "Yes!"

She went herself to fetch Lottie.

Lottie was in her room darning stockings.

"Put the mending basket down, Lottie," said Sister Ursula. "Brush your hair and wash your hands. Hurry! There are visitors in the parlor who wish to see you."

Lottie stared at Sister Ursula.

"Visitors for me? Oh no, there must be some mistake, Sister Ursula! There could not be visitors for me. For Sophie or Amélie, or Thérèse, perhaps, but not for me, because in all the world I have no one."

Sister Ursula smiled gently.

"Do as I say, Lottie. Make yourself tidy. Sometimes *le bon Dieu* sends us friends when we least expect them."

Lottie went downstairs in a daze. Who could be waiting for her? She had never been in the parlor before. It had curtains of rich starched lace. It had pictures of saints in gold frames. It had wax flowers in glass cases. It had a red velvet carpet. But do you think Lottie noticed those things? No. All she saw as she stood timidly in the doorway were the good kind faces of Mama and Papa Duval.

Mama smiled and gave Lottie the bag of macaroons. "For you, *petite*," she said, opening the bag and popping a cake into Lottie's astonished mouth. "Eat them all. They are good, no?"

51

Papa smiled and bowed, and took the gold coins from his pocket.

"For you, Mademoiselle Lottie. For you because you were kind to my Coo-Coo. Because you took care of my beautiful pigeon and sent her safely home. Ah yes, little one! We know all about it, from Sister Ursula here. And my thanks to you, Mademoiselle, with all my heart!"

Lottie gulped down the macaroon, and took the gold coins in bewilderment. She stood speechless, staring at these strange people. Her valentine people! She had never been called Mademoiselle before. She did not know what to do or say. Sister Ursula came to the rescue. She took Lottie's hands and put them into Mama and Papa Duval's hands.

"Listen to me, child," she said. "Once you were left at the gates here, long ago. You were not wanted. You were wrapped in rags. No one knew from where you came, no one knew to whom you belonged. But today, Lottie, you will go out through that same gate into a new life. Now you are wanted. Now you will be loved. You have been chosen out of all the little girls in the world. You will belong to Mama and Papa Duval, and they will belong to you. Tell me Lottie, do you want to go and live with them? Do you think you will be happy with them? It is your choice to make, my dear."

Lottie looked up at Mama and Papa. She liked their kind smiles and the jolly twinkle in their eyes. It was not hard to make up her mind.

"Yes, Sister Ursula, I want to go with them. I want to belong to them."

And, as simply as that, the matter was settled.

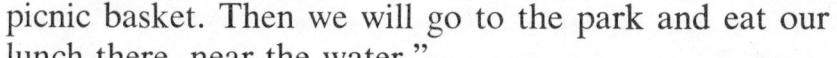

ONE cool summer morning Andrewshek's Auntie Katushka said, "Andrewshek, I think I will put some sandwiches and some cottage cheese and some poppy seed cakes and two eggs in our picnic basket. Then we will go to the park and eat our lunch there, near the water."

"May I go with you, Auntie Katushka?" said Andrewshek.

"Of course you may go to the park with me," said Auntie Katushka. "But first we have a great many things to do, before we can start to the park. I must go into the garden and catch the white goat. I will tie her up so she will not run away. Please find the kitten, Andrewshek, and put her in the cellar, so she will not worry the chickens while we are gone."

The Picnic Basket

BY MARGERY CLARK

Illustrated by Maud and Miska Petersham

"Yes, indeed, I will find the kitten and put her in the cellar," said Andrewshek, "so she will not worry the chickens while we are gone."

But all Andrewshek really did was to lift up the red and white napkin which Auntie Katushka had laid over the picnic basket and look at the eggs and the poppy seed cakes and touch the sandwiches and taste the cottage cheese.

The goat was not easy to catch. The goat wanted to go to the park, too. She galloped round and round the garden.

53

At last Auntie Katushka caught her and tied her firmly to a post.

Then Auntie Katushka went into the house to get Andrewshek and the lunch basket. She saw Andrewshek peeping under the red and white napkin and tasting the cottage cheese. He had forgotten all about the kitten.

The kitten was nowhere to be found. "I think she must be paying a visit to the Mouse family," said Auntie Katushka.

Then Auntie Katushka put on her bright shawl and took her umbrella with the long crooked handle under one arm. Then she picked up the lunch basket with the red and white napkin on top and she and Andrewshek started for the park.

They went down the hill and across the tracks and past the market and down a long street until they came to the park by the water.

Andrewshek sat down on the grass beside a little stream. Andrewshek's Auntie Katushka laid her umbrella with the long crooked handle and the basket of lunch on the grass beside Andrewshek.

"Andrewshek," said Auntie Katushka, "I must go to the spring and get some water for us to drink. Please watch the basket with the eggs and the sandwiches and poppy seed cakes and cottage cheese while I am gone."

"Yes, indeed, I will watch the basket of lunch," said Andrewshek.

But what Andrewshek really did was to say to himself, "I would like to take off my shoes and my stockings and wade in the little stream. I believe I will!"

Andrewshek took off his shoes and his stockings and went wading in the little stream.

A big white swan came floating calmly down the

54

stream. He saw the picnic basket lying on the grass. He stopped and stretched and stretched his long neck, till he could touch the basket. "Honk! honk! honk!" said he. "I wonder what is under the red and white napkin."

The big white swan lifted the napkin with his red bill and looked in the basket. "Oh, oh, oh! Won't Mother Swan be pleased with this nice lunch!" said he. "Sandwich bread makes fine food for baby swans."

He picked up the basket in his strong red bill and floated it ahead of him down the stream.

Andrewshek could not wade after the big white swan. The water was too deep.

"Stop! stop! White Swan!" cried Andrewshek. "That is my Auntie Katushka's picnic basket and it has our lunch in it. Please put it back on the grass."

"No, indeed! I will not put the basket back," honked the big white swan. "Sandwich bread makes fine food for baby swans and I have ten baby swans to feed."

The big white swan gave the picnic basket a little push with his red bill. The basket floated on down the little stream, lazily. The big white swan floated calmly behind it.

Just then Andrewshek's Auntie Katushka came hurrying up with the spring water. She saw the big white swan floating down the stream, with the lunch basket floating ahead of him.

Little Andrewshek stood in the middle of the stream, crying.

Auntie Katushka picked up her umbrella with the long crooked handle. Auntie Katushka ran along the shore until she overtook the big white swan, with the lunch basket floating ahead of him.

She caught the handle of the picnic basket in the crook of her long handled umbrella. She drew the basket safely to shore.

"Well! well!" said Auntie Katushka, as she spread the red and white napkin on the grass, and laid the sandwiches and the poppy seed cakes and the cottage cheese and the eggs upon it. "It always pays to carry an umbrella to a picnic."

56

THERE are trails
　　　that a lad may follow
　When the years
　　of his boyhood slip,
But I shall soar like a swallow
　　On the wings of a silver ship,

Guiding my bird of metal,
　　One with her throbbing frame,
Floating down like a petal,
　　Roaring up like a flame;

　Winding the wind that scatters
　　　Smoke from the chimney's lip,
Tearing the clouds to tatters
　　With the wings
　　　of a silver ship;

Grazing the broad
　　blue skylight
　Up where the falcons fare,
Riding the realms of twilight,
　Brushed by a comet's hair;

Silver Ships

BY MILDRED PLEW MEIGS

Illustrated by Judith Brown

　Snug in my coat of leather,
　　Watching the skyline swing,
Shedding the world like a feather
　　From the tip of a tilted wing.

　There are trails that a lad may travel
　　When the years of his boyhood wane,
But I'll let a rainbow ravel
　　Through the wings of my silver plane.

Foreign Lands

BY ROBERT LOUIS STEVENSON

Illustrated by Alexander Dobkin

UP into the cherry tree
Who should climb but little me?
I held the trunk with both my hands
And looked abroad on foreign lands.

I saw the next-door garden lie,
Adorned with flowers, before my eye,
And many pleasant places more
That I had never seen before.

I saw the dimpling river pass
And be the sky's blue looking-glass;
The dusty roads go up and down
With people tramping in to town.

If I could find a higher tree
Farther and farther I should see,
To where the grown-up river slips
Into the sea among the ships,

To where the roads on either hand
Lead onward into fairy land,
Where all the children dine at five,
And all the playthings come alive.

A Boy's Song

BY JAMES HOGG

WHERE the pools are bright and deep,
Where the grey trout lies asleep,
Up the river and over the lea,
That's the way for Billy and me.

Where the blackbird sings the latest,
Where the hawthorn blooms the sweetest,
Where the nestlings chirp and flee,
That's the way for Billy and me.

Where the mowers mow the cleanest,
Where the hay lies thick and greenest,
There to trace the homeward bee,
That's the way for Billy and me.

Where the hazel bank is steepest,
Where the shadow falls the deepest,
Where the clustering nuts fall free,
That's the way for Billy and me.

Why the boys should drive away
Little sweet maidens from the play,
Or love to banter and fight so well,
That's the thing I never could tell.

But this I know, I love to play
Through the meadow, among the hay;
Up the water and over the lea,
That's the way for Billy and me.

Roads

BY RACHEL FIELD

Illustrated by Joseph Low

A ROAD might lead to anywhere—
    To harbor towns and quays,
Or to a witch's pointed house
    Hidden by bristly trees.
It might lead past the tailor's door,
    Where he sews with needle and thread,
Or by Miss Pim, the milliner's,
    With her hats for every head.
It might be a road to a great, dark cave
    With treasure and gold piled high,
Or a road with a mountain tied to its end,
    Blue-humped against the sky.
Oh, a road might lead you anywhere—
    To Mexico or Maine.
But then, it might just fool you, and—
    Lead you back home again!

U P the airy mountain,
  Down the rushy glen,
We daren't go a-hunting
  For fear of little men;
Wee folk, good folk,
  Trooping all together;
Green jacket, red cap,
  And white owl's feather!

Down along the rocky shore
  Some make their home,
They live on crispy pancakes
  Of yellow tide-foam;
Some in the reeds
  Of the black
    mountain lake,
With frogs for
    their watchdogs,
  All night awake.

High on the hill-top
  The old King sits;
He is now so old and gray
  He's nigh lost his wits.

The Fairies

BY

WILLIAM ALLINGHAM

Illustrated by
Dorothy P. Lathrop

With a bridge of white mist
  Columbkill he crosses,
On his stately journeys
  From Slieveleague to Rosses;
Or going up with music
  On cold starry nights
To sup with the Queen
  Of the gay Northern Lights.

They stole little Bridget
    For seven years long;
When she came down again
    Her friends were all gone.
They took her lightly back,
    Between the night and morrow,
They thought that she was fast asleep,
    But she was dead with sorrow.
They have kept her ever since
    Deep within the lake,
On a bed of flag-leaves,
    Watching till she wake.

By the craggy hill-side,
    Through the mosses bare,
They have planted thorn-trees
    For pleasure here and there.
If any man so daring
    As dig them up in spite,
He shall find their sharpest thorns
    In his bed at night.

Up the airy mountain,
    Down the rushy glen,
We daren't go a-hunting
    For fear of little men;
Wee folk, good folk,
    Trooping all together;
Green jacket, red cap,
    And white owl's feather!

COME listen to me,
　　you gallants so free,
　　All you that love mirth for to hear,
　　And I will tell you of a bold outlaw,
　　　That lived in Nottinghamshire.

As Robin Hood in the forest stood,
　　All under the greenwood tree,
　　There he was ware of a brave young man,
　　　As fine as fine might be.

The youngster was clothed
　　in scarlet red,
　　　In scarlet fine and gay:
And he did frisk it
　　over the plain,
　　And chanted a roundelay.

As Robin Hood
　　next morning stood,
　　　Amongst the leaves so gay,
There did he espy
　　the same young man
　　Come drooping along
　　　the way.

Robin Hood and Allen-a-Dale

FOLK BALLAD

Illustrated by
Serge Hollerbach

The scarlet he wore the day before,
　　It was clean cast away;
And at every step he fetcht a sigh,
　　"Alack and well a day!"

Then stepped forth brave Little John,
　　And Nick the miller's son,

64

Which made the young man bend his bow,
    When as he see them come.

"Stand off, stand off," the young man said,
    "What is your will with me?"
"You must come before our master straight,
    Under yon greenwood tree."

And when he came bold Robin before,
    Robin askt him courteously,
"O hast thou any money to spare
    For my merry men and me?"

"I have no money," the young man said,
    "But five shillings and a ring;
And that I have kept this seven long years,
    To have it at my wedding.

"Yesterday I should have married a maid,
    But she is now from me ta'en
And chosen to be an old knight's delight,
    Whereby my poor heart is slain."

"What is thy name?" then said Robin Hood,
    "Come tell me, without any fail."
"By the faith of my body," then said the young man,
    "My name it is Allen-a-Dale."

"What wilt thou give me," said Robin Hood,
    "In ready gold or fee,
To help thee to thy true-love again,
    And deliver her unto thee?"

"I have no money," then quoth the young man.
    "No ready gold nor fee,
But I will swear upon a book
    Thy true servant for to be."

"How many miles is it to thy true-love?
    Come tell me without any guile."
"By the faith of my body," then said the young man,
    "It is but five little mile."

Then Robin he hasted over the plain,
    He did neither stint nor lin,
Until he came unto the church,
    Where Allen should keep his wedding.

"What dost thou do here?" the bishop he said,
    "I prithee now tell to me."
"I am a bold harper," quoth Robin Hood,
    "And the best in the north country."

"O welcome, O welcome," the bishop he said,
    "That musick best pleaseth me."
"You shall have no musick," quoth Robin Hood,
    "Till the bride and the bridegroom I see."

With that came in a wealthy knight,
    Which was both grave and old,
And after him a finikin lass,
    Did shine like the glistening gold.

66

"This is not a fit match," quoth bold Robin Hood,
    "That you do seem to make here;
For since we are come unto the church,
    The bride shall chuse her own dear."

Then Robin Hood put his horn to his mouth,
    And blew blasts two or three;
When four and twenty bowmen bold
    Came leaping over the lea.

And when they came into the churchyard,
    Marching all on a row,
The first man was Allen-a-Dale,
    To give bold Robin his bow.

"This is thy true-love," Robin he said,
    "Young Allen, as I hear say;
And you shall be married at this same time,
    Before we depart away."

"That shall not be," the bishop he said,
    "For thy word shall not stand;
They shall be three times askt in the church,
    As the law is of our land."

Robin Hood pulled off the bishop's coat,
    And put it on Little John;
"By the faith of my body," then Robin said,
    "This cloath doth make thee a man."

When Little John went into the quire,
    The people began for to laugh;
He askt them seven times in the church,
    Lest three times should not be enough.

"Who gives me this maid?" then said Little John.
    Quoth Robin, "That do I,
And he that takes her from Allen-a-Dale
    Full dearly he shall her buy."

And thus having ended this merry wedding,
    The bride lookt as fresh as a queen,
And so they returned to the merry greenwood,
    Amongst the leaves so green.

CAPTAIN Joe sailed north in his steamship.

He sailed and sailed.

One day he saw ice in the sea.

The next day he saw some more ice. Every day he saw more and more ice in the sea.

Then one day he saw something on some ice. He took out his binoculars to look.

Sure enough! There was a big Eskimo boy waving his arms. The Eskimo waved and waved. "Poor Eskimo," said Captain Joe. "He is afraid I don't see him. He is afraid I will sail away and leave him on the ice."

Captain Joe sailed near. "Hello," called Captain Joe. "Hello, Eskimo boy. How did you get here?"

"I fell asleep," called the Eskimo boy, "and the ice carried me away." "Do you want to go home?" asked Captain Joe.

"Yes, thank you," called the Eskimo.

Captain Joe and the Eskimo

BY VEOTTA McKINLEY ADAMS

Illustrated by Barney Tobey

"Then we must think how to get you on my ship. Can you climb?" called Captain Joe.

"Up an iceberg?" called the Eskimo.

"No," called Captain Joe. "Up a rope."

"I don't know," called the Eskimo. "What is a rope?"

"This," called Captain Joe, and he threw out a big rope.

He waited and waited.

69

Why was the Eskimo so long?

The Eskimo boy was sitting on the ice!

"Why are you sitting there?" called Captain Joe.

"I am waiting for you to throw more rope down to me. When I stick my sharp bone knife into the rope, the rope breaks and I fall back on the ice."

"That is not the way to climb," called Captain Joe.

"That is the way I climb," called the Eskimo.

Captain Joe did not know what to say. He had never heard of such a way to climb. How could he get the Eskimo onto his ship? He thought and thought.

Then he said, "I know what I will do! I will throw down a life preserver."

"Hold onto the life preserver," called Captain Joe. "I will pull you up." Then Captain Joe called over the side of his ship, "Are you ready?"

"Yes," called the Eskimo.

Captain Joe pulled and pulled and pulled and pulled.

The rope came up with nothing on the end.

70

Captain Joe looked and looked for the Eskimo.

"Where are you?" he called over the side of the ship.

"Sailing around on the little boat," called the Eskimo. "I am waiting for you to pull me up."

"But you untied the life preserver!" called Captain Joe.

"I like it for a boat," called the Eskimo. "I never had a round boat."

"But how can I pull you up?" called Captain Joe. Captain Joe was getting cross. "I know what I will do," he said. "See this barrel?" he called to the Eskimo.

"Where did you find all that wood?" called the Eskimo.

"You climb into that barrel, and I will pull you up," called Captain Joe.

"Are you ready?"

"I am very busy," called the Eskimo.

"What are you doing?" called Captain Joe.

"I am making a paddle for my new boat out of the wood you gave me."

Captain Joe looked down. The Eskimo was sitting on the ice with the life preserver beside him. He was making a paddle out of some of the wood with his sharp bone knife.

Captain Joe was angry. "I do not think you want to come on my ship."

"I would like very much to come on your ship," called the Eskimo, "but it is very hard to get on your ship."

"We will try once more," called Captain Joe, and he went to the ship's kitchen and he got out a big bucket. "Climb into this old bucket," called Captain Joe to the Eskimo. "I will pull you up."

"What is in the bucket?" called the Eskimo.

"Nothing," called Captain Joe, "but it once had lard in it."

Captain Joe waited and waited. At last he called, "Are you ready?"

"No," called the Eskimo, "I am eating."

"Eating?" called Captain Joe.

"Yes," called the Eskimo, "I am eating the lard that is on the sides of this bucket. I like this lard very much. It tastes something like blubber. Do you have any blubber for me to eat?"

"No," called Captain Joe, "and I am tired of trying to help you. You cut my rope with your sharp bone knife.

72

You use my life preserver for a boat. You cut a paddle from my barrel. You keep me waiting while you sit eating lard out of my old bucket. Now if you want to come on my ship, you climb inside that bucket and I will pull you up."

The Eskimo sat still. "Hurry," called Captain Joe. "I do not want to wait all day!"

"Well," called the Eskimo, "maybe you better go. I do not think I need to come on your ship after all.

"I have a new round boat.

"I have a new wooden paddle.

"I have some lard to eat."

"But you cannot stay there and eat lard," called Captain Joe.

"Oh, no," called the Eskimo, "I will take some home in my new little boat. Thank you for my boat and paddle and the lard."

Captain Joe slapped his hand to his forehead.

WHAT AN ESKIMO!

The Eskimo climbed onto the life preserver and sat down.

He waved good-bye to Captain Joe. Away he went, sitting on the life preserver with Captain Joe's lard bucket on his lap!

I WISH I could travel
  to Elephant-land.
 High in the dark
  of the tree
I would watch the monkeys
  go hand over hand,
 Throwing coconuts
  down to me.

On the elephant's top, in a jiggety seat
 With cushions of soft-feeling silk,
I'd nibble away at the coconut meat
 And suck out
  the coconut milk.

The elephant's trunk
  would carry me up
When we started
  from Elephant-town.
And when I got home and
  said Hup-a-hup-HUP!
He would lift me
  so carefully down.

Elephant-Town

BY MARION EDEY

Illustrated by

Nola Langner

 His trunk would be gray
  and his name would be Jim,
  His toes would be painted with black.
 It would always be lovely
  to gallop with him
  And to look at the world from his back.

THE forest was dark and very quiet.
Not a creature was stirring.
Even the wind had stopped breathing.
Not a leaf was falling, not a blade of
grass was moving.

And do you know why this was so?

Because it was just the time between night and day,
when night was ending and day was about to begin.

Night in the forest is very dark, and it creeps away
slowly.

At the time this story begins it was still very dark
in the forest. It was also very warm.

All the creatures were very
quiet. But the quietest of all
was the tiger.

The tiger was lying at the
foot of a tree by the side of a
road that divided the forest in
half.

It would have been very
hard to see the tiger for he was
hidden by leaves, flowers, vines
and grasses. He was hidden
also by the darkness.

The Camel Who Took a Walk

BY JACK TWORKOV

Illustrated by Roger Duvoisin

Suddenly the first glimmer of light trembled in the
sky. The sky, the forest, and even the air began to turn
blue.

Just then, on the road that divided the forest in half,
far, far up that road—right near the horizon, which is
where the sky and the ground meet—something—yes,
something was moving.

Now the tiger might have been sleeping! But if you could have looked into his face you would have seen that one eye, the eye facing the thing that was moving, was open just the tiniest, tiniest crack.

And when a tiger's eye is open the tiniest crack, then you know that the tiger is not sleeping as he would have you believe. But—he is watching and thinking.

Now this thing that was moving, and that the tiger was watching, was drawing nearer and nearer. The sky was getting bluer and bluer. The light on the road had turned pink, so you could see that the thing was———you will be surprised! a very beautiful camel.

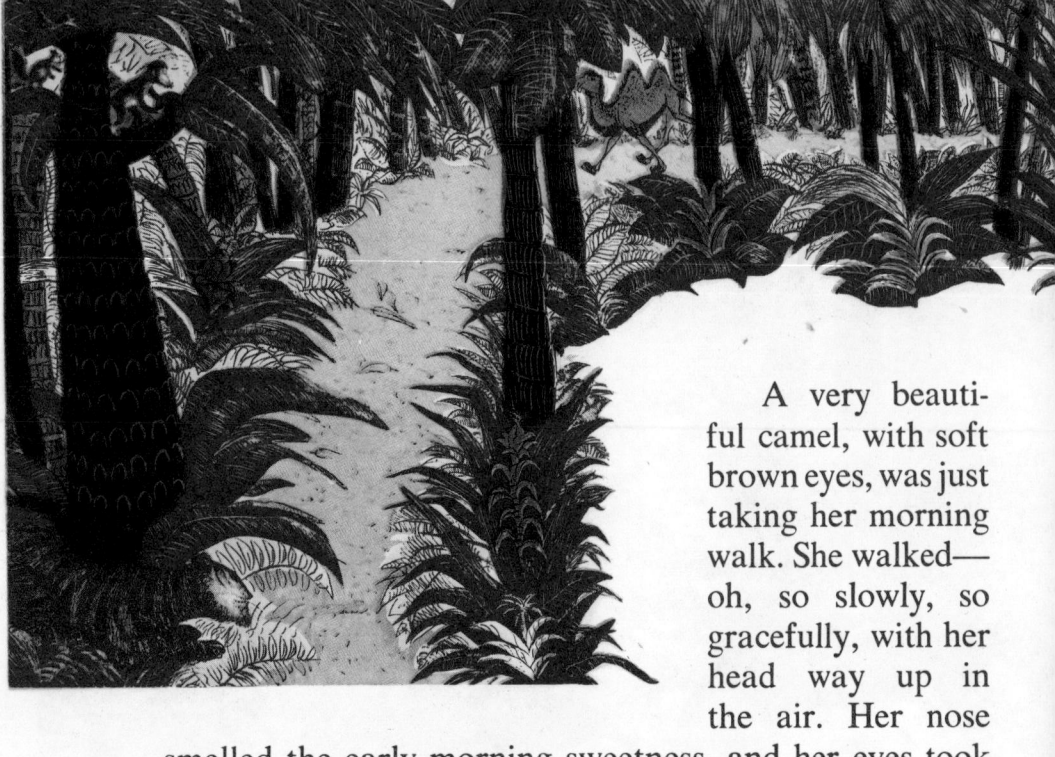

A very beautiful camel, with soft brown eyes, was just taking her morning walk. She walked— oh, so slowly, so gracefully, with her head way up in the air. Her nose smelled the early morning sweetness, and her eyes took in all the blue and pink colors of the sky.

And the tiger who was lying at the foot of the tree was thinking, "As soon as this beautiful camel comes to where the shadow of the tree falls across the road—I am going to pounce on her!"

But the tiger was not the only one who saw the camel walking down the road.

'Way up in the tree, on a branch directly over the tiger, sat a little monkey! And he knew what the tiger was thinking about! And so he, very quietly, reached for a cocoanut and held it in his

78

hands. And he said to himself, "Just as soon as the tiger is about to pounce on the camel—I will drop this cocoanut on his head."

And all the while the beautiful camel walked gracefully down the road, turning her pretty head this way and that, while the sky got brighter and brighter.

But the tiger and the monkey were not the only ones who saw the beautiful camel.

On the same tree a little squirrel with its bright little eyes had seen what was going on. And the little squirrel, very quietly, crept right up behind the monkey's tail. And the little squirrel said to himself, "As soon as the monkey is ready to drop the cocoanut on the tiger's head—I will bite his tail!"

All the while, the beautiful camel walked gracefully down the road turning her pretty head, this way and that, while the sky grew brighter and brighter.

But the tiger, the monkey, and the squirrel were not the only ones who saw the beautiful camel. A little bird was watching what the tiger, the monkey, and the squirrel were up to. And the little bird said to himself, "Aha! I know what I shall do— As soon as the squirrel is ready to bite the monkey's tail, I shall pounce, with my sharp claws, upon his tiny head."

And now the tiger was so excited—so excited, he forgot to keep his tail still. He swished it from side to side, this way and that way.

Meanwhile, the camel was getting nearer and

nearer, and the sun was getting hotter and hotter, and the camel was getting warmer and warmer. And just as the camel had almost reached the shadow of the tree and the tiger and the monkey and the others were all getting ready —the camel suddenly stopped, and stretched her pretty neck 'way up in the sky. And she opened her mouth— oh, so wide, and—she let out an awful YAWN, and said sweetly in an ordinary sort of voice, "I think I'll go back."

The tiger was so flabbergasted—which means he was so surprised—that, just when he should have—

He didn't pounce on the camel.

And the monkey didn't drop his cocoanut.

The squirrel didn't bite the monkey's tail.

And the bird didn't pounce on the squirrel's head.

And they didn't do all of these things all in the same instant.

For just a tiny second no one said anything, and not a sound was heard.

80

Then the little bird burst into a peal of laughter that pierced the forest.

The squirrel began to chatter and the monkey began jumping up and down with such glee, that all the creatures in the forest woke up crying, "What happened? What happened?"

But you know what happened. *Nothing* happened. The beautiful camel just turned around and walked back the same way she had come. The tiger *slinked* away into the deep dark forest. And the sun shone like brass in the sky.

THIS is the story of the great war that Rikki-tikki-tavi fought single-handed, through the bathrooms of the big bungalow in Segowlee cantonment. . . .

He was a mongoose, rather like a little cat in his fur and his tail, but quite like a weasel in his head and his habits. His eyes and the end of his restless nose were pink; he could scratch himself anywhere he pleased, with any leg, front or back, that he chose to use; he could fluff up his tail till it looked like a bottle-brush, and his war-cry as he scuttled through the long grass was: *"Rikk-tikk-tikki-tikki-tchk!"*

Rikki-tikki-tavi

BY

RUDYARD KIPLING

Illustrated by Kurt Wiese

One day, a high summer flood washed him out of the burrow where he lived with his father and mother, and carried him, kicking and clucking, down a roadside ditch. He found a little wisp of grass floating there, and clung to it till he lost his senses. When he revived, he was lying in the hot sun on the middle of a garden path, very draggled indeed, and a small boy was saying: "Here's a dead mongoose. Let's have a funeral."

"No," said his mother; "let's take him in and dry him. Perhaps he isn't really dead."

They took him into the house, and a big man picked him up between his finger and thumb and said he was not dead but half choked; so they wrapped him in cotton-wool, and warmed him, and he opened his eyes and sneezed.

"Now," said the big man (he was an Englishman who

had just moved into the bungalow); "don't frighten him, and we'll see what he'll do."

It is the hardest thing in the world to frighten a mongoose, because he is eaten up from nose to tail with curiosity. The motto of all the mongoose family is, "Run and find out"; and Rikki-tikki was a true mongoose. He looked at the cotton-wool, decided that it was not good to eat, ran all round the table, sat up and put his fur in order, scratched himself, and jumped on the small boy's shoulder.

"Don't be frightened, Teddy," said his father. "That's his way of making friends."

"Ouch! He's tickling under my chin," said Teddy.

Rikki-tikki looked down between the boy's collar and neck, snuffed at his ear, and climbed down to the floor, where he sat rubbing his nose.

"Good gracious," said Teddy's mother, "and that's a wild creature! I suppose he's so tame because we've been kind to him."

"All mongooses are like that," said her husband. "If Teddy doesn't pick him up by the tail or try to put him in a cage, he'll run in and out of the house all day long. Let's give him something to eat."

They gave him a little piece of raw meat. Rikki-tikki liked it immensely, and when it was finished he went out into the veranda and sat in the sunshine and fluffed up his fur to make it dry to the roots. Then he felt better.

"There are more things to find out about in this house," he said to himself, "than all my family could find out in all their lives. I shall certainly stay and find out."

He spent all that day roaming over the house. He nearly drowned himself in the bath-tubs, put his nose into the ink on a writing-table, and burned it on the end of the big man's cigar, for he climbed up in the big man's lap to see how writing was done. At nightfall he ran into Teddy's nursery to watch how kerosene lamps were lighted, and when Teddy went to bed Rikki-tikki climbed up too; but he was a restless companion, because he had to get up and attend to every noise all through the night, and find out what made it.

One day Rikki-tikki went out into the garden to see what was to be seen. It was a large garden, only half cultivated, with bushes as big as summer-houses of Marshal Niel roses, lime and orange trees, clumps of bamboos, and thickets of high grass. Rikki-tikki licked his lips. "This is a splendid hunting-ground," he said, and his tail grew bottle-brushy at the thought of it, and he scuttled up and down the garden, snuffing here and there till he heard very sorrowful voices in a thornbush.

It was Darzee, the tailor-bird, and his wife. They had made a beautiful nest by pulling two big leaves together and stitching them up the edges with fibers, and had filled the hollow with cotton and downy fluff. The nest swayed to and fro, as they sat on the rim and cried.

"What is the matter?" asked Rikki-tikki.

"We are very miserable," said Darzee. "One of our babies fell out of the nest yesterday and Nag ate him."

"H'm!" said Rikki-tikki, "that is very sad—but I am a stranger here. Who is Nag?"

Darzee and his wife only cowered down in the nest without answering, for from the thick grass at the foot of the bush there came a low hiss—a horrid cold sound that made Rikki-tikki jump back two clear feet. Then inch by inch out of the grass rose up the head and spread hood of Nag, the big black cobra, and he was five feet long from tongue to tail. When he had lifted one-third of

84

himself clear of the ground, he stayed balancing to and
fro exactly as a dandelion-tuft balances in the wind, and
he looked at Rikki-tikki with the wicked snake's eyes that
never change their expression, whatever the snake may be
thinking of.

"Who is Nag?" he said, "*I* am Nag. The great god of
Brahm put his mark upon all our people when the first
cobra spread his hood to keep the sun off Brahm as he
slept. Look, and be afraid!"

He spread out his hood more than ever, and Rikki-
tikki saw the spectacle-mark on the back of it that looks
exactly like the eye part of a hook-and-eye fastening. He
was afraid for the minute; but it is impossible for a mon-

goose to stay frightened for any length of time, and though Rikki-tikki had never met a live cobra before, his mother had fed him on dead ones, and he knew that all a grown mongoose's business in life was to fight and eat snakes. Nag knew that too, and at the bottom of his cold heart he was afraid.

"Well," said Rikki-tikki, and his tail began to fluff up again, "marks or no marks, do you think it is right for you to eat fledglings out of a nest?"

Nag was thinking to himself, and watching the least little movement in the grass behind Rikki-tikki. He knew that mongooses in the garden meant death sooner or later for him and his family; but he wanted to get Rikki-tikki off his guard. So he dropped his head a little, and put it on one side.

"Let us talk," he said. "You eat eggs. Why should not I eat birds?"

"Behind you! Look behind you!" sang Darzee.

Rikki-tikki knew better than to waste time in staring. He jumped up in the air as high as he could go, and just under him whizzed by the head of Nagaina, Nag's wicked wife. She had crept up behind him as he was talking, to make an end of him; and he heard her savage hiss as the stroke missed. He came down almost across her back, and if he had been an old mongoose he would have known that then was the time to break her back with one bite; but he was afraid of the terrible lashing return-stroke of the cobra. He bit, indeed, but did not bite long enough, and he jumped clear of the whisking tail, leaving Nagaina torn and angry.

"Wicked, wicked Darzee!" said Nag, lashing up as high as he could reach toward the nest in the thornbush;

86

but Darzee had built it out of reach of snakes, and it only swayed to and fro.

Rikki-tikki felt his eyes growing red and hot (when a mongoose's eyes grow red, he is angry), and he sat back on his tail and hind legs like a little kangaroo, and looked all around him, and chattered with rage. But Nag and Nagaina had disappeared into the grass.

That night Teddy carried him off to bed, and insisted on Rikki-tikki sleeping under his chin. Rikki-tikki was too well bred to bite or scratch, but as soon as Teddy was asleep he went off for his nightly walk round the house. Rikki-tikki listened. The house was as still as still, but he thought he could just catch the faintest *scratch-scratch* in the world—a noise as faint as that of a wasp walking on a window-pane—the dry scratch of a snake's scales on brickwork.

"That's Nag or Nagaina," he said to himself, "and he is crawling into the bathroom sluice. You're right, Chuchundra; I should have talked to Chua."

He stole off to Teddy's bathroom, but there was nothing there, and then to Teddy's mother's bathroom. At the bottom of the smooth plaster wall there was a brick pulled out to make a sluice for the bath water, and as Rikki-tikki stole in by the masonry curb where the bath is put, he heard Nag and Nagaina whispering together outside in the moonlight.

"When the house is emptied of people," said Nagaina to her husband, "*he* will have to go away, and then the garden will be our own again. Go in quietly, and remember that the big man who killed Karait is the first one to bite. Then come out and tell me, and we will hunt for Rikki-tikki together."

"But are you sure that there is anything to be gained by killing the people?" said Nag.

"Everything. When there were no people in the bungalow, did we have any mongoose in the garden? So long as the bungalow is empty, we are king and queen of the garden; and remember that as soon as our eggs in the melon-bed hatch (as they may tomorrow), our children will need room and quiet."

"I had not thought of that," said Nag. "I will go, but there is no need that we should hunt for Rikki-tikki afterward. I will kill the big man and his wife, and the child if I can, and come away quietly. Then the bungalow will be empty, and Rikki-tikki will go."

Rikki-tikki tingled all over with rage and hatred at this, and then Nag's head came through the sluice, and his five feet of cold body followed it. Angry as he was, Rikki-tikki was very frightened as he saw the size of the big cobra. Nag coiled himself up, raised his head, and looked into the bathroom in the dark, and Rikki could see his eyes glitter.

"Now, if I kill him here, Nagaina will know; and if I fight him on the open floor, the odds are in his favor. What am I to do?" said Rikki-tikki-tavi.

Nag waved to and fro, and then Rikki-tikki heard him drinking from the biggest water-jar that was used to fill the bath. "That is good," said the snake. "Now, when Karait was killed, the big man had a stick. He may have that stick still, but when he comes in to bathe in the morning he will not have a stick. I shall wait here till he comes. Nagaina—do you hear me?—I shall wait here in the cool till daytime."

There was no answer from outside, so Rikki-tikki

knew Nagaina had gone away. Nag coiled himself down, coil by coil, round the bulge at the bottom of the water-jar, and Rikki-tikki stayed still as death. After an hour he began to move, muscle by muscle, toward the jar. Nag was asleep, and Rikki-tikki looked at his big back, wondering which would be the best place for a good hold. "If I don't break his back at the first jump," said Rikki, "he can still fight; and if he fights—O Rikki!" He looked at the thickness of the neck below the hood, but that was too much for him; and a bite near the tail would only make Nag savage.

"It must be the head," he said at last; "the head above the hood; and, when I am once there, I must not let go."

Then he jumped. The head was lying a little clear of the water-jar, under the curve of it; and, as his teeth met, Rikki braced his back against the bulge of the red earthenware to hold down the head. This gave him just one second's purchase, and he made the most of it. Then he was battered to and fro as a rat is shaken by a dog—to and fro on the floor, up and down, and round in great circles; but his eyes were red, and he held on as the body cart-whipped over the floor, upsetting the tin dipper and the soap-dish and the fleshbrush, and banged against the tin side of the bath. As he held, he closed his jaws tighter and tighter, for he made sure he would be banged to death, and, for the honor of his family, he preferred to be found with his teeth locked. He was dizzy, aching, and felt shaken to pieces when something went off like a thunderclap just behind him; a hot wind knocked him senseless and red fire singed his fur. The big man had been wakened by the noise, and had fired both barrels of a shot-gun into Nag just behind the hood.

Rikki-tikki held on with his eyes shut, for now he was quite sure he was dead; but the head did not move, and the big man picked him up and said: "It's the mongoose again, Alice; the little chap has saved *our* lives now."

One day Rikki scuttled to the veranda. Teddy and his mother and father were there at early breakfast; but Rikki-tikki saw that they were not eating anything. They sat stone-still, and their faces were white. Nagaina was coiled up on the matting by Teddy's chair, within easy striking distance of Teddy's bare leg, and she was sway-ing to and fro singing a song of triumph.

"Son of the big man that killed Nag," she hissed, "stay still. I am not ready yet. Wait a little. Keep very still, all you three. If you move I strike, and if you do not move I strike. Oh, foolish people, who killed my Nag!"

Teddy's eyes were fixed on his father, and all his father

could do was to whisper, "Sit still, Teddy. You mustn't move. Teddy, keep still."

Then Rikki-tikki came up and cried: "Turn round, Nagaina; turn and fight!"

"All in good time," said she, without moving her eyes. "I will settle my account with *you* presently. Look at your friends, Rikki-tikki. They are still and white; they are afraid. They dare not move, and if you come a step nearer I strike."

"Look at your eggs," said Rikki-tikki, "in the melon-bed near the wall. Go and look, Nagaina."

The big snake turned half round, and saw the egg on the veranda. "Ah-h! Give it to me," she said.

Rikki-tikki put his paws one on each side of the egg, and his eyes were blood-red. "What price for a snake's egg? For a young cobra? For a young king-cobra? For the last—the very last of the brood? The ants are eating all the others down by the melon-bed."

Nagaina spun clear round, forgetting everything for the sake of the one egg; and Rikki-tikki saw Teddy's father shoot out a big hand, catch Teddy by the shoulder and drag him across the little table with the tea-cups, safe and out of reach of Nagaina.

"Tricked! Tricked! Tricked! *Rikk-tchk-tchk!*" chuckled Rikki-tikki. "The boy is safe, and it was I—I—I that caught Nag by the hood last night in the bathroom." Then he began to jump up and down, all four feet together, his head close to the floor. "He threw me to and fro, but he could not shake me off. He was dead before the big man blew him in two. I did it. *Rikki-tikki-tchk-tchk!* Come then, Nagaina. Come and fight with me. You shall not be a widow long."

Nagaina saw that she had lost her chance of killing Teddy, and the egg lay between Rikki-tikki's paws. "Give me the egg, Rikki-tikki. Give me the last of my eggs, and I will go away and never come back," she said, lowering her hood.

"Yes, you will go away, and you will never come back; for you will go to the rubbish-heap with Nag. Fight, widow! The big man has gone for his gun! Fight!"

Rikki-tikki was bounding all round Nagaina, keeping just out of the reach of her stroke, his little eyes like hot coals. Nagaina gathered herself together, and flung out at him. Rikki-tikki jumped up and backward. Again and again and again she struck, and each time her head came

with a whack on the matting of the veranda and she gathered herself together like a watch-spring. Then Rikki-tikki danced in a circle to get behind her, and Nagaina spun round to keep her head to his head, so that the rustle of her tail on the matting sounded like dry leaves blown along by the wind.

He had forgotten the egg. It still lay on the veranda, and Nagaina came nearer and nearer to it, till at last, while Rikki-tikki was drawing breath, she caught it in her mouth, turned to the veranda steps, and flew like an arrow down the path, with Rikki-tikki behind her. When the cobra runs for her life, she goes like a whiplash flicked across a horse's neck.

Rikki-tikki knew that he must catch her, or all the trouble would begin again. She headed straight for the long grass by the thornbush. . . .

Then the grass by the mouth of the hole stopped waving, and Darzee said: "It is all over with Rikki-tikki! We must sing his death-song. Valiant Rikki-tikki is dead! For Nagaina will surely kill him underground."

So he sang a very mournful song that he made up all on the spur of the minute, and just as he got to the most touching part the grass quivered again, and Rikki-tikki, covered with dirt, dragged himself out of the hole leg by leg, licking his whiskers. Darzee stopped with a little shout. Rikki-tikki shook some of the dust out of his fur and sneezed. "It is all over," he said. "The widow will never come out again." And the red ants that live between the grass stems heard him, and began to troop down one after another to see if he had spoken the truth.

Rikki-tikki curled himself up in the grass and slept where he was—slept and slept till it was late in the afternoon, for he had done a hard day's work.

ONE cold rainy day when my father was a little boy, he met an old alley cat on his street. The cat was very drippy and uncomfortable so my father said, "Wouldn't you like to come home with me?"

This surprised the cat—she had never before met anyone who cared about old alley cats—but she said, "I'd be very much obliged if I could sit by a warm furnace, and perhaps have a saucer of milk."

"We have a very nice furnace to sit by," said my father, "and I'm sure my mother has an extra saucer of milk."

My father and the cat became good friends but my father's mother was very upset about the cat. She hated cats, particularly ugly old alley cats. "Elmer Elevator," she said to my father, "if you think I'm going to give that cat a saucer of milk, you're very wrong. Once

My Father's Dragon

BY RUTH
STILES GANNETT

Illustrated by

Ruth Chrisman Gannett

you start feeding stray alley cats you might as well expect to feed every stray in town, and I am *not* going to do it!"

This made my father very sad, and he apologized to the cat because his mother had been so rude. He told the cat to stay anyway, and that somehow he would bring her a saucer of milk each day. My father fed the cat for three weeks, but one day his mother found the cat's saucer in the cellar and she was extremely angry. She whipped my father and threw the cat out the door, but later on my father sneaked out and found the cat. To- gether they went for a walk in the park and tried to think of nice things to talk about. My father said, "When I grow up I'm going to have an airplane. Wouldn't it be wonderful to fly just anywhere you might think of!"

"Well," said the cat, "if you'd really like to fly that much, I think I know of a sort of a way you might get to fly while you're still a little boy."

"You mean you know where I could get an airplane?"

"Well, not exactly an airplane, but something even better. As you can see, I'm an old cat now, but in my younger days I was quite a traveler. My traveling days are over but last spring I took just one more trip and sailed to the Island of Tangerina, stopping at the port of Cranberry. Well, it just so happened that I missed the boat, and while waiting for the next I thought I'd look around a bit. I was particularly interested in a place called Wild Island, which we had passed on our way to Tangerina. Wild Island and Tangerina are joined to- gether by a long string of rocks, but people never go to Wild Island because it's mostly jungle and inhabit- ed by very wild animals. So, I de- cided to go across the rocks and ex- plore it for myself. It certainly is an interesting place,

but I saw something there that made me want to weep.

"Wild Island is practically cut in two by a very wide and muddy river," continued the cat. "This river begins near one end of the island and flows into the ocean at the other. Now the animals there are very lazy, and they used to hate having to go all the way around the beginning of this river to get to the other side of the island. It made visiting inconvenient and mail deliveries slow, particularly during the Christmas rush. Crocodiles could have carried passengers and mail across the river, but crocodiles are very moody, and not the least bit dependable, and are always looking for something to eat. They don't care if the animals have to walk around the river, so that's just what the animals did for many years.

"One day about four months before I arrived on Wild Island a baby dragon fell from a low-flying cloud onto the bank of the river. He was too young to fly very well, and besides, he had bruised one wing quite badly, so he couldn't get back to his cloud. The animals found him soon afterwards and everybody said, 'Why, this is just exactly what we've needed all these years!' They tied a big rope around his neck and waited for the wing to get well. This was going to end all their crossing-the-river troubles.

"They started training him to carry passengers, and even though he is just a baby dragon, they work him all day and all night too sometimes. They make him carry loads that are much too heavy, and if he complains, they twist his wings and beat him. He's always tied to a stake on a rope just long enough to go across the river. His only friends are the crocodiles, who say 'Hello' to him once a week if they don't forget. Really, he's the most

96

miserable animal I've ever come across. When I left I promised I'd try to help him someday, although I couldn't see how. The rope around his neck is about the biggest, toughest rope you can imagine, with so many knots it would take days to untie them all.

"Anyway, when you were talking about airplanes, you gave me a good idea. Now, I'm quite sure that if you were able to rescue the dragon, which wouldn't be the least bit easy, he'd let you ride him most anywhere, provided you were nice to him, of course. How about trying it?"

"Oh, I'd love to," said my father, and he was so angry at his mother for being rude to the cat that he didn't feel the least bit sad about running away from home for a-while.

That very afternoon my father and the cat went down to the docks to see about ships going to the Island of Tangerina. They found out that a ship would be sailing the next week, so right away they started planning for the rescue of the dragon. The cat was a great help in suggesting things for my father to take with him, and she told him everything she knew about Wild Island. Of course, she was too old to go along.

The night before my father sailed he borrowed his father's knapsack and he and the cat packed everything very carefully. He took chewing gum, two dozen pink lollipops, a package of rubber bands, black rubber boots, a compass, a tooth brush and a tube of tooth paste, six magnifying glasses, a very sharp jackknife, a comb and a hairbrush, seven hair ribbons of different colors, an empty grain bag with a label saying "Cranberry," some clean clothes, and enough food to last my father while

he was on the ship. He couldn't live on mice, so he took twenty-five peanut butter and jelly sandwiches and six apples, because that's all the apples he could find in the pantry.

When everything was packed my father and the cat went down to the docks to the ship. A night watchman was on duty, so while the cat made loud queer noises to distract his attention, my father ran over the gangplank onto the ship. He went down into the hold and hid among some bags of wheat. The ship sailed early the next morning.

My father hid in the hold for six days and nights. Twice he was nearly caught when the ship stopped to take on more cargo. But at last he heard a sailor say that the next port would be Cranberry.

After my father left the ship he walked until he came to a crossroads and he stopped to read the signs. Straight ahead an arrow pointed to the Beginning of the River; to the left, to the Ocean Rocks; and to the right, to the Dragon Ferry.

He hurried on but it was farther away than he had judged. He finally came to the river bank in the late afternoon and looked all around, but there was no dragon anywhere in sight. He must have gone back to the other side.

My father sat down under a palm tree and was trying to have a good idea when something big and black and hairy jumped out of the tree and landed with a loud crash at his feet.

"Well?" said a huge voice.

"Well what?" said my father, for which he was very sorry when he looked up and discovered he was talking to an enormous and very fierce gorilla.

"Well, explain yourself," said the gorilla. "I'll give you till ten to tell me your name, business, your age and what's in that pack," and he began counting to ten as fast as he could.

My father didn't even have time to say "Elmer Elevator, explorer," before the gorilla interrupted, "Too slow! I'll twist your arms the way I twist that dragon's wings, and then we'll see if you can't hurry up a bit." He grabbed my father's arms, one in each fist, and was just about to twist them when he suddenly let go and began scratching his chest with both hands.

"Blast those fleas!" he raged. "They won't give you a moment's peace, and the worst of it is that you can't even get a good look at them. Rosie! Rhoda! Rachel! Ruthie! Ruby! Roberta! Come here and get rid of this flea on my chest. It's driving me crazy!"

Six little monkeys tumbled out of the palm tree, dashed to the gorilla, and began combing the hair on his chest.

"Well," said the gorilla, "it's still there!"

"We're looking, we're looking," said the six little monkeys, "but they're awfully hard to see, you know."

"I know," said the gorilla, "but hurry. I've got work to do," and he winked at my father.

"Oh, Gorilla," said my father, "in my knapsack I have

six magnifying glasses. They'd be just the thing for hunting fleas." My father unpacked them and gave one to Rosie, one to Rhoda, one to Rachel, one to Ruthie, one to Ruby, and one to Roberta.

"Why, they're miraculous!" said the six little monkeys. "It's easy to see the fleas now, only there are hundreds of them!" And they went on hunting frantically.

A moment later many more monkeys appeared out of a nearby clump of mangroves and began crowding around to get a look at the fleas through the magnifying glasses. They completely surrounded the gorilla, and he could not see my father nor did he remember to twist his arms.

My father walked back and forth along the bank trying to think of some way to cross the river. He found a high flagpole with a rope going over to the other side. The rope went through a loop at the top of the pole and then down the pole and around a large crank. A sign on the crank said:

TO SUMMON DRAGON, YANK THE CRANK

REPORT DISORDERLY CONDUCT

TO GORILLA

From what the cat had told my father, he knew that the other end of the rope was tied around the dragon's neck, and he felt sorrier than ever for the poor dragon. If he were on this side, the gorilla would twist his wings until it hurt so much that he'd have to fly to the other side. If he were on the other side, the gorilla would crank the rope until the dragon would either choke to death or fly back to this side. What a life for a baby dragon!

My father knew that if he called to the dragon to come across the river, the gorilla would surely hear him, so he thought about climbing the pole and going across on the rope. The pole was very high, and even if he could get to the top without being seen he'd have to go all the way across hand over hand. The river was very muddy, and all sorts of unfriendly things might live in it, but my father could think of no other way to get across. He was about to start up the pole when, despite all the noise the mon-

keys were making, he heard a loud splash behind him. He looked all around in the water but it was dusk now, and he couldn't see anything there.

"It's me, Crocodile," said a voice to the left. "The water's lovely, and I have such a craving for something sweet. Won't you come in for a swim?"

A pale moon came out from behind the clouds and my father could see where the voice was coming from. The crocodile's head was just peeping out of the water.

"Oh, no thank you," said my father. "I never swim after sundown, but I do have something sweet to offer you. Perhaps you'd like a lollipop, and perhaps you have friends who would like lollipops, too?"

103

"Lollipops!" said the crocodile. "Why, that is a treat! How about it, boys?"

A whole chorus of voices shouted, "Hurrah! Lollipops!" and my father counted as many as seventeen crocodiles with their heads just peeping out of the water.

"That's fine," said my father as he got out the two dozen pink lollipops and the rubber bands. "I'll stick one here in the bank. Lollipops last longer if you keep them out of the water, you know. Now, one of you can have this one."

The crocodile who had first spoken swam up and tasted it. "Delicious, mighty delicious!" he said.

"Now if you don't mind," said my father, "I'll just walk along your back and fasten another lollipop to the tip of your tail with a rubber band. You don't mind, do you?"

"Oh no, not in the least," said the crocodile.

"Can you get your tail out of the water just a bit?" asked my father.

"Yes, of course," said the crocodile, and he lifted up his tail. Then my father ran along his back and fastened another lollipop with a rubber band.

"Who's next?" said my father, and a second crocodile swam up and began sucking on that lollipop.

"Now, you gentlemen can save a lot of time if you just line up across the river," said my father, "and I'll be along to give you each a lollipop."

So the crocodiles lined up right across the river with their tails in the air, waiting for my father to fasten on the rest of the lollipops. The tail of the seventeenth crocodile just reached the other bank.

When my father was crossing the back of the fifteenth

104

crocodile with two more lollipops to go, the noise of the monkeys suddenly stopped, and he could hear a much bigger noise getting louder every second. Then he could hear seven furious tigers and one raging rhinoceros and two seething lions and one ranting gorilla along with countless screeching monkeys, led by two extremely irate wild boars, all yelling, "It's a trick! It's a trick! There's an invasion and it must be after our dragon. Kill it! Kill it!" The whole crowd stampeded down to the bank.

As my father was fixing the seventeenth lollipop for the last crocodile he heard a wild boar scream. "Look, it came this way! It's over there now, see! The crocodiles made a bridge for it," and just as my father leapt onto the other bank one of the wild boars jumped onto the back of the first crocodile. My father didn't have a moment to spare.

By now the dragon realized that my father was coming to rescue him. He ran out of the bushes and jumped up and down yelling, "Here I am! I'm right here! Can you see me? Hurry, the boar is coming over on the crocodiles, too. They're all coming over! Oh, please hurry, hurry!" The noise was simply terrific.

My father ran up to the dragon, and took out his very sharp jackknife. "Steady, old boy, steady. We'll make it. Just stand still," he told the dragon as he began to saw through the big rope.

By this time both boars, all seven tigers, the two lions, the rhinoceros, and the gorilla, along with the countless screeching monkeys, were all on their way across the crocodiles and there was still a lot of rope to cut through.

"Oh, hurry," the dragon kept saying, and my father again told him to stand still.

"If I don't think I can make it," said my father, "we'll fly over to the other side of the river and I can finish cutting the rope there."

Suddenly the screaming grew louder and madder and my father thought the animals must have crossed the river. He looked around, and saw something which surprised and delighted him. Partly because he had finished his lollipop, and partly because crocodiles are very moody and not the least bit dependable and are always looking for something to eat, the first crocodile had turned away from the bank and started swimming down the river. The second crocodile hadn't finished yet, so he followed right

after the first, still sucking his lollipop. All the rest did the same thing, one right after the other, until they were all swimming away in a line. The two wild boars, the seven tigers, the rhinoceros, the two lions, the gorilla, along with the countless screeching monkeys, were all riding down the middle of the river on the train of crocodiles sucking pink lollipops, and all yelling and screaming and getting their feet wet.

My father and the dragon laughed themselves weak because it was such a silly sight. As soon as they had recovered, my father finished cutting the rope and the dragon raced around in circles and tried to turn a somersault. He was the most excited baby dragon that ever lived. My father was in a hurry to fly away, and when the dragon finally calmed down a bit my father climbed up onto his back.

"All aboard!" said the dragon. "Where shall we go?"

"We'll spend the night on the beach, and tomorrow we'll start on the long journey home. So, it's off to the shores of Tangerina!" shouted my father as the dragon soared above the dark jungle and the muddy river and all the animals bellowing at them and all the crocodiles licking pink lollipops and grinning wide grins. After all, what did the crocodiles care about a way to cross the river, and what a fine feast they were carrying on their backs!

As my father and the dragon passed over the Ocean Rocks they heard a tiny excited voice scream, "Bum cack! Bum cack! We dreed our nagon! I mean, we need our dragon!"

But my father and the dragon knew that nothing in the world would ever make them go back to Wild Island.

ALL the young folk in the village called him "Fish." It wasn't a good nickname, far from it. But Fish had plenty of grit and was bound he'd live the name down.

For an Eskimo boy of twelve Fish was unusually big and strong. He could throw a harpoon and shoot a bow almost as skilfully as a man. In time he'd make a top-notch hunter. He had the patience and endurance for it, and he was quick and eager to learn. Already he knew more than most of the older boys about the habits of animals.

As far back as he could remember, the one thing his heart had been set on was to be a whale hunter. Nothing in the world could be more exciting, thought Fish and every other boy in the village, than to join the men when they put out to sea in their kayaks after a bowhead whale.

Boy with a Harpoon

BY WILLIAM LIPKIND

Illustrated by

Nicolas Mordvinoff

It was almost taken for granted, before he got his nickname, that Fish would be the first boy in the village to go on a whale hunt. Everybody could see how old One Eye, the chief shaman of the village, felt about Fish. And it was One Eye, after all, who picked the whale hunters.

But now Fish's chances didn't look so good. It was his own fault, at least in part: he *had* been clumsy. In part it was bad luck.

Fish had been practicing in his father's kayak. He'd

108

been paddling round and round a small stretch of water. Some of the young folk were playing close by on the shore ice.

Fish was about to make a turn. He drove the kayak close to the shore ice. Perhaps too close. The kayak brushed against the edge of the ice and wobbled. One good stroke of the paddle would be enough to set it straight. But Fish tried too hard and lost his balance. The kayak tipped and rolled over. Splash! Into the water went Fish with the kayak on top of him. Before he could collect his wits, he'd swallowed a mouthful of water and dropped his paddle.

One of his friends, a young man by the name of Dance, ran to the edge of the ice. Reaching out with a long harpoon shaft, he righted the kayak and dragged the boy, dripping and ashamed, onto the ice.

"Look at the fish I've caught. Isn't he a beauty?" Dance never missed a chance for fun.

Boys and girls crowded around, laughing. "How do you like it out of the water, Fish?" "Take your scales off, Fish, they're dripping wet." Everybody had a remark. Even Fish could not help laughing, though the joke was on him.

From that time on, the name stuck. Only his grown-up relatives still used the kin names. Everybody else said "Fish" and Fish knew he'd have to do something out of the ordinary if he was to have a chance at the whale hunt. Fish didn't mope or sulk. He kept his eyes open for a chance to make a new name for himself.

One clear day in early spring Fish took his harpoon and line, and headed north across the shore ice.

Here and there a hole in the ice looked promising

109

Ordinarily, he'd have stopped and waited for a seal to come up to breathe. Not this day, though. Somehow he felt he could do better.

On and on he trudged, farther from the village than he'd gone before. Suddenly, way out on the sea ice, he saw a black dot.

"If that's a seal," said Fish to himself, "it's a big one."

The ice looked solid all the way, but Fish didn't take any chances. Every few steps he tested it, tap-tap, with the butt of his harpoon.

About three hundred yards from the seal Fish stopped. Seals have poor eyesight, he knew. Still, there was no point in taking the risk of being spotted.

He looked the seal over. It was an oogrug, a bearded seal, the largest member of the seal family. With growing excitement he noted that it was full-grown, the biggest oogrug he had ever seen.

The oogrug was basking in the sun near the hole in the ice through which it had come. It seemed to be fast asleep. But Fish knew that seals only take short naps on the ice, waking every minute or two to make sure no enemy is near.

Suddenly the oogrug twisted up its head and peered around. It could see nothing dangerous and it dropped back into its nap.

Fish looked over the lay of the land. Behind the oogrug the ice sloped upward slightly and then dropped away slowly. A long stone's throw beyond that, there was another hole in the ice. Fish saw that he had a chance if he used his wits and had plenty of luck.

He made a great circle around the place where the seal was. He moved quickly and quietly, keeping his eyes on the seal. When the oogrug lifted its head and looked around, Fish stopped and waited till the seal settled back to its doze.

It took a long time to reach the spot he had picked, the hole in the ice far beyond the seal. The slight rise against which the oogrug lay cut off the view. Fish could just make out the edge of the hole, but he could not see the oogrug.

He looked over his harpoon. Everything was in good shape. The line was solid. The end of the line was securely knotted behind the small wooden plug to which it was attached.

Fish touched the hood of his parka to make sure his hunting charm was safely there. He did not make a sound, but in his mind he hummed the hunting song his father had taught him. It was good to keep in touch with the hunting luck of his family and this song to Polar Bear was magically strong.

"Kiya ayaga." Most of the words that sang in his mind meant nothing, but they had power in them. Then came a few words that had meaning: "Give the oogrug a good sleep." Polar Bear, the great slayer of oogrugs, might hear the song and help.

Fish dipped the line and plug into the water. He kept them in a few minutes to make sure they were thoroughly soaked. Then, dropping to the ice, Fish began to creep toward the oogrug. Nothing existed in the world but the seal in front of him and the song in his mind.

For all his excitement there was no haste. He crawled slowly and carefully, keeping his body slightly sideways. A side view, Fish knew, would look to the seal like another seal. A head-on view might arouse its suspicion.

From time to time Fish stopped, lifted his head and looked around. He was acting like a seal so completely that he almost felt like a seal.

Fish was just at the top of the rise when he heard a splash. The oogrug had rolled over and plopped into the water for a dip.

Fish did not waste a minute. He went to work with feverish energy. He dug his knife into the ice and scooped out a deep but narrow hole, just big enough to admit the plug on his line. He shoved the plug down into the hole. On top he rammed down bits of snow and ice, stuffing the hole firmly. It wouldn't take long for the wet plug and line to freeze solidly into the ice.

Fish squirmed as close as he could get to the top of the rise without being spotted by the oogrug when it came out. He held his harpoon ready and waited intently. "Would the oogrug come up again? Had it sensed danger?"

The wait was not long. While Fish was still wondering whether the oogrug would come back, its head cut sleekly through the surface of the water. The oogrug looked around warily.

The coast seemed clear. With one heave the oogrug shot its great body smoothly out of the water and onto the ice. Shaking the water from its glistening hide, it clambered clumsily up the small slope.

This was his chance. Fish sprang to his feet, his harpoon poised at his shoulder. The oogrug seemed enormous. But this was no time for hesitation. Fish struck out with all his might and with perfect aim.

The barb of the harpoon sank deep into the upper curve of the oogrug's shoulder. With marvelous swiftness the bulky animal rolled over and into the water.

112

A wave of water sloshed the ice at the boy's feet and a length of line swept by him. But there was still line to spare when the pull eased off. Instead of going straight away, the oogrug, confused by pain, was swimming in circles in its frenzied attempt to get away from the barb in its shoulder.

From the moment he struck, Fish had been singing his hunting song out loud. Now, as fast as he could, he carved a big slab out of the ice of the slope and slid it down into the hole so that it jammed the line. He cut another slab and shoved that on top.

He did not stop until he was sure that the line was as safe as he could make it. If it were cut by rubbing against the edge of the ice, the oogrug would get away and all his work would go for nothing.

The next thing to do was to get help. Fish started for the village at a good clip. His hunting luck had held till now. He kept singing his song as he went: "Kiya ayaga."

He was in sight of the village when he met Bigfoot. Bigfoot was Dance's older brother, a goodnatured man of middle age. A store of meat and oil would be welcome to him.

"Can you help me carry some meat, uncle?" They were not close kin, but Fish had always called Bigfoot uncle.

"What have you caught, small nephew?" asked Bigfoot.

"I left my harpoon in a little seal. If it hasn't got loose, it's still there."

"Good," said Bigfoot. "Lead the way."

"Not so fast, uncle," said Fish. "You will need a sled."

"It must be something big then."

"If it hasn't shrunk, it will be more than we can carry."

They turned back to the village and Bigfoot went after his dogs and sled. Fish could see only a few old people and little children in the village. All the others were out hunting.

Luckily, just as Bigfoot was harnessing his dogs to the sled, Dance turned up and joined them. The two brothers were big men and noted for their strength. Bigfoot started his dogs with a shout. Fish rode the sled and the two men ran behind.

They reached the place of the hunt and after one look Bigfoot said: "It seems the line is still here, little nephew. Let's see if there is anything at the other end of the line."

Bigfoot cut the ice away from around the plug, freeing the end of the line. He tied it tightly to the back of his sled. Dance, meanwhile, cleared the ice from the top of the hole.

"Now, little nephew, start the dogs slowly."

Fish sent the dog team slowly forward, while Bigfoot and Dance eased the line away from the ice. Fish waited tensely, afraid that the oogrug had got away.

In a moment the body of the oogrug broke the surface of the water. Harpoon and line had held. The oogrug had worn itself out in the struggle to escape.

Dance and Bigfoot let out a shout. The huge bulk of the oogrug surprised them. It had never occurred to them that a boy would have the courage and skill to bring down a full-grown oogrug. They knew that no animal of the north, except perhaps the polar bear and the whale, is as hard to capture. This would have been a triumph for a man. It was the first oogrug of that spring season.

"Hold the sled," shouted Bigfoot. Dance and he pulled

with all their force and dragged the body of the oogrug out to the open ice.

"Younger brother," said Bigfoot to Dance, "it would be a pity to cut up a monster like this on the ice, as we usually do. Our nephew has done a big thing; we ought to do a little something too."

"You are right, older brother," said Dance with a grin. "Perhaps we can summon up a little strength just this once."

"Hold the dogs, little nephew," said Bigfoot, "and we'll see if we can find room for this big oogrug on the sled."

The boy had trouble holding the hungry dogs back. Dance and Bigfoot strained to lift the head and shoulders of the oogrug on to the back of the sled. The weight of the oogrug tipped the front of the sled upward.

Little by little, grunting and putting forth their strength together, Bigfoot and Dance inched the carcass up on the sled. The head flopped over the front, the tail hung down in back between the runners.

Dance and Bigfoot tied a number of thongs around to keep the carcass secure on the sled. The dogs were whining in their eagerness to go. They sensed the good meal ahead. The carcass was barely tied to the sled when they made off without waiting for a signal.

All the way to the village the men and the boy sang as they ran. Just outside the village a few children were playing. When they saw the sled coming, the little boys raced for it. The first to reach it would get a prize of meat, the others would get pieces of blubber.

The hunters had come back to the village by this time,

but there was no catch to compare with this. All the young men ran down to the beach to help unload the sled.

Fish could see that his father and mother were proud, though they said nothing.

Bigfoot spoke to them. "I have always called him little nephew."

Dance broke in: "I've heard another name too." The young folk laughed.

Bigfoot went on. "He did not speak of the oogrug. He said he had put his harpoon in a little seal. I will call him Little Seal."

"A good name." The boy's father spoke quietly. "Now I must get ready a drum." He turned to go, hiding his satisfaction.

The boys crowded around, joking. Now their jokes did not sting at all. "Little Seal, now you can sleep on the ice. Keep an eye out for Polar Bear." He was not Fish any longer; he had won a good name.

Little Seal's heart gave a leap. The drum was for him too, he knew. Catching the oogrug had brought him closer to being a man. Soon he would be able to drum at the dances, with the men and older boys.

NOW living in a jungle is very much like living next door to the zoo, except that the animals are not in cages, which makes quite a difference. Sometimes at night Kintu would lie awake and listen to the strange sounds made by wild creatures in the jungle, and be very afraid.

There was an insect which ticked all night long like a little watch, and an insect which made a loud noise like an alarm clock. There were the excited voices of suddenly awakened monkeys, and the croaking of big frogs which sounded like old men talking together in deep hoarse voices. There were panthers and leopards whose snarls were like the sound of thick canvas being torn. And there were the grunts of hippopotami who left the river and walked on land at night. There were noises made by nightjars and cicadas, and all the other hundreds of creatures who preferred to do their talking after dark.

Magic

BY
ELIZABETH ENRIGHT

*Illustrated by
Elizabeth Enright*

Kintu would lie on his hard earthen bed and shake with fright, because he knew that when he was older his father would expect him to hunt in the jungle and to know it as well as he knew his own village. It would never do for a chief's son to be afraid!

It worried Kintu badly, and finally he decided to go and see the witch doctor and ask him for a spell to make him braver.

118

So one morning, after breakfast, he stole away from his brothers and sisters and playmates, and all by himself walked to the witch doctor's hut.

It was set apart from the rest of the village, and on either side of the door were little idols carved of black wood. One had a very ugly, cross face, and one grinned from ear to ear showing a double row of square, ivory teeth. Kintu bowed and raised his spear to each of them, then he entered the hut and came face to face with the witch doctor.

The witch doctor was very old and very wise, and he wore a derby hat, which he had got from the same trader who brought the telephone wire. From his great height he looked down at Kintu, without smiling, and Kintu would have shaken in his shoes if he had any to shake in.

"Chief's son," said the witch doctor, "why have you come to see me?"

"Witch doctor," began Kintu bravely, "I am in great trouble. I am afraid of the jungle!" He paused, and glanced up to see if the witch doctor looked disapproving, but there was no change in the old man's expression, so he continued. "Yes, I'm afraid of it. All of it. Its beasts, its noises and its huge trees. I don't even like the way it smells. How can I ever be a great chief like my father when I am such a coward?"

He hung his head for he was very much ashamed.

"This is bad!" said the witch doctor. "I must think." And he sat down on the floor, pulled his derby hat over his nose and thought. Kintu leaned against the wall and watched him almost without breathing, he was so terribly excited.

After several minutes (long ones, they seemed) the

witch doctor stood up, pushing back his hat. Still without smiling he looked down at Kintu.

"Chief's son," he said, "I believe I have a cure for you."

He leaned down, took something out of a red earthenware bowl, and put it into Kintu's little black hand.

"Take this," he said, "and tomorrow, when the sun is at its highest, walk three hundred paces into the jungle towards the east. After you have walked for three hundred paces, plant this charm at the foot of the first baobab tree you find; then, when you have buried it, say these words—" (But what the words were I cannot tell you for they were black magic, and a secret.)

"In the jungle? All by myself?" asked Kintu in a timid voice.

"All by yourself, chief's son," said the witch doctor firmly.

Kintu walked slowly home. Once he stopped and opened his hand to see what the charm was like; it was nothing but the dry stone of a fruit and didn't look as though it had much magic in it; but the witch doctor had said it had, and Kintu believed him.

That evening he couldn't eat his supper and his mother was worried about him.

"You have been eating between meals again," she said. "When *will* you learn to leave that monkey-bread tree alone?"

But Kintu only sighed, and said nothing. Very late that night he lay awake and listened to the jungle sounds which seemed louder and more terrifying than ever. He thought the cicadas were chanting a jeering song: "Afraid, afraid, afraid," they cried, over and over again.

"Perhaps after tomorrow you'll be singing another song," whispered Kintu into the darkness; and feeling a little more cheerful, he went to sleep.

The next day dawned bright and very hot; and Kintu went through his duties in a daze.

When, soon after their morning meal, the sun had ridden to its highest point, and everybody else had gone to sleep in the shade, Kintu picked up his spear (ekonga), and holding the charm in his other hand, tiptoed through the drowsy village and into the jungle.

It was hot and steamy under the great trees; it smelled like the inside of a greenhouse, warm and damp. Everywhere the silk cotton trees raised their great trunks; and high, high overhead a whole, separate airy world existed: parrots called in cross voices, a thousand birds sang different songs, and monkeys leapt nimbly along the boughs, chattering and scolding.

121

Counting all the time, and forgetting to be afraid, Kintu looked up and stubbed his toe badly on a root. By this time he had walked his first hundred paces and was beginning his second hundred. The farther he walked the wilder the jungle grew, and he had to beat back the undergrowth and tear apart the vines which hung, covered with flowers, from every tree.

Once he surprised a group of little brown monkeys who were sitting sociably on the ground in a circle, eating berries. They simply leapt up the trunk of a palm tree when they saw him, and sat high in the leaves telling him what they thought of him till long after he had passed.

Great moths flew blindly into his face; and once he came upon a hibiscus bush so beautiful, with its flaming red flowers, that he stopped and stared at it.

All this time he had forgotten about being afraid, but now as he came to the middle of his last hundred paces the shadows seemed suddenly darker, and the trees taller than before, and he found himself counting more and more rapidly.

"Two hundred and eighty," said Kintu, leaping over a log, "two hundred and eighty-one—eighty-two—eighty-three . . ." On his right something gave a squeal and plunged into the bushes.

"Eighty-four, eighty-five," shouted Kintu in a loud, bold voice (he was running now), "eighty-six, eighty-seven, eighty-eight, eighty-nine . . ."

At last the three hundred paces were behind him, and he began to look about for a baobab tree.

There were silk cotton trees, and gum trees, and pandanus trees, and borassus trees, and ebony trees, and rubber trees, and mahogany trees, and kakula trees; but there was not a single baobab tree in sight!

122

Kintu sighed; his heart was beating like a tom-tom and the palms of his hands felt cold and damp; but he had come this far and he simply couldn't turn back till he had buried the magic fruit pit.

So he hunted and he hunted, and went farther and farther into the jungle, and at last he came upon an enormous baobab tree standing all by itself in a clearing.

He felt safer somehow now that he had found it, and with relief he knelt among its great roots and scooped out a hole in the ground with the head of his spear; he buried the charm and covered it with earth. After that, he said the words of black magic which the witch doctor had taught him.

Then he picked up his spear and started back.

It had taken him a long time to find the baobab tree and by now it was the middle of the afternoon; the shadows were growing longer.

A crowd of little gnats circled around his head as he walked, buzzing in high thin voices till his ears rang and he felt dizzy. He kept waving his spear at them to drive them away, but they didn't mind it in the least and came back again as soon as he stopped.

On and on stumbled Kintu, among flowers, and tendrils, and great leaves. He realized that he had lost his way, and that so far the magic had not worked, because he felt more frightened than ever.

He thought about his family all safe together in the village, and wondered when they would miss him and begin to look for him. He thought about the stories told by the old hunters of fierce lions who sometimes came into the jungle at night, of hyenas whose cry is like the

124

laughter of a devil-god, of great elephants with tusks of ivory who can uproot small trees with their trunks. He thought about the buried fruit pit and the magic words, and they seemed small protection against the jungle and its many dangers. He wished that he had never gone to see the witch doctor at all, and that he had allowed himself to be a coward in peace.

Kintu began to cry quietly, because he was sure that he would never see his family again, and he was terribly afraid. He stopped walking and stood very still among great ferns like giant feather dusters; it seemed foolish to go on when whatever direction he took was bound to be the wrong one.

It was growing darker now, and already the tree toads had begun their evening conversation. "Wack-a-wack-a-wack," they cried in harsh voices from every tree. The gnats, fortunately, had got tired of Kintu's waving spear and had all gone off together to find some other creature to torment; so except for the remarks of the tree toads, and the occasional cry of a bird, it seemed very still.

Then, all at once, quite near, he heard a sound like that of thick canvas being torn in two. The snarl of a leopard!

It no longer seemed useless to go on; in fact, it seemed most necessary to go somewhere very quickly; and Kintu, spear in hand, began to run faster than he had ever run before.

Ahead of him, six little monkeys, who had also heard the dangerous sound, went leaping and skipping along the ground at great speed. Kintu, feeling somehow that they were his friends, followed them; and when they came to a huge tree hung with creepers which the monkeys swarmed up neatly, like little sailors climbing up a rigging, he went right after them as fast as he could go.

Up and up he struggled, with his spear between his strong teeth, and his little black fingers and toes curling around the thick vine almost as cleverly as the monkeys' did. The creeper looped itself over one of the lower branches and returned to earth on the other side, so Kintu began climbing up the boughs; stretch, pull, swing! stretch, pull, swing!—till he had nearly reached the top of the tree, and then he sat down on a huge limb with

his shoulder against the broad trunk, and his spear across his knees. His heart was thumping like anything and he was out of breath, but he felt slightly safer.

The six little monkeys, who didn't seem to mind him at all, sat on a branch just above him, and said things very fast in monkey language about leopards. Kintu wished that he could understand them and join in their conversation; he wanted to ask them if leopards were very good at climbing trees. Still, even if he couldn't speak to them, it was a comfort just to have them there, and he hoped they wouldn't go away.

All about him stretched the strange leaves and branches of jungle trees, and below him he saw the great ferns and flowers through which he had beaten his way. Overhead the sky was a darker blue, with a little purple in it, and already there was a star, pale and cold, shining just over the place where the sun had set.

The air was filled with queer smells. A clump of yellow orchids bloomed in a deserted bird's nest several feet below him and gave off a perfume so strong and heavy that he grew tired of it very soon. There were big red berries on a tree nearby that had an odor rather like cough medicine; and you've been in the monkey house at the zoo, haven't you? So you know how the monkeys smelled.

It was really twilight now, and Kintu saw the bright busy lights of fireflies everywhere. Huge mosquitoes came whining out of the shadows, cicadas sang at the tops of their voices, and the tree toads almost screamed at each other. An evening wind stirred for a moment in the feathery treetops and moved the branch above Kintu where the monkeys were dozing in a row. It woke them up, and they chattered anxiously at each other for a minute. But they soon went back to sleep; and Kintu, feeling like the loneliest person on earth, continued to stare at the sparkling patterns made by fireflies against the darkness.

Presently the moon rose, huge and lopsided, above the world; each leaf glittered in its light, and the brass bracelets on Kintu's ankle looked as if they were made of purest gold.

The night was full of sounds: rustling sounds and scratchings and scamperings; squeaks and grunts in the darkness below; the singing of the night birds in the leaves above.

Then Kintu heard another sound—a new one. He heard the heavy, soft footsteps of an enormous creature stepping quietly; the snapping of shrubs and the squelching sound of wet earth under huge feet. He leaned forward and peered still more intently into the blackness below him. A tremendous shape, darker than the shadows from which it came, moved gently and ponderously towards the tree where he was hidden. Bigger than a house, it looked; almost as big as a mountain, Kintu thought. Slowly, slowly the Thing approached; then paused directly below him. Suddenly there was a faint sound of scraping, and the tree began to quiver as though in an earthquake; the monkeys jabbered nervously, and Kintu knew that an elephant, the largest of all wild creatures, was scratching his back on a branch.

Then slowly, as before, the great beast went on its way; the noise of snapping twigs and heavy tread grew fainter, and it was seen no more.

Hours passed; the moon was high in the sky; and Kintu, too tired to think of fear any longer, settled himself against the tree trunk and slept with the monkeys.

128

PICKEN was wide awake and listening intently.

"Tom-toms!" he exclaimed. Tom-toms are native drums. By gripping them in certain ways with one arm and beating with the other hand you can make high notes and low notes. By means of these sounds, messages can be sent. Often the use of tom-toms is called the Bush Telegraph. In the still tropical air, you can hear the sound a great distance and bushmen pick up messages from one village, tap them out on their tom-toms, and so on from village to village.

Picken understood the language of the tom-toms, so he listened very carefully. He wondered if he was needed at home because this was the only way in which a message could be sent to him. But no, it was not for him. Tap-tap-tap, TAP-TAP, tap-tap-tap, TAP-TAP, on and on went the message, repeated time and time again.

Picken Goes in Search of Gold

BY NORMAN DAVIS

Illustrated by Winslade

Picken couldn't make out every word, but this is roughly what it meant.

"Listen, everyone. Bojang, the Safu of Busumbala is sad and downcast. A messenger, bringing him a beautiful golden bracelet for his favorite daughter, has been set upon by thieves who have stolen the bracelet. Anyone finding it and returning it to the Safu will be greatly rewarded."

129

Picken was thrilled; he knew well what a great man the Safu was, even more powerful and important than an Alkali like his father.

"If only I could find the missing bracelet," said Picken to himself, "how wonderful to hand it to the Safu and claim the reward and then I could return in triumph to my father."

Suddenly he made up his mind. "I'm going to try to find it," he said aloud, but how to make a start, that was the difficulty. Judging from the sound of the tom-toms, Busumbala could only be a mile or two from where he was resting in his canoe, but the thieves could be hidden anywhere in the dense jungle which stretched for miles and miles in all directions. They might even now have reached the great river and made off in a boat.

Picken thought of all these possibilities, but was not discouraged. So keen was he on the idea of finding the bracelet that he wouldn't wait a minute.

"Come on, Benjie, we are going to find the stolen treasure."

Benjie woke up, stretched himself, yawned and leapt on to Picken's shoulder, ready for anything. Picken patted him.

"Listen, Benjie, we will first of all try to find the village of Busumbala and there we can ask in which direction the thieves are thought to have gone."

Benjie playfully bit Picken's ear, which seemed to mean that anything he said would suit Benjie!

"As we may be away for a day or two we must take provisions," said Picken. So he filled his pockets with rice. He then made sure his knife was safely fixed at his side and "I'd better take my bow and arrows," he said. "You never know in strange parts like these. We must also see that the canoe is safely moored in case someone tries to steal it."

So, paddling the canoe slowly as near to the bank as possible, Picken looked for a likely spot. He soon found a tiny creek where, during the rainy season, a stream had poured its waters into the bigger creek.

"This will do," thought Picken, and skilfully he steered for the opening. Palms and mangroves overhung so densely that in a short time the canoe was completely hidden.

Having made fast the canoe, Picken, with Benjie still clinging to his shoulder, scrambled ashore to look for an opening in the dense bush that might lead to the village.

. . . Picken hesitated. It was rather frightening really to venture into this jungle tunnel. Benjie was obviously uneasy, jumping from one shoulder to another, chattering nervously.

Picken didn't hesitate long, because his keenness to find the missing gold bracelet drove all his fears away.

"Cheer up, Benjie, I can look after you," said Picken bravely.

In they went. It grew darker and darker. . . .

"Better give up for the night," thought Picken. He didn't like the idea of spending the night so deep in the jungle, but there was nothing else for it. Benjie was frankly afraid and started one of his shivering fits. Picken decided that as snakes usually like the lower branches of trees and leopards don't climb very high, the best thing he could do was to climb up a good big tree and settle down in one of the upper branches.

He was a good climber and after selecting the right

tree, he was up it with an agility that almost equalled
Benjie's. He soon found a suitable branch, with thick
foliage so that he could not easily fall off. Benjie seemed
more settled now and wrapping his long tail round a
smaller branch for safety, he snuggled up to Picken and
promptly fell asleep.

It was pitch dark now, save for a few stars that Picken
could see above him. The day noises of the jungle had
died down and the night noises had hardly begun. It was
weirdly still. Picken didn't like it much, but he was a
brave boy and made the best of it. He was very tired and
soon he, too, was fast asleep.

It was the sound of voices that woke him up and, as
he had quite forgotten where he was, he very nearly fell
out of the tree! It was only Benjie clinging on to him, his
tail well coiled round the branch, that saved him.

Picken peered down from the tree and to his astonishment he could see four men lit up by a flaming torch
carried by one of them.

They were talking quite loudly and Picken could hear
plainly what they said, but the words were in a strange
language. Though Picken couldn't understand their language, he knew from the sound that they belonged to
the dreaded tribe known as Futankis. "Beware of the
Futankis, Picken," he had often heard his father say;
"they be thief men, plenty bad."

The moon was well up now and a few pale rays
struggled through the rich foliage. Picken could just see
the path below him. He had decided the best thing to do
was to keep quiet where he was, so as not to attract the
men's attention.

Picken was curious. Why should men, particularly
Futankis, be walking along this lonely disused path at
such a late hour? Then it dawned on him. Were they not
thief men? Probably they were just the thieves they were
seeking!

Picken was wildly excited, but he knew he must go
carefully. To see and not be seen, to hear and not to be
heard was his motto. With great speed, but silently and
skilfully he clambered down the tree, Benjie lightly skipping after him. His bare feet made no sound as he padded
lightly behind the four men. They were walking in single
file, the foremost carrying the flaming torch. Picken
paused for breath every now and then. The men were
moving lightly but quickly and he wanted to keep them in
view, but not to get near enough to be seen or heard.

On and on they went; the path that was still narrow
and winding seemed never to end.

133

Suddenly, the men screamed out in fright and broke into a run. Amidst all the palaver, Picken could hear a hissing sound. He stopped dead. How well he knew that sound. "Sah!" he said under his breath. "Sah" means snake, and snakes could be very very dangerous.

Benjie, who had been hopping along behind leapt up to his shoulder and hung on as he always did when danger was about. Cautiously Picken moved forward, peering into the pale darkness. He stopped again, looking intently upwards. There from a low bough a wicked-looking snake was hanging. It was swaying angrily backwards and forwards, its tail firmly twisted round the bough.

The moon pierced the gloom at this point and shone full on the snake. It was about five feet long, judged Picken, and its skin shone in the moonlight like dull steel. "A black mamba!" he whispered. Sure enough, here was one of the jungle's deadliest snakes, angry at missing its prey.

It would be folly to try to run, for it wouldn't be likely to miss a second time. One bite, Picken knew, would be the end of him. He had got his ju-ju, of course, and that should protect him. However, even a good ju-ju like the one Picken had might not work if he took such a foolish risk.

He was only a few yards away from the snake now, who was absolutely still. Very stealthily, Picken unhooked his bow from his shoulder, selected a sharp arrow from his quiver and took careful aim. He simply must not miss and, what was more important, he must hit the snake through the head, otherwise he might only make it more angry, and also give away where he was. That might well be the end of Picken and Benjie too.

134

He waited until the shining wavy head was still. He could clearly see its cruel eyes and deadly fangs. With all his strength, he drew back the bow string; Benjie kept perfectly still. "Fs-s-s-s-s," went the arrow, straight as a die. It was a perfect shot, clean through the head of the snake. It was quite dead and its body slowly unwound itself from the branch and fell with a thud almost at Picken's feet.

"Well, that's that," said Picken; "there is no time to be lost." So he bent down and made sure the snake was really quite dead. Then he picked out the arrow and carefully replaced it in his quiver. As nobody need be afraid of a dead snake, he hung it round his neck. This was a fearful shock for Benjie, who leapt off Picken's shoulder, chattering and making the most awful faces at him.

"Don't be so silly, Benjie," laughed Picken, "it can't hurt you now and I've an idea that this snake may help us later on. Just you see."

But Benjie didn't like the idea one bit and continued for some time to show how shocked he was.

"We must push on as quickly as possible now or else we may miss the thieves."

Picken started to run swiftly and silently; Benjie, still chunnering, followed a few paces behind. The thieves, having got over their fright, had settled down to walking again, so it didn't take long for Picken to catch sight of them and slowing down, he followed as before.

At last, the journey came to an end. The path had led them to the creek again, some miles farther away from Picken's canoe. They had paused at quite a large clearing which sank gently to the water, and there, moored at the bank under an overhanging tree, was a big canoe with a square sail.

The thieves jumped into the boat and Picken's heart sank. He dare not call out to them.

"After all this tracking, I shall lose them," sighed Picken.

But the men showed no signs of departing. Instead, they got out some food and some palm wine and were soon feasting merrily. One of them leapt on to the bank and made a fire. The feasting continued, which made Picken, who had climbed the overhanging tree and hidden himself, very very hungry.

After eating and drinking their fill, the thieves settled down in the canoe. One of them, who had been carrying the torch and who appeared to be their leader, drew out of his pocket a small bag made of goatskin. The others gathered round him. Slowly he opened it and in the light of the fire Picken, who was peering from above, could see him bring out of it the loveliest golden bracelet you have ever seen. It shone and glistened in the firelight as though it, too, were on fire.

"Fine—fine past everything," murmured Picken to himself. "I was right, these are the thieves who have stolen the Safu's bracelet."

Now Benjie, who had been peeping too, loved bright things as all monkeys do. He trembled with excitement and to Picken's horror, without warning, Benjie dropped on to the canoe, right into the middle of the astonished men. He snatched the bracelet and like a flash, he leapt back into the tree! The men jumped up shouting angrily and drew their knives. If they caught sight of him, Picken realized, they would not rest until he was captured.

The men were now peering up into the tree, but so far the thick wide leaves kept Picken and Benjie from view. Benjie was quite unaware of the danger and was carefully examining the bracelet by the light of the moon. Picken realized he must act quickly if he were to escape. Very gently he uncoiled the dead snake from his shoulders and holding it by its tail, he lowered it head first, bit by bit, through the thick leaves, swinging it slightly from side to side.

Lower and lower went the ugly head. Suddenly one of the men saw it and stood petrified with fear. Very soon, the other three saw it, too, and for a moment they all stood rooted to the spot. Picken let go of the tail and the snake fell with a plop into their midst!

There was pandemonium! With loud yells, the men scattered in all directions and vanished into the dark jungle.

"Come on, Benjie," shouted Picken, and in a second or two they were in the canoe. One slash from Picken's knife at the moorings and the large craft was free and floating gently into the middle of the creek. There was a fair breeze and, adjusting the sail, they moved silently and swiftly on their way. Picken's plan was to land as soon as there were signs of a village and find out the way to Busumbala.

Picken suddenly remembered the bracelet; Benjie was still clutching it and was most reluctant to hand it to Picken.

"It would be safer with me, Benjie," said Picken, and after much persuasion Benjie gave it to him. It was certainly a lovely thing, very heavy in solid gold, and most beautifully carved. Picken carefully put it into his pocket. Benjie tried to take it out several times, and in the end Picken had to smack his hand!

The moon had nearly set now and it was getting too dark to see, so Picken furled the sail and moored at the opposite bank in a well-hidden spot. He was dead tired after all the excitement and loss of sleep. Benjie was very tired, too. They had hardly closed their eyes, before they were fast asleep.

THIS time, no one came out to wish the hunters a speedy journey. From within the *igloo* no sound could be heard except the fretful crying of little Noota, curved against his mother's back. The whip cracked in the biting air. The dogs leaped forward. Tuktu felt his arms pulled almost from their sockets as he struggled to hold his place beside his father. He knew that Pum-yuk would pick up the tracks of *nanook* that they had seen that morning. The tracks would be easy to follow in the snow by the light of the flickering sky, for they were fresh. This very day *nanook* had made his way out to the dangerous sea ice.

As the sled leaped and slid over the rough snow, Tuktu remembered to whistle to the Spirits of the Aurora Borealis. And looking upward, he knew that the gods had heard, for the lights flared suddenly brighter.

"*Nanook! Nanook!*" Pum-yuk shouted to the dogs.

One Day with Tuktu

BY
ARMSTRONG SPERRY

Illustrated by

Armstrong Sperry

The animals were panting with eagerness and excitement. The greatest moment in the life of the husky is when he comes face to face with the polar bear. *Nanook* is the most powerful animal in the North Land. The sled crunched past the place where the seal had been killed that morning. How long ago that seemed, thought Tuktu. Now they were approaching the edge of the dangerous sea ice. Out here the world was filled with sound. As the sled rattled along, Tuktu could hear the grinding crunch of ice, the splash of frightened seals, the bellow of the walrus. There came the whir and beat of wings as a flock of geese flew overhead. This was the first time in his young life that Tuktu had ever been allowed way out here. He was so thrilled that he forgot the danger of it.

"*Nanook! Nanook!*" Pum-yuk was urging his dogs on.

Their noses never left the snow. Their flying heels threw back clouds of it, like powder. Suddenly Kingmik began a furious barking. The others took it up. The tracks of *nanook* were clearer now. He could not be far off. With fresh speed the dogs leaped onward.

Nanook saw them first. He had killed a seal, and he rose to his feet with an angry roar. What enemy was this, invading his kingdom? The dogs stopped in their tracks. Looking over the top of the sled, Tuktu's eyes fell on the biggest animal he had ever seen. *Nanook* towered white and ghostly against the night sky. The little boy caught his breath when he saw the long, narrow head, the gleaming teeth, the bits of foam dripping from his open jaws. *Nanook* stood upright on his hind legs, his great paws outstretched.

Pum-yuk stooped and cut the thong that held the traces of the dog harness. Instantly the huskies leaped to the attack. Savage snarls and howls filled the air. The dogs formed a circle about the bear. Those in front darted in whenever they saw an opening. Then they retreated before the sweeping paws, while those in the rear snapped at the animal's shaggy hind legs.

Now *nanook* dropped on all fours, roaring his rage. He stretched out his long neck, holding his head low. His powerful legs thrashed a circle around him. Again the dogs fell back. *Nanook* rose on his hind legs . . . up, up he towered. Tuktu was breathless with excitement. He clutched his bow and arrows as tightly as he could. He saw his father advancing toward the bear with his two harpoons.

Then it was that Kingmik, the leader dog, sprang for *nanook's* throat. The bear turned aside to strike at him.

142

At that second, Pum-yuk hurled his harpoon. It buried itself in the bear's ribs, just over the heart. With a sweep of his paw, *nanook* broke off the wooden handle. He advanced, bellowing with pain and rage. Again Kingmik sprang for him. A sweeping paw hurled the dog through the air, to fall twenty feet away.

But it gave Pum-yuk his chance. He threw his second harpoon. Swift and eager, the weapon struck its mark. But a terrible thing happened: as he hurled the heavy weapon, Pum-yuk lost his footing on the ice. He fell—his right leg cracking under him.

The bear plunged forward—straight for Pum-yuk. *Nanook* was mortally wounded but his strength was great.

"Tuktu!" shouted Pum-yuk. "Tuktu! Your arrows!"

Tuktu's icy hands raised the bow. His eye ran along the arrow. All his strength went into that pull on the cord. The wide-open jaws of *nanook* were almost upon his father.

"Quick, Tuktu! Quick!"

Pinnnng! went the snap of the bowstring. Clean and straight the arrow found its mark. Into the wide-open jaws of *nanook*. Up through the roof of his mouth.

With a thundering cough the bear fell forward, not a foot from Pum-yuk. It was a shot to warm a hunter's heart. Pum-yuk himself could have done no better. Men would talk about it when Tuktu was old.

The dogs rushed in, eager to tear the bear limb from limb.

"Back, Kingmik! Back, Apek!" Tuktu seized the walrus whip and fought off the dogs. They retreated and squatted on their haunches, licking their chops. Tuktu ran to his father's side.

"*Ai-a!*" cried Pum-yuk. "I have broken my leg. We are lost, my son. You can never drive the dog team back to the *igloo*. We shall perish out here on the sea ice!"

But Tuktu laughed. Victory sang in his heart. "Do you think I'm afraid of Kingmik!" he cried. "I can manage the dogs. Come, let me help you to the sled."

Pum-yuk was weak with pain. He dragged himself to the sled with his son's help, then sank down exhausted. Tuktu caught up the traces. He cracked the whip and shouted at the dogs. Kingmik eyed him slyly, as if to say, "You don't think I'm going to pay any attention to you, do you!" Nevertheless the leader dog slunk into place in the team. Then Tuktu ran back to *nanook*. His knife flashed right and left as he cut off as much meat as he thought the dogs could pull with the added weight of Pum-yuk. Then he dragged it to the sled and loaded it on as best he could. It took every ounce of strength in his young arms to lift the heavy burden. His father was powerless to help him.

Tuktu stood up very straight and rapped with the whip on the sled handle. Instantly the dogs leaped to their feet—all except Kingmik. He took his time about it.

"You, Kingmik! Up and go!" Tuktu cried.

With a "*houk!*" and an "*ai-a-ai!*" they were off, clattering over the rough ice. Before they had gone many paces, Tuktu knew that Kingmik was lagging.

"Keep the traces taut, you Kingmik!" he shouted in his loudest voice.

But the leader dog looked back over his shoulder

144

and it seemed that he grinned with scorn. When the leader lags, the other dogs will lag, too. Tuktu cracked the whip through the air. Not for nothing had he practiced with this walrus whip. The lash was twenty feet long, but the boy snapped it so skilfully that the tip nicked a piece out of Kingmik's ear.

With a howl of pain the leader dog stopped. Then he sat down. Every other dog sat down, too. The sled skidded and came to a halt. The moment had come. Kingmik must learn who was master. Tuktu left the back of the sled and advanced toward the wolf dog. The animal crouched and bared his teeth. With a terrible crack, Tuktu brought the heavy whip handle down over the dog's nose. Yelping with pain and astonishment, Kingmik buried his nose in his paws. Then he fawned at Tuktu's feet.

"You, Kingmik!" the little boy cried. "I am master, do you hear! Now up! Up and go!"

The dogs leaped to their feet and strained forward. No longer did Kingmik shirk his job. He set his fastest

pace. Over the ice they tore at a great clip. Tuktu was so warm with his exertion that he threw back the hood of his fur shirt.

Then, for the first time, he noticed that there were pools of water on the sea ice. The water hadn't been there on the trip out . . . The crunch and grind of the ice floe took on new meaning. The sea ice—it was preparing to break away from the land ice! Tuktu knew a moment of panic. His heart sank. But still he cracked the whip and urged the dogs onward. Pum-yuk seemed to have fainted with pain. He huddled, silent and still, on top of the sled. There was no help to be had from him.

There was still far to go. How many miles, the boy did not know. Through the shallow pools they splashed. Now cracks were appearing in the ice—black holes through which Tuktu could see the dark waters below.

"On, Kingmik! On, Apek! Keep the traces taut!"

The sled swung crazily over the black cracks. The noise of the crunching ice was terrible now. Oh, oh, would they never reach the shore ice? The cracks were getting wider and wider. The dogs whined as they leaped and ran.

"On, Kingmik! On, Apek! Keep the traces taut!"

One mile . . . two . . . how many more?

Suddenly a different sound came from under the runners. A solid sound. Here it was—the shore ice! Joy sang in Tuktu's heart as they sped over the rough surface. They were safe now. Safe! Once again that day he passed the hole where he and Pum-yuk had killed the seal. Almost before he knew it, they were again within sight of the *igloo*.

The barking of the dogs threw the *igloo* into confusion. Even above the uproar, Tuktu could hear the happy shouts of his family. They all came running out. They were worried when they saw Pum-yuk, but joyous when they found that he had nothing worse than a broken leg.

"And what—what is *that!*" exclaimed Bearded Seal, pointing to the bundle on top of the sled.

"Oh, just a little bear that happened to get in our way," answered Tuktu, with the modesty becoming an Eskimo hunter. "He was a very stupid bear. He did not know how to run away."

Inside the *igloo* the lamps had been filled with flaming oil. Tuktu must tell the whole story, over and over again. Pum-yuk's leg was bound with strong thongs to the shaft of a harpoon. Soon, promised Bearded Seal, it would grow well and straight again. In the meantime the family would be provided for. There was a new hunter in the family. Tuktu was a man! Little Oopik's eyes were as round as coffee cups. He seemed about to burst with pride as he looked at his brother. Even Hiki chewed down the young hunter's boots with a new show of respect.

Then it was that Tuktu gave them his biggest surprise. From within the fold of his coat, he brought forth the red heart of *nanook!* Even in the excitement of defending his father, he had not forgotten the reason for their hunt. The boy's mother wept as she dropped the precious object into the boiling kettle.

Now the *igloo* rang with laughter and fun. Soon little Noota would be well again. This was the most wonderful day of their lives! They would sing and dance and tell stories. They would have a feast—a big feast! Boiled seal and bear steaks. Caribou fat and frozen caribou meat.

Dried fish and slices of frozen reindeer stomachs filled with moss and twigs for "salad." Cylinders of marrow cracked from the leg bones. And *mak-kak,* the greatest tidbit of all—the outer covering of white porpoise skin. (It tastes like gelatin or like boiled white of egg.) Mmmmm! How delicious!

"*Ka-poon-ga!* I am hungry!" cried Bearded Seal.

"*Ka-poon-ga! Ka-poon-ga!*" cried everyone else, all at the same time.

The lamps flared and the kettles boiled. The snow ceiling melted and dripped on everybody, and no one minded, even though they had put on their best furs for the celebration. Grandmother had on her dancing boots of softest seal, edged with ermine. Hiki was wearing her jacket of delicate lemming, decorated with bands of Arctic hare.

Bearded Seal was composing a new song in Tuktu's honor. Pum-yuk had recovered his strength. He was lying on the bed platform, cracking marrow from reindeer legs. Oopik was popping huge pieces of steaming bear meat into his mouth, and chewing them as if he could never get enough. Tuktu was so tired with the excitement of the day that he could scarcely keep his eyes open. But he was the hero of the hour. Every moment someone was pressing a new tidbit upon him.

"Will you eat this choice bite, O Tuktu?"

"Will you taste this bit of gizzard, O mighty hunter?"

But at last he could not sit upright any longer. He crawled into his sleeping bag and snuggled down next to his father. Pum-yuk reached over and laid his hand for a moment upon the little boy's forehead. That was the man's way of saying how proud he was of this fine son. Outside, the wind howled and whistled across the Arctic ice fields. The dogs sent up their mournful chorus to the fading sky. But how soft and warm the reindeer sleeping bag felt! Oh! the little boy wished that he might sleep for days and days.

"Look, Tuktu!" Mother's voice sounded in his ear. "Look, my son, at the little one."

Tuktu struggled to open his eyes. His mother was holding back her hood for Tuktu to see. There, warm against her body, lay little Noota, sleeping sweetly.

"The heart of the Great White One has done its work," his mother whispered. "See how sweetly he sleeps! He has not cried once. O Tuktu, I—"

But Tuktu did not hear. Sleep weighted his eyelids. He was dreaming of the summer to come. Then, for two short months, flowers would glow yellow and purple and white against the ridges, and salmon would be swimming in the clear streams.

149

SHERWOOD in the twilight,
    is Robin Hood awake?
Grey and ghostly shadows
    are gliding through the brake,
Shadows of the dappled deer,
    dreaming of the morn,
Dreaming of a shadowy man
    that winds a shadowy horn.

Robin Hood is here again: all his merry thieves
Hear a ghostly bugle-note shivering through the leaves,
Calling as he used to call, faint and far away,
In Sherwood, in Sherwood,
    about the break of day.

Merry, merry England
    has kissed the lips of June;
All the wings of fairyland
    were here beneath the
      moon,
Like a flight of rose-leaves
    fluttering in a mist
Of opal and ruby
    and pearl and amethyst.

A Song
of Sherwood

BY ALFRED NOYES

Illustrated by
Alexander Dobkin

Merry, merry England is waking as of old,
With eyes of blither hazel and hair of brighter gold;
For Robin Hood is here again beneath the bursting spray
In Sherwood, in Sherwood, about the break of day.

Love is in the greenwood building him a house
Of wild rose and hawthorn and honeysuckle boughs;

150

Love is in the greenwood, dawn is in the skies,
And Marian is waiting with a glory in her eyes.

Hark! The dazzled laverock climbs the golden steep!
Marian is waiting; is Robin Hood asleep?
Round the fairy grass-rings frolic elf and fay,
In Sherwood, in Sherwood, about the break of day.

Oberon, Oberon,
    rake away the gold,
Rake away the red leaves,
    roll away the mould,
Rake away the gold leaves,
    roll away the red,
And wake Will Scarlett
    from his leafy forest bed.

Friar Tuck and Little John are riding down together
With quarter-staff and drinking-can
   and grey goosefeather.
The dead are coming back again,
   the years are rolled away
In Sherwood, in Sherwood, about the break of day.

Softly over Sherwood the south wind blows.
All the heart of England hid in every rose
Hears across the greenwood the sunny whisper leap,
Sherwood in the red dawn, is Robin Hood asleep?

Hark, the voice of England wakes him as of old
And, shattering the silence with a cry of brighter gold,
Bugles in the greenwood echo from the steep,
Sherwood in the red dawn, is Robin Hood asleep?

Where the deer are gliding down the shadowy glen
All across the glades of fern he calls his merry men—
Doublets of the Lincoln green glancing through the May
In Sherwood, in Sherwood, about the break of day—

Calls them and they answer: from aisles of oak and ash
Rings the *Follow! Follow!* and the boughs begin to crash,
The ferns begin to flutter and the flowers begin to fly,
And through the crimson dawning the robber band goes by.

Robin! Robin! Robin! All his merry thieves
Answer as the bugle-note shivers through the leaves,
Calling as he used to call, faint and far away,
In Sherwood, in Sherwood, about the break of day.

152

Maps

BY DOROTHY BROWN THOMPSON

Illustrated by Joseph Low

Hᴵᴳᴴ adventure
    And bright dream—
Maps are mightier
    Than they seem:

Ships that follow
    Leaning stars—
Red and gold of
    Strange bazaars—

Ice floes hid
    Beyond all knowing—
Planes that ride where
    Winds are blowing!

Train maps, maps of
    Wind and weather,
Road maps—taken
    Altogether

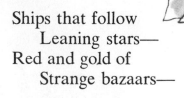

Maps are really
    Magic wands
For home-staying
    Vagabonds!

153

Pirate Story

BY ROBERT
LOUIS STEVENSON

Illustrated by
Tasha Tudor

THREE of us afloat in the meadow by the swing,
  Three of us aboard in the basket on the lea.
Winds are in the air, they are blowing in the spring,
  And waves are on the meadow like the waves there
    are at sea.

Where shall we adventure, to-day that we're afloat,
  Wary of the weather and steering by a star,
Shall it be to Africa, a-steering of the boat,
  To Providence, or Babylon, or off to Malabar?

Hi! but here's a squadron a-rowing on the sea—
  Cattle on the meadow a-charging with a roar!
Quick, and we'll escape them, they're as mad as they
    can be,
The wicket is the harbor and the garden is the shore.

154

Where Go the Boats?

BY ROBERT
LOUIS STEVENSON

Illustrated by
Dorothy P. Lathrop

Dark brown is the river,
 Golden is the sand.
It flows along forever,
 With trees on either hand.

Green leaves a-floating,
 Castles of the foam,
Boats of mine a-boating—
 Where will all come home?

On goes the river
 And out past the mill,
Away down the valley,
 Away down the hill.

Away down the river,
 A hundred miles or more,
Other little children
 Shall bring my boats ashore.

155

LITTLE Tim lived in a house by the sea.

He wanted very much to be a sailor.

When it was fine he spent the day on the beach playing in and out of the boats, or talking to his friend the old boatman who taught him all about the sea and ships.

Sometimes Tim astonished his parents by saying, "That's a Cunarder," or "Look at that Barquentine on the port bow."

When it was wet Tim would visit Captain McFee, who would tell him about his voyages and sometimes give him a sip of his grog, which made Tim want to be a sailor more than ever.

But alas for Tim's hopes. When he asked his mummy and his daddy if he could be a sailor they laughed and said he was much too young, which made Tim very sad.

He was so sad that he resolved to run away to sea.

One day the old boatman

Little Tim and the Brave Sea Captain

BY

EDWARD ARDIZZONE

Illustrated by

Edward Ardizzone

told Tim that he was going out in his motor boat to a steamer which was anchored some way out. Would Tim like to come, too? Tim was overjoyed.

The boatman went on to say that the Captain of the steamer was a friend of his, and, as the steamer was about to sail, he wanted to say good-bye to him.

156

Tim helped the boatman to launch the boat and off they went.

Tim got more and more excited as they neared the steamer as he had never been in one before.

When they arrived alongside they clambered on board. Tim was left on the deck while the boatman went to see the Captain who was in his cabin.

Now Tim had a great idea. He would hide and when the boatman left, not seeing Tim, he would forget all about him.

This is exactly what happened.

Off went the boatman and away went the steamer with Tim on board.

When Tim thought that there was no chance of being put on shore he showed himself to a sailor.

"Oi," said the sailor. "What are you doing here? Come along with me, my lad. The Captain will have something to say to you."

When the Captain saw Tim he was furious, and said Tim was a stowaway and must be made to work his passage.

So they gave Tim a pail and a scrubbing brush and made him scrub the deck, which Tim found very hard work. It made his back ache and his fingers sore. He cried quite a lot and wished he had never run away to sea.

After what seemed hours to Tim the sailor came and said he could stop work and that he had not done badly for a lad of his size. He then took Tim to the galley where the cook gave him a mug of cocoa.

Tim felt better after the cocoa and when the sailor found him a bunk he climbed in and was soon fast asleep.

He was so tired that he did not even bother to take off his clothes.

Tim soon got accustomed to life on board. As he was a bright boy, and always ready to make himself useful, it was not long before he became popular with the crew. Even the Captain said that he was not too bad for a stowaway.

Tim's best friend was the cook who was a family man. Tim would help him in the galley and in return get any nice tidbits that were going.

158

Besides helping the cook Tim would run errands and do all sorts of odd jobs, such as taking the Captain his dinner and the second mate his grog, helping the man at the wheel, and sewing buttons on the sailors' trousers.

One morning the wind started to blow hard and the sea became rough which made the steamer rock like anything. Poor Tim felt very sick and could not eat any of the tidbits that the cook gave him.

All that day the wind blew harder and harder and the sea got rougher and rougher, till by nightfall it was blowing a terrible gale.

In the middle of the night there was a fearful crash. The ship had struck a rock.

The sailors rushed on deck shouting, "We are sinking. To the boats. To the boats." With great difficulty they launched the boats and away they went in the raging sea.

160

BUT—they had quite forgotten Tim. He was so small and frightened that nobody had noticed him.

Tim crept onto the bridge where he found the Captain who had refused to leave the ship.

"Hullo, my lad," said the Captain. "Come, stop crying and be a brave boy. We are bound for Davy Jones's locker, and tears won't help us now."

So Tim dried his eyes and tried not to be too frightened. He felt he would not mind going anywhere with the Captain, even to Davy Jones's locker.

They stood hand in hand waiting for the end.

Just as they were about to sink beneath the waves

Tim gave a great cry. "We're saved! We're saved!" He had seen the lifeboat coming to rescue them.

The lifeboat came alongside and a life line was thrown to them, down which, first Tim and then the Captain were drawn to safety.

Hardly had they left the steamer when it sank beneath the waves.

When the lifeboat came into the harbor, the crowd which had gathered on the quay to watch its return gave a great cheer. They had seen Tim and the Captain, and realized that the lifeboat had made a gallant rescue.

When the lifeboat docked, Tim was lifted out and he and the Captain were taken to the nearest house, where they were wrapped in blankets and sat in front of the fire with their feet in tubs of hot water. Then having got nice and warm they were put to bed where they slept hours and hours.

The next morning Tim
sent a telegram to his parents
saying that he was taking
the train home and that the
Captain was coming too. Then he and the Captain, after
thanking the lifeboatmen and the kind people who had
put them up, went to the station and caught their train.

Tim's parents were at the garden gate to give them a
great welcome when they arrived. Captain McFee and
the boatman were there, too. You can imagine how
pleased Tim was to see his daddy and his mummy and his
old friends again.

The Captain told Tim's parents all about their adventures and how brave Tim had been and he asked them
if they would let Tim come with him on his next voyage
as he felt that Tim had the makings of a fine sailor.

Tim was very pleased and happy to hear his parents
say yes.

The lifeboatmen were pleased, too, as they were pre-
sented by the Mayor with medals for bravery.

Freight Boats

BY JAMES S. TIPPETT

Illustrated by Hans A. Mueller

BOATS that carry sugar
And tobacco from Havana;
Boats that carry coconuts
And coffee from Brazil;
Boats that carry cotton
From the city of Savannah;
Boats that carry anything
From any place you will.

Boats like boxes loaded down
With tons of sand and gravel;
Boats with blocks of granite
For a building on the hill;
Boats that measure many thousand
Lonesome miles of travel,
As they carry anything
From any place you will.

Ferryboats

BY JAMES S. TIPPETT

Illustrated by Hans A. Mueller

OVER the river,
Over the bay,
Ferryboats travel
Every day.

Most of the people
Crowd to the side
Just to enjoy
Their ferryboat ride.

Watching the sea gulls,
Laughing with friends,
I'm always sorry
When the ride ends.

165

Pirate Wind

BY MARY JANE CARR

Illustrated by Susanne Suba

THE autumn wind's a pirate,
　　Blustering in from sea;
With a rollicking song, he sweeps along,
　　Swaggering boist'rously.

His skin is weather-beaten;
　　He wears a yellow sash,
With a handkerchief red about his head,
　　And a bristling black mustache.

He laughs as he storms the country,
　　A loud laugh and a bold;
And the trees all quake and shiver and shake,
　　As he robs them of their gold.

The autumn wind's a pirate,
　　Pillaging just for fun;
He'll snatch your hat as quick as that,
　　And laugh to see you run!

The Wave   BY HARRY BEHN

1 THERE were lonesome birds on a misty shore,
2 And a kind of a far-off rumbling roar,
3 And creatures that dig in the sand to hide,
4 And empty shells at the edge of a tide.
all The water was blue and smooth and wide—
      Only a tired old sea.

all Then slowly a big wave grew and grew,
all A white wave spilled from the top of the blue
solo And roared up the shore to splash me! Instead,
all It splashed itself, and curled back to its bed
      Like a tired old dragon not quite dead—
            solo But dragons don't frighten me!

O Sailor, Come Ashore
BY CHRISTINA ROSSETTI

O SAILOR, come ashore,
   What have you brought for me?
Red coral, white coral,
   Coral from the sea.

            I did not dig it from the ground,
               Nor pluck it from a tree;
            Feeble insects made it
               In the stormy sea.

167

Once there was a very young little dog whose name was Angus, because his mother and father came from Scotland.

Although the rest of Angus was quite small, his head was very large and so were his feet.

Angus was curious about many places and many things:

He was curious about what lived under the sofa and in dark corners and who was the little dog in the mirror.

He was curious about Things-Which-Come-Apart and those Things-Which-Don't-Come-Apart, such as slippers and gentlemen's suspenders and things like that.

Angus was also curious about Things-Outdoors but he could not find out much about them because of a leash.

The leash was fastened at one end to the collar around his neck and at the other end to somebody else.

Angus and the Ducks

BY MARJORIE FLACK

Illustrated by
Marjorie Flack

But Angus was most curious of all about a noise which came from the other side of the large green hedge at the end of the garden.

The noise usually sounded like this: Quack! Quack! Quackety! Quack!!

But sometimes it sounded like this: Quackety! Quackety! Quackety! Quack!!

168

One day the door between outdoors and indoors was left open by mistake; and out went Angus without the leash or somebody else.

Down the little path he ran until he came to the large green hedge at the end of the garden.

He tried to go around it but it was much too long. He tried to go over it but it was much too high. So Angus went under the large green hedge and came out on the other side.

There, directly in front of him, were two white

ducks. They were marching forward, one-foot-up and one-foot-down. Quack! Quack! Quackety! Quack!!!

Angus said: WOO-OO-OOF!!!

Away went the ducks all of a flutter. Quackety! Quackety! Quackety! Quackety! Quackety!!!

Angus followed after.

Soon the ducks stopped by a stone watering trough under a mulberry tree.

Angus   stopped,   too.
Each duck dipped a yellow
bill in the clear cool water.
Angus watched. Each duck

170

took a long drink of the cool clear water. Still Angus watched. Each duck took another long drink of cool clear water.

Then Angus said: WOO-OO-OOF!!!

Away the ducks scuttled and Angus lapped the cool clear water.

Birds sang in the mulberry tree.

The sun made patterns through the leaves over the grass.

The ducks talked together: Quack! Quack! Quack! Then: HISS-S-S-S-S-S-S!!! HISS-S-S-S-S-S-S!!!

The first duck nipped Angus's tail! HISS-S-S-S-S-S-S!!! HISS-s-s-s-s-s-s!!! The second duck flapped his wings!

Angus scrambled under the large green hedge, scurried up the little path, scampered into the house and crawled under the sofa.

For exactly three minutes by the clock, Angus was not curious about anything at all.

Jippy and Jimmy

BY LAURA E. RICHARDS

JIPPY and Jimmy
    were two little dogs.
They went to sail
    on some floating logs;
The logs rolled over,
    the dogs rolled in,
And they got very wet,
    for their clothes were thin.

Jippy and Jimmy
    crept out again.
They said, "The river
    is full of rain!"
They said, "The water
    is far from dry!
Ki-hi! ki-hi!
    ki-*hi*-yi! ki-hi!"

Jippy and Jimmy
    went shivering home.
They said, "On the river
    no more we'll roam;
And we won't go to sail
    until we learn how,
Bow-wow! bow-wow!
    bow-*wow*-wow! bow-wow!"

OH, wind, blow softly over my sheep
Away from the lion
And over the lamb
Blow softly.

Over the grasses
And pointed flowers
Blow softly.

Oh, wind, blow softly out of the blue
Over the white
And the black sheep, too.
Blow softly.

Little Lost Lamb

BY GOLDEN MacDONALD

Illustrated by Leonard Weisgard

HIGH in the mountains where the green grass ends and the snow begins, the shepherd was singing.

Below him in the green grass huddled the sheep—a great gray moving field of young lambs with their mothers. And in all that soft flock of moving gray was one little black smudge.

It was the black sheep born in every flock. A sweet little black lamb kicking up his stiff young legs—leaping with the gray lambs in the small dances of baby animals.

The shepherd laughed to himself as he watched over the foolish lambs. He listened to the baa's of the mother sheep calling the strayed lambs after them as they nosed their way toward greener grass.

173

As the snows melted, the green grass blades sprang up, higher and higher toward the white peaks.

And every day the little shepherd brought his sheep up here to the mountain meadows.

This day was a soft, warm, windy day.

There was the smell of new green grass and mountain flowers that grow up out of the snow.

And here in the grassy meadows the little shepherd watched his sheep during the cool early sunlight of the day. He watched to see that they didn't stray away from the flock. And when they did, he whistled for his dog to go and get them.

That little black sheep was always skipping off by himself.

And then as the sunlight grew warmer he led them higher up into the mountains, with the little wobbly black sheep bringing up the rear.

They went to a little green valley right in the mountain peaks.

This valley was at a place higher up in the mountains than they had ever gone before.

And the grass was so green and tender here that the mother sheep almost forgot to baa for their lambs as they munched the new green grass blades.

The shepherd boy was busy cutting himself a whistle from a hollow stick of mountain ash.

His dog was sleepy and dozed alongside a lizard on a warm, sun-baked rock.

They did not see the little black sheep go frisking off by himself.

They did not see his little heels kick sideways as he

darted higher up the mountain on the other side of the valley.

And when his mother lifted her head to baa for him, he wasn't there.

And when the shepherd looked for him, he couldn't see him.

And when the old dog was sent bounding after him,
He couldn't find him.

The little black sheep didn't know it.

But the little black sheep was lost. For all the little black sheep cared, it was the sheep and the shepherd who were lost.

The mother sheep ran this way and that way—BAA, BAA, BAA—

She was so nervous that soon she had the other sheep baa-ing too.

BAAAAAAAAAAAH
BAH BAH

And the little lambs answered in their high, shaking voices.

b-a-a-a-a-a-a
BAH—BAAH
b-a-a-a-a-a-a

But the little black sheep didn't answer, and though the shepherd boy called and called and called and blew on his whistle and the old dog ran sniffing and barking about, they couldn't find that little black sheep.

And the little black sheep didn't come back.

He was having too good a time off by himself.

And then the sun began to go down. And though the shepherd waited as long as he could, he had to take the other sheep down to the lower valley before dark.

That was what a shepherd had to do. And so he did it.

He led the sheep back to the flock in the valley.

Here dogs and men would guard them all night in the lower pastures of the mountain.

Here they were safe.

Safe from mountain lions that leapt and prowled among the rocks higher up.

Safe from the cold of the high mountains at night, as the sheep huddled together in a great bleating flock. Here all together they were warm, like a blanket.

And here in the valley they were safe from the great jagged lightning and the black thunder clouds of rain that were ripped open on the mountain crags.

The stars came out, and the wind blew cold. The shepherd boy went to bed, but he didn't sleep. He kept thinking—

My black sheep is up there. He may need me. And he told himself—a sheep will stray. You have done all you could. Wait until morning and you will find your black sheep. In the morning you will find your little lost lamb.

But the little shepherd could not sleep. And, like a shadow, he and his dog crept from the hut and went back through the cold and the starlight up the side of the mountain.

Around them they heard the little whistles of rock rabbits and small rocks and pebbles trickling down the mountain side and the quiet scampering of small animals in the dark.

High up they heard the scream of a mountain lion.

But the little shepherd was more afraid for his black sheep than he was afraid for himself. And so he went on, up toward the jagged mountain peaks and the stars.

And then as he came into the high valley where he had lost his sheep he heard the crash of a lion and the bleat of a lamb.

But his dog heard too. And there was a scuffling of stones as the mountain lion was chased away into the night.

Then there was a soft little bleat, and the baby black sheep stood there by the cold gray rocks.

The little lost lamb was found.

The shepherd boy picked up his little black sheep and carried him in his arms down the mountain side back to the flock. And he sang to the night—

Oh, wind, blow softly over my sheep
Away from the lion
And over the lamb
Blow softly.

Over the grasses
And pointed flowers
Blow softly.

Oh, wind, blow softly out of the blue
Over the white
And the black sheep, too.
Blow softly.

MY two white rabbits
Chase each other
With humping, bumping backs.
They go hopping, hopping,
And their long ears
Go flopping, flopping.
And they
Make faces
With their noses
Up and down.

Today
I went inside their fence
To play rabbit with them.
And in one corner
Under a loose bush
I saw something shivering
the leaves.
And I pushed
And looked.
And I found—

Rabbits

BY

DOROTHY W. BARUCH

Illustrated by

Judith Brown

There
In a hole
In the ground—
Three baby rabbits
Hidden away.
And *they*
Made faces
With their noses
Up and down.

180

ALMOST a full moon ago, when Apodemus was a very young Mouse still living in the nest, his mother had brought him to the Giants' cave. She had been explaining the dangers that beset Field Mice. She warned him about Owls, who look so clumsy and dive so fast. She warned him about Cats, with their big green eyes and sharp claws. Apodemus had shivered and promised to remember.

But Giants had to be seen to be believed.

So Apodemus had crouched with his mother underneath a spray of beach plum blossom to see with his own eyes this greatest danger of all. He had never been so frightened in his life. The Giants were livelier than grasshoppers, and so big he could hardly believe it. They whirled round and round till he was dizzy and fairly deafened him with their shrieks and howls.

A Field Mouse Visits School

BY PATRICIA GORDON

Illustrated by Garry MacKenzie

Apodemus could never say he had not been warned.

Today everything was quiet, except for a steady hum inside the Giants' cave, but Apodemus knew it was perilous to linger. He was all ready to run—but his nose wouldn't let him. It twitched and it quivered, for the Most Beautiful Smell came from somewhere near the cave.

It wasn't a smell of grass or grain. It wasn't a smell of sea or flowers. It wasn't a smell he knew at all. But his

181

nose had never failed him. If his nose said, "Breakfast!" then it *was* breakfast.

His nose said, "BREAKFAST!"

Apodemus crept closer. The hum grew louder. The cave grew larger. And the Smell grew stronger.

He scurried over to the base of the cave and then began to climb. He climbed right up to the Giants' door. The door was closed, and outside it were Smells, all in a row. Apodemus darted from one to another, his nose twitching and his whiskers quivering.

The first Smell reminded him of the honey in morning-glory trumpets.

The second Smell made him think of birds for some reason. Eggs, that was it. It was like the sea-gull eggs he had found in nests in the salt meadow, only not so fishy.

The third and fourth Smells were too dull to bother about.

But the *fifth* . . .

"BREAKFAST!" said his nose.

Apodemus began to nibble.

"P-fui!" he said two seconds later.

He thought his nose had failed him for once. The Smell was beautiful, but the taste was brown and crackly.

But his nose kept right on saying "BREAKFAST!" And Apodemus remembered the story of hickory nuts his mother used to keep for special treats. Nut shells were like that, brown and crackly. You had to nibble through them to get at the delicious meats inside.

Apodemus went back to the Smell and nibbled through the brown, crackly outside, spitting out bits as he went along. Next he came to something that made him think of seeds. The Smell had some sort of a rind

182

as well as a shell. He chewed through and swallowed the rind, just to be rid of it.

Then he reached the Most Beautiful Smell.

His nose had been perfectly right, as always. The Most Beautiful Smell was an even More Breakfasty Taste. Apodemus wondered what it might be called.

It was so breakfasty that it tickled his nose and tickled his whiskers. Apodemus simply had to sneeze for joy.

"Ah-ah-ah-*cheese!*" he sneezed.

Somehow that sounded just right. He would name it Ah-Cheese.

Apodemus nibbled straight through to the other rind. He took a deep breath and gnawed his way back again. Back and forth he went till the Ah-Cheese looked like yellow meadow rue, and his little white stomach was as tight as any cranberry in the bog.

At last he couldn't nibble another nibble. He couldn't gnaw another gnaw. He sighed happily and sat up to wash his face and comb his whiskers with his front paws, as any well brought-up young field mouse should.

But as any well brought-up young field mouse should *never* do, he forgot to watch and listen for danger. He no longer heard the hum in the Giants' cave. He didn't hear when it changed. He didn't hear anything at all till the Giants burst out with a whoop and a roar and a shriek.

Apodemus froze where he sat, too frightened even to shiver. But a good deal was going on inside his head, and his Bump of Caution took its customary gloomy view of the situation.

"If you hadn't followed your nose," it told him severely, "you would be better off."

Apodemus was not so sure of that. It seemed to him that the situation would be worse on an empty stomach. Much worse. He thought about the Ah-Cheese, and in spite of his peril, his pink tongue flickered out to see if he mightn't have overlooked just one crumb when he washed his face. He had.

"You'd have done better to stay in your nice safe home," his Bump of Caution persisted, "even if you had to swim in your sleep."

"Botheration on all this caution!" squeaked Apodemus, and he twitched his whiskers crossly. Was he Mouse or was he Minnow?

Here he was, a fine upstanding young Field Mouse. A Mouse could always make a dash for safety. Or, if he couldn't dash, he might dive—

Directly in front of Apodemus's scared black eyes loomed a dark cave. Not a Giants' cave that was almost too big to see, but a little cave just mouse-size. Head first, Apodemus Sylvaticus dived into it.

It was the most peculiar hole he had ever been in, squishy and nearly as soft as his own fur. It might even turn out to be the home he had been hunting, though it did have a few undesirable features.

It was located rather too close to the Giants for comfort, and he would have preferred it airier and with a bit of a view. But then, as his Bump of Caution was forever telling him, we can't have everything. It *was* dry and *cozy,* and it *was* delightfully near the Ah-Cheese. Apodemus settled down for a nap.

He hadn't got his forty winks, not even ten, before his new house sprang into the air, tumbling Apodemus right over on his nose.

"Ooof!" he gasped. Before he
could get his balance, it happened
again.

The mouse-size cave went on
jumping up and down and fairly
set his wits to wambling.

To say nothing of his stomach.

186

A Nuthatch, and a very sensible fellow in spite of his name, had once told Apodemus, with shudders, about riding out a storm on a piece of driftwood on the Great South Bay. Seasick, the Nuthatch called it, and Apodemus decided that cave-sick was every bit as bad. He shuddered too, but that was a mistake. Cave-sick with shudders was twice as bad as cave-sick plain.

The bouncing stopped just in time to save his lovely Ah-Cheese breakfast. When the cave moved again, it was more sedately. It was rather soothing, in fact, except for a noise like a herd of Giants marching along together.

Apodemus didn't like that. Bad enough to find yourself in a cave that behaved as if it were alive, without having it move in such shocking company. But the situation improved. The cave dipped suddenly and then was still. A wonderful stillness without a solitary giantish sound to spoil it.

Apodemus had a quick think. He had to decide whether to leave now or take that interrupted nap. The way things were going, a Mouse could not be sure what might happen next, and probably he had better keep up his strength to meet it.

He wriggled down in his little cave, tucked in his paws, and curled his tail over his nose.

But, alackaday, what might happen next began to happen that very minute.

He uncurled his tail as a bright slit appeared at the top of his hole. Something pink and plump and a most peculiar wigglish shape crept in and fastened itself around him. Not until he was pulled out into the daylight could Apodemus see that a Giant's paw was holding him.

Even his Bump of Caution had no time to worry, for

187

the paw did not hold him long. He found himself flying through the air and his ears rang with the screech that followed him.

"R-A-A-A-A-T-S!"

It was a pity Apodemus did not know the language of the Giants. He had once met a water rat, and he would have been enormously set up to be mistaken for such a fine big fellow.

His poor wits rattled in his head as the scream was taken up by one Giant after another. There was no doubt about it—Apodemus Sylvaticus was inside the Giants' giant cave, a fearful predicament for even the most upstanding young Field Mouse.

The Giants came all sorts and sizes. Funny-looking ones with long hair, perching on top of peculiar logs. Skinny ones jumping up and down. A fat one holding his sides. The biggest Giant crouched over the biggest log, and his mouth kept opening and shutting although no sound could be heard above the squeaking and screeching and shouting of the others.

"R-A-A-A-A-T-S!"

It was enough to drive a mouse out of his senses. Something frightful must have scared them. Apodemus was glad he could not see what it was. If it was big enough and horrible enough to scare Giants; it was no sight for a Mouse.

He wanted to run, but something held his legs fast to the ground. Stiffening of the joints, maybe. His great-great-uncle on his mother's side got that in his old age. But it seemed too much for a young Mouse to come down with it when he needed his legs as never before.

The biggest Giant banged a round shiny thing in

front of him that made a noise like the bell buoys out in the Bay, and he shouted in a voice that was a deep growl instead of a shriek.

It must have been the signal that the danger was past, because the little Giants stopped screaming and sat down on their logs.

That is, all the other Giants but one, who was making straight for Apodemus, walking on its hind legs the way Giants did. Apodemus kept telling his feet to run, but that stiffening of the joints, or whatever it was, was worse than before. Only the very tip of his nose would move at all, and that was twitching much too rapidly. A paw, skinnier and browner than the first one, closed over him.

"I hope you're satisfied," his Bump of Caution grumbled. "Now just see what you got us into."

For all the Giant's paw was so huge, it was very gentle. And this new Giant's growl was a cheerful sort of humming, something like the buzzing of Bumble Bee when he found a particularly tasty honeysuckle blossom. Slowly the paw lifted Apodemus up to a big face that was as freckled as a mackerel.

"Our last minute has come," said his Bump of Caution with gloomy satisfaction.

"*Will* you be quiet?" squeaked Apodemus furiously. If he had to end as Breakfast-for-a-Giant, he would meet his fate like a Mouse.

It wasn't his last minute, after all. The Giant kept on buzzing as he carried him over to one of the logs. Apodemus could not see what was going on, but he found himself dropped into another small-size cave as brown as the shell of Ah-Cheese and smelling a little bit like Ah-Cheese too. He was just wishing it was not quite so dark when the Giant pushed something bright through the sides here and there to make little windows.

"Now, that was most considerate," Apodemus told his Bump of Caution. He found that his stiffening of the joints had disappeared and he felt really remarkably well. And not nearly so much frightened as curious. That annoyed his Bump of Caution and it stopped speaking to him.

The roof of the cave opened and crumbs of seedy-smelling Ah-Cheese rind rained in on him. Apodemus thought it unfair—they didn't hurt, of course, but it was not nice to pelt him with things. Now, if it had been Ah-Cheese . . .

It *was* Ah-Cheese. The roof opened a second time and delicious snippets fell all around him. That was quite different.

"BREAKFAST!" said his nose, and Apodemus didn't say anything at all till he had swallowed the last crumb and his white fur waistcoat was a tighter fit than it had ever been before.

190

"Not bad!" said Apodemus as he washed his face. "Not bad at all!" He combed his whiskers neatly.

"Just what the inner Mouse needed!" he added and yawned with full contentment.

His Bump of Caution heard him, but it didn't say a word.

Apodemus strolled across to a cave-window for a quick Mouse's-eye view of the Giants before settling down to his nap.

But Giant-watching proved so fascinating that he forgot all about sleep. The biggest Giant, facing all the others over his log, would growl something in an asking sort of voice; and one after another the smaller Giants would get up on their hind legs and growl back at him.

Apodemus could even recognize the one he was beginning to think of as his Own Particular Giant. He was sure he would have known his growl from all the others, even if he couldn't see him. It was such a nice buzzy growl to listen to, except when the Giants stood up together and all the growls became sing-y and high, like a million mosquitoes around one pair of ears. That was terrible.

When it was over, and none too soon, the biggest Giant banged on his bell buoy. The other Giants began growling to each other all at once and stowing things away. Then they got up and marched to the mouth of the cave. Apodemus's Own Particular Giant picked up the little brown cave and carried it outdoors with him.

"You see, now!" Apodemus told his Bump of Caution. "There was no need for you to take on so. He's going to let me go out here where it is safe."

His Bump of Caution was still sulking and wouldn't answer.

Tom's Little Dog

BY WALTER DE LA MARE

Illustrated by Dorothy P. Lathrop

TOM told his dog called Tim to beg,
And up at once he sat,
His two clear amber eyes fixed fast,
His haunches on his mat.

Tom poised a lump of sugar on
His nose; then, "Trust!" says he;
Stiff as a guardsman sat his Tim;
Never a hair stirred he.

"Paid for!" says Tom; and in a trice
Up jerked that moist black nose;
A snap of teeth, a crunch, a munch,
And down the sugar goes!

The Hippopotamus

BY GEORGIA ROBERTA DURSTON

IN the squdgy river,
   Down the oozely bank,
Where the ripples shiver,
   And the reeds are rank.

Where the purple Kippo
   Makes an awful fuss,
Lives the hip-hip-hippo
   Hippo-pot-a-mus!

Broad his back and steady;
   Broad and flat his nose;
Sharp and keen and ready
   Little eyes are those.

You would think him dreaming
   Where the mud is deep.
It is only seeming—
   He is not asleep.

Better not disturb him,
   There'd be an awful fuss
If you touched the Hippo,
   Hippo-pot-a-mus.

BUTTERCUP, the cow,
had a new baby calf,
a fine baby calf,
a strong baby calf,
Not strong like his mother
But strong for a calf,
For *this* baby calf
was so *new!*

Buttercup licked him with her strong warm tongue,
Buttercup washed him with her strong warm tongue,
Buttercup brushed him with her strong warm tongue,
And the new baby calf
liked that!

The new baby calf
took a very little walk,
a tiny little walk,
a teeny little walk,
But his long legs wobbled
When he took a little walk,
And the new baby calf
fell down.

The New
Baby Calf

BY EDITH H. NEWLIN

Illustrated by
Nils Hogner

Buttercup told him
with a low soft "Moo-oo!"
That he was doing very well
for one so very new
And she talked very gently,
as mother cows do,
And the new baby calf
liked that!

The new baby calf took
another little walk,
a little longer walk,
a little stronger walk,
He walked around his mother
And he found the place to drink.
And the new baby calf liked *that!*

Buttercup told him with another low moo
That drinking milk from mother was a fine thing to do,
That she had lots of milk for him and for the farmer too,
And the new baby calf liked *that!*

The new baby calf drank milk every day,
His legs grew so strong that he could run and play,
He learned to eat grass and then grain and hay.
And the big baby calf grew fat!

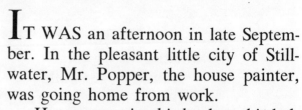

IT WAS an afternoon in late September. In the pleasant little city of Stillwater, Mr. Popper, the house painter, was going home from work.

He was carrying his buckets, his ladders, and his boards so that he had rather a hard time moving along. He was spattered here and there with paint and calcimine, and there were bits of wallpaper clinging to his hair and whiskers, for he was rather an untidy man.

The children looked up from their play to smile at him as he passed, and the housewives, seeing him, said, "Oh dear, there goes Mr. Popper. I must remember to ask John to have the house painted over in the spring."

No one knew what went on inside of Mr. Popper's head, and no one guessed that he would one day be the most famous person in Stillwater.

He was a dreamer. Even when he was busiest smoothing down the paste on the wallpaper, or painting the outside of other people's houses, he would forget what he was doing. Once he had painted three sides of a kitchen green, and the other side yellow. The housewife, instead of being angry and making him do it over, had liked it so well that she had made him leave it that way. And all the other housewives, when they saw it, admired it too, so that pretty soon everybody in Stillwater had two-colored kitchens.

Out of the Antarctic

BY RICHARD AND FLORENCE ATWATER

Illustrated by Robert Lawso

The reason Mr. Popper was so absent-minded was that he was always dreaming about far-away countries. He had never been out of Stillwater. Not that he was unhappy. He had a nice little house of his own, a wife whom he loved dearly, and two children, named Janie and Bill. Still, it would have been nice, he often thought, if he could have seen something of the world before he met Mrs. Popper and settled down. He had never hunted tigers in India, or climbed the peaks of the Himalayas, or dived for pearls in the South Seas. Above all, he had never seen the Poles.

That was what he regretted most of all. He had never seen those great shining white expanses of ice and snow. How he wished that he had been a scientist, instead of a house painter in Stillwater, so that he might have joined some of the great Polar expeditions. Since he could not go, he was always thinking about them.

Whenever he heard that a Polar movie was in town, he was the first person at the ticket-window, and often he sat through three shows. Whenever the town library had a new book about the Arctic or the Antarctic—the North Pole or the South Pole—Mr. Popper was the first to borrow it. Indeed, he had read so much about Polar explorers that he could name all of them and tell you what each had done. He was quite an authority on the subject.

His evenings were the best time of all. Then he could sit down in his little house and read about those cold regions at the top and bottom of the earth. As he read he could take the little globe that Janie and Bill had given him the Christmas before, and search out the exact spot he was reading about.

So now, as he made his way through the streets, he

was happy because the day was over, and because it was the end of September.

When he came to the gate of the neat little bungalow at 432 Proudfoot Avenue, he turned in.

"Well, my love," he said, setting down his buckets and ladders and boards, and kissing Mrs. Popper, "the decorating season is over. I have painted all the kitchens in Stillwater; I have papered all the rooms in the new apartment building on Elm Street. There is no more work until spring, when people will want their houses painted."

Mrs. Popper sighed. "I sometimes wish you had the

kind of work that lasted all year, instead of just from spring until fall," she said. "It will be very nice to have you at home for a vacation, of course, but it is a little hard to sweep, with a man sitting around reading all day."

"I could decorate the house for you."

"No, indeed," said Mrs. Popper firmly. "Last year you painted the bathroom four different times, because you had nothing else to do, and I think that is enough of that. But what worries me is the money. I have saved a little, and I daresay we can get along as we have other winters. No more roast beef, no more ice cream, not even on Sundays."

"Shall we have beans every day?" asked Janie and Bill, coming in from play.

"I'm afraid so," said Mrs. Popper. "Anyway, go wash your hands for supper. And Papa, put away this litter of paints, because you won't be needing them for quite a while."

That evening, when the little Poppers had been put to bed, Mr. and Mrs. Popper settled down for a long, quiet evening. The neat living room at 432 Proudfoot Avenue was much like all the other living rooms in Stillwater, except that the walls were hung with pictures from the *National Geographic Magazine.* Mrs. Popper picked up her mending, while Mr. Popper collected his pipe, his book, and his globe.

From time to time Mrs. Popper sighed a little as she thought about the long winter ahead. Would there really be enough beans to last, she wondered.

Mr. Popper was not worried, however. As he put on his spectacles, he was quite pleased at the prospect of a whole winter of reading travel books, with no work to interrupt him. He set his little globe beside him and began to read.

"What are you reading?" asked Mrs. Popper.

"I am reading a book called *Antarctic Adventures*. It is very interesting. It tells all about the different people who have gone to the South Pole and what they have found there."

"Don't you ever get tired of reading about the South Pole?"

"No, I don't. Of course I would much rather go there than read about it. But reading is the next best thing."

"I think it must be very boring down there," said Mrs. Popper. "It sounds very dull and cold, with all that ice and snow."

"Oh, no," answered Mr. Popper. "You wouldn't think it was dull if you had gone with me to see the movies of the Drake Expedition at the Bijou last year."

"Well, I didn't, and I don't think any of us will have any money for movies now," answered Mrs. Popper, a little sharply. She was not at all a disagreeable woman, but she sometimes got rather cross when she was worried about money.

"If you had gone, my love," went on Mr. Popper, "you would have seen how beautiful the Antarctic is. But I think the nicest part of all is the penguins. No wonder all the men on that expedition had such a good time playing with them. They are the funniest birds in the world. They don't fly like other birds. They walk erect like little men. When they get tired of walking they just lie down on their stomachs and slide. It would be very nice to have one for a pet."

"Pets!" said Mrs. Popper. "First it's Bill wanting a

200

dog and then Janie begging for a kitten. Now you and penguins! But I won't have any pets around. They make too much dirt in the house, and I have enough work now, trying to keep this place tidy. To say nothing of what it costs to feed a pet. Anyway, we have the bowl of goldfish."

"Penguins are very intelligent," continued Mr. Popper. "Listen to this, Mamma. It says here that when they want to catch some shrimps, they all crowd over to the edge of an ice bank. Only they don't just jump in, because a sea leopard might be waiting to eat the penguins. So they crowd and push until they manage to shove one penguin off, to see if it's safe. I mean if he doesn't get eaten up, the rest of them know it's safe for them all to jump in."

"Dear me!" said Mrs. Popper in a shocked tone. "They sound to me like pretty heathen birds."

"It's a queer thing," said Mr. Popper, "that all the polar bears live at the North Pole and all the penguins at the South Pole. I should think the penguins would like the North Pole, too, if they only knew how to get there."

At ten o'clock Mrs. Popper yawned and laid down her mending. "Well, you can go on reading about those heathen birds, but I am going to bed. Tomorrow is Thursday, September thirtieth, and I have to go to the first meeting of the Ladies' Aid and Missionary Society."

"September thirtieth!" said Mr. Popper in an excited tone. "You don't mean that tonight is Wednesday, September twenty-ninth?"

"Why, yes, I suppose it is. But what of it?"

Mr. Popper put down his book of *Antarctic Adventures* and moved hastily to the radio.

"What of it!" he repeated, pushing the switch. "Why, this is the night the Drake Antarctic Expedition is going to start broadcasting."

"That's nothing," said Mrs. Popper. "Just a lot of men at the bottom of the world saying 'Hello, Mamma. Hello, Papa.' "

"*Sh!*" commanded Mr. Popper, laying his ear close to the radio.

There was a buzz, and then suddenly, from the South Pole, a faint voice floated out into the Popper living room.

"This is Admiral Drake speaking. Hello, Mamma. Hello, Papa. Hello, Mr. Popper."

"Gracious goodness," exclaimed Mrs. Popper. "Did he say 'Papa' or 'Popper'?"

"Hello, Mr. Popper, up there in Stillwater. Thanks for your nice letter about the pictures of our last expedition. Watch for an answer. But not by letter, Mr. Popper. Watch for a surprise. Signing off. Signing off."

"*You* wrote to Admiral Drake?"

"Yes, I did," Mr. Popper admitted. "I wrote and told him how funny I thought the penguins were."

"Well, I never," said Mrs. Popper, very much impressed.

Mr. Popper picked up his little globe and found the Antarctic. "And to think he spoke to me all the way from there. And he even mentioned my name. Mamma, what do you suppose he means by a surprise?"

"I haven't any idea," answered Mrs. Popper, "but I'm going to bed. I don't want to be late for the Ladies' Aid and Missionary Society meeting tomorrow."

What with the excitement of having the great Admiral Drake speak to him over the radio, and his curiosity about the Admiral's message to him, Mr. Popper did not sleep very well that night. He did not see how he could possibly wait to find out what the Admiral meant. When morning came, he was almost sorry that he had nowhere to go, no houses to paint, no rooms to paper. It would have helped to pass the time.

"Would you like the living room papered over?" he asked Mrs. Popper. "I have quite a lot of Paper Number 88, left over from the Mayor's house."

"I would not," said Mrs. Popper firmly. "The paper on now is plenty good enough. I am going to the first meeting of the Ladies' Aid and Missionary Society today and I don't want any mess around to clean up when I get home."

"Very well, my love," said Mr. Popper meekly, and he settled down with his pipe, his globe, and his book of *Antarctic Adventures*. But somehow, as he read today, he could not keep his mind on the printed words. His thoughts kept straying away to Admiral Drake. What could he have meant by a surprise for Mr. Popper?

Fortunately for his peace of mind, he did not have so very long to wait. That afternoon, while Mrs. Popper was still away at her meeting, and Janie and Bill had not yet come home from school, there was a loud ring at the front door.

"I suppose it is just the postman. I won't bother to answer it," he said to himself.

The bell rang again, a little louder this time. Grumbling to himself, Mr. Popper went to the door.

It was not the postman who stood there. It was an expressman with the largest box Mr. Popper had ever seen.

"Party by the name of Popper live here?"

"That's me."

"Well, here's a package that's come Air Express all the way from Antarctica. Some journey, I'll say."

Mr. Popper signed the receipt and examined the box. It was covered all over with markings. *"Unpack At Once,"* said one. *"Keep Cool,"* said another. He noticed that the box was punched here and there with air holes.

You can imagine that once he had the box inside the house, Mr. Popper lost no time in getting the screwdriver, for by this time, of course, he had guessed that it was the surprise from Admiral Drake.

He had succeeded in removing the outer boards and part of the packing, which was a layer of dry ice, when from the depths of the packing case he suddenly heard a faint *"Ork."* His heart stood still. Surely he had heard that sound before at the Drake Expedition movies. His hands were trembling so that he could scarcely lift off the last of the wrappings.

There was not the slightest doubt about it. It was a penguin.

Mr. Popper was speechless with delight.

But the penguin was not speechless. *"Ork,"* it said again, and this time it held out its flippers and jumped over the packing debris.

It was a stout little fellow about two and a half feet high. Although it was about the size of a small child, it looked much more like a little gentleman, with its smooth white waistcoat in front and its long black tailcoat dragging a little behind. Its eyes were set in two white circles in its black head. It turned its head from one side to the

other, as first with one eye and then with the other it examined Mr. Popper.

Mr. Popper had read that penguins are extremely curious, and he soon found that this was true, for stepping out the visitor began to inspect the house. Down the hall it went and into the bedrooms, with its strange, pompous little strut. When it, or he—Mr. Popper had already begun to think of it as he—got to the bathroom, it looked around with a pleased expression on its face.

"Perhaps," thought Mr. Popper, "all the white tiling reminds him of the ice and snow at the South Pole. Poor thing, maybe he's thirsty."

Carefully Mr. Popper began to fill the bathtub with cold water. This was a little difficult because the inquisitive bird kept reaching over and trying to bite the faucets with its sharp red beak. Finally, however, he succeeded in getting the tub all filled. Since the penguin kept looking over, Mr. Popper picked it up and dropped it in. The penguin seemed not to mind.

"Anyway, you're not shy," said Mr. Popper. "I guess you've got sort of used to playing around with those explorers at the Pole."

When he thought the penguin had had enough of a bath, he drew out the stopper. He was just wondering what to do next when Janie and Bill burst in from school.

"Papa," they shouted together at the bathroom door. "What is it?"

"It's a South Pole penguin sent to me by Admiral Drake."

"Look!" said Bill. "It's marching."

The delighted penguin was indeed marching. With little pleased nods of his handsome black head he was parading up and down the inside of the bathtub. Sometimes he seemed to be counting the steps it took—six steps for the length, two steps for the width, six steps for the length again, and two more for the width.

"For such a big bird he takes awfully small steps," said Bill.

"And look how his little black coat drags behind. It almost looks as if it were too big for him," said Janie.

But the penguin was tired of marching. This time, when it got to the end of the tub, it decided to jump up the slippery curve. Then it turned, and with outstretched flippers, tobogganed down on its white stomach. They could see that those flippers, which were black on the outside, like the sleeves of a tailcoat, were white underneath.

"*Gook! Gook!*" said the penguin, trying its new game again and again.

"What's his name, Papa?" asked Janie.

"*Gook! Gook!*" said the penguin, sliding down once more on his glossy white stomach.

"It sounds something like 'Cook,' " said Mr. Popper. "Why, that's it, of course. We'll call him Cook—Captain Cook."

"Call who Captain Cook?" asked Mrs. Popper, who had come in so quietly that none of them had heard her.

"Why, the penguin," said Mr. Popper. "I was just saying," he went on, as Mrs. Popper sat down suddenly on the floor to recover from her surprise, "that we'd name him after Captain Cook. He was a famous English explorer who lived about the time of the American Revolution. He sailed all over where no one had ever been before. He didn't actually get to the South Pole, of course, but he made a lot of important scientific discoveries about the Antarctic regions. He was a brave man and a kind leader. So I think Captain Cook would be a very suitable name for our penguin here."

"Well, I never!" said Mrs. Popper.

"*Gork!*" said Captain Cook, suddenly getting lively again. With a flap of his flippers he jumped from the tub to the washstand, and stood there for a minute surveying the floor. Then he jumped down, walked over to Mrs. Popper, and began to peck her ankle.

"Stop him, Papa!" screamed Mrs. Popper, retreating into the hallway with Captain Cook after her, and Mr. Popper and the children following. In the living room she paused. So did Captain Cook, for he was delighted with the room.

Now a penguin may look very strange in a living room, but a living room looks very strange to a penguin. Even Mrs. Popper had to smile as they watched Captain Cook, with the light of curiosity in his excited circular eyes, and his black tailcoat dragging pompously behind his little pinkish feet, strut from one upholstered chair to another, pecking at each to see what it was made of. Then he suddenly turned and marched out to the kitchen.

"Maybe he's hungry," said Janie.

Captain Cook immediately marched up to the refrigerator.

"*Gork?*" he inquired, turning to slant his head wisely at Mrs. Popper, and looking at her pleadingly with his right eye.

"He certainly is cute," she said. "I guess I'll have to forgive him for biting my ankle. He probably only did it out of curiosity. Anyway, he's a nice clean-looking bird."

"*Ork?*" repeated the penguin, nibbling at the metal

208

handle of the refrigerator door with his upstretched beak.

Mr. Popper opened the door for him, and Captain Cook stood very high and leaned his sleek black head back so that he could see inside. Now that Mr. Popper's work was over for the winter, the icebox was not quite so full as usual, but the penguin did not know that.

"What do you suppose he likes to eat?" asked Mrs. Popper.

"Let's see," said Mr. Popper, as he removed all the food and set it on the kitchen table. "Now then, Captain Cook, take a look."

The penguin jumped up onto a chair and from there onto the edge of the table, flapping his flippers again to recover his balance. Then he walked solemnly around the table, and between the dishes of food, inspecting every-thing with the greatest in-terest, though he touched

nothing. Finally he stood still, very erect, raised his beak to point at the ceiling, and make a loud, almost purring sound. *"O-r-r-r-h, o-r-r-r-h,"* he trilled.

"That's a penguin's way of saying how pleased it is," said Mr. Popper, who had read about it in his Antarctic books.

Apparently, however, what Captain Cook wanted to show was that he was pleased with their kindness, rather than with their food. For now, to their surprise, he jumped down and walked into the dining room.

"I know," said Mr. Popper. "We ought to have some seafood for him, canned shrimps or something. Or maybe he isn't hungry yet. I've read that penguins can go for a month without food."

"Mamma! Papa!" called Bill. "Come see what Captain Cook has done."

Captain Cook had done it all right. He had discovered the bowl of goldfish on the dining-room window sill. By the time Mrs. Popper reached over to lift him away, he had already swallowed the last of the goldfish.

"Bad, bad penguin!" reproved Mrs. Popper, glaring down at Captain Cook.

Captain Cook squatted guiltily on the carpet and tried to make himself look small.

"He knows he's done wrong," said Mr. Popper. "Isn't he smart?"

"Maybe we can train him," said Mrs. Popper. "Bad, naughty Captain," she said to the penguin in a loud voice. "Bad, to eat the goldfish." And she spanked him on his round black head.

Before she could do that again, Captain Cook hastily waddled out to the kitchen.

There the Poppers found him trying to hide in the

still opened refrigerator. He was squatting under the ice-cube coils, under which he could barely squeeze, sitting down. His round, white-circled eyes looked out at them mysteriously from the dimness of the inside of the box.

"I think that's about the right temperature for him, at that," said Mr. Popper. "We could let him sleep there, at night."

"But where will I put the food?" asked Mrs. Popper.

"Oh, I guess we can get another icebox for the food," said Mr. Popper.

"Look," said Janie. "He's gone to sleep."

Mr. Popper turned the cold control switch to its coldest so that Captain Cook could sleep more comfortably. Then he left the door ajar so that the penguin would have plenty of fresh air to breathe.

"Tomorrow I will have the icebox service department send a man out to bore some holes in the door, for air," he said, "and then he can put a handle on the inside of the door so that Captain Cook can go in and out of his refrigerator, as he pleases."

"Well, dear me, I never thought we would have a penguin for a pet," said Mrs. Popper. "Still, he behaves pretty well, on the whole, and he is so nice and clean that perhaps he will be a good example to you and the children. And now, I declare, we must get busy. We haven't done anything but watch that bird. Papa, will you just help me to set the beans on the table, please?"

"Just a minute," answered Mr. Popper. "I just happened to think that Captain Cook will not feel right on the floor of that icebox. Penguins make their nests of pebbles and stones. So I will just take some ice cubes out of the tray and put them under him. That way he will be more comfortable."

THE gingham dog and the calico cat
Side by side on the table sat;
'Twas half past twelve,
and (what do you think!)
Nor one nor t'other had slept a wink!
The old Dutch clock
and the Chinese plate
Appeared to know as sure as fate
There was going to be a terrible spat.
(I wasn't there: I simply state
What was told to me by the Chinese plate!)

The gingham dog went,
"Bow-wow-wow!"
And the calico cat
replied, "Mee-ow!"
The air was littered,
an hour or so,
With bits of gingham
and calico,
While the old Dutch clock in the chimney place
Up with its hands before its face,
For it always dreaded a family row!
(Now mind: I'm only telling you
What the old Dutch clock declares is true!)

The Chinese plate looked very blue,
And wailed, "Oh, dear! what shall we do!"
But the gingham dog and the calico cat
Wallowed this way and tumbled that,

The Duel

BY EUGENE FIELD

Illustrated by Meg Wohlberg

Employing every tooth and claw
  In the awfullest way you ever saw—
And, oh! how the gingham and calico flew.
   (Don't fancy I exaggerate—
   I got my news from the Chinese plate!)

Next morning, where the two had sat
They found no trace of dog or cat:
And some folks think unto this day
That burglars stole the pair away!
  But the truth about the cat and pup
  Is this: they ate each other up!
Now what do you really think of that!
   (The old Dutch clock it told me so,
   And that is how I came to know.)

Old Log House

BY
JAMES S. TIPPETT

Illustrated by
Joseph Cellini

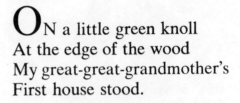

ON a little green knoll
At the edge of the wood
My great-great-grandmother's
First house stood.

The house was of logs
My grandmother said
With one big room
And a lean-to shed.

The logs were cut
And the house was raised
By pioneer men
In the olden days.

I like to hear
My grandmother tell
How they built the fireplace
And dug the well.

They split the shingles;
They filled each chink;
It's a house of which
I like to think.

Forever and ever
I wish I could
Live in a house
At the edge of a wood.

214

WHEN Eric swung away from the deserted camp beside the river and turned his pony's head toward the hills, he knew exactly why he chose that special direction. The men were looking for the vanished Sioux Indians and the lost little girl all across the great plain to the west and south. Why did the boy seek to find her in the broken country toward the north? This was what he was thinking, if his thoughts had been put into words:

"Gray Eagle carried Mary Anne away because he was a friend, not an enemy. So when he and his people ran away from the Arickaree horse thieves they would take Mary Anne to the very safest place they knew."

And where would she be more securely hidden than in those broken hills just showing in the faint starlight so far away to the north? Sancho was tired, but he seemed to have forgotten his laziness for the time being, and to know as well as his rider that theirs was a pressing errand. He stretched his weary legs to the new trail and loped forward.

The Willow Whistle

BY CORNELIA MEIGS

Illustrated by E. Boyd Smith

The sun came up and showed them the way more plainly, though the hills seemed no nearer. It was one of those hot, heavy days that come at the beginning of summer. They stopped as they crossed a shallow-running creek, and both of them drank. Eric munched some bread and cheese that his grandfather had slipped into his

215

pocket before he set out. Sancho cropped a few mouth-
fuls of grass and would have liked to linger, but went on
obediently when Eric slid into the saddle once more.

By noon they had reached uneven, barren country
where the edge of the great grassy plain had just begun to
break up into cracks and ravines. The sun was fiercely
hot overhead and the sky was without a cloud. Both boy
and pony were so worn out that it was plain they must

216

rest a little before they could possibly go forward. They came to a wide creek-bed, so nearly empty of water that it held only a series of pools instead of a running stream. Its course bent around a broad sandy curve where grew a dense and tangled thicket of young poplar trees.

It was the trees that decided Eric to stop here to eat, drink, and rest. Any patch of shade looked welcome indeed after the blinding brightness of the beating sun. He

217

guided Sancho carefully down the steep bank into the sandy bottom lands, skirted the poplar grove—and stopped short.

A vast, shaggy beast came splashing and snorting through the shallow water and out on the sand. It was a great bull buffalo, big-shouldered and heavy-horned, with the shaft of an Indian arrow standing out from a wound in his neck. An ordinary grazing buffalo is fairly peaceable, but a wounded bull is a bellowing whirlwind of stupid rage. The moment his glinting eyes caught sight of Eric and the tired pony, he dropped his horns and charged at them.

Swift Sancho fled along the sandy level, keeping close to the poplar thicket. An angry buffalo can gallop faster than a tired pony, but this buffalo was fortunately floundering in the heavy sand. How long he had carried that tormenting arrow in his shoulder Eric could not know. It was only plain to him that the great beast knew that a human hunter had hurt him, and that now he was going to hurt someone in his turn.

They rounded the end of the poplar grove and Eric saw the steep bank rise before him. The worn-out pony could never scramble up it, not even when he was driven by terror of the furious animal at his heels. There was nothing to do but swing about, still skirting the edge of the poplars, and ride in a wide curve down the stream again.

The buffalo's big clumsy feet had stumbled and sunk deeper in the sand than Eric had thought. Snorting and angry, their pursuer was still following them, but more and more slowly. The boy and the pony had come in a circle all the way around the grove of trees and had galloped so much faster than the buffalo that they were

218

now behind him instead of in front. Eric was breathless and knew that they were still in danger, but in spite of that he almost laughed aloud.

A buffalo viewed from behind is very different from a buffalo seen from in front. When one looks at his huge shoulders, at the hump behind them covered with a shaggy mane of hair, at his heavy head and short thick horns, he seems a terrible beast indeed. But observed from the rear, he shows a sloping back and such small hind legs that he does not seem terrible at all, but even a little ridiculous.

At the sound of the horse's hoofs behind him, the big bull did not wheel about, but only struggled harder and harder to plunge forward through the sand. The hunter whose arrow had wounded his shoulder had shot him from the rear and now, in his dull buffalo mind, the big creature could only think that he was being pursued again. He snorted with terror, though a minute before he had been bellowing with rage. Eric shouted, to drive him still faster. With a scramble of hasty hoofs and a rattle of stones all about him, the great beast went climbing up the bank to the level above. The arrow caught on a branch of poplar and was jerked free. In wonder and relief but still in a tremendous fright, the buffalo, with his head lowered and his tail straight up in the air, went galloping away across the plain and disappeared.

Eric slipped out of the saddle, sat down on the sand, and drew a long breath. The pony wasted no time in wondering over their escape but waded into the water and dropped his head to take a long cool drink. All about them the sand was torn and trampled by those clumsy cloven feet, but the danger was safely past. Eric loosened

219

the cinch on Sancho's saddle, and lifted the saddle off. The grateful pony scrambled up the bank to the green level above and rolled gloriously on the soft grass. Then he fell to snatching a hasty dinner, while Eric lay at full length on the sand in the shade of the poplars, closed his eyes, and listened to the whispering of the lightly hung leaves and the comfortable munching of Sancho on the bank above his head. He must go on in a few minutes to look for Mary Anne, but he knew enough to keep lazily quiet and to rest completely as he lay for that short time upon the sand. Sancho came obediently at his whistle when it was necessary to saddle and ride on once more.

Eric traveled more slowly now, looking anxiously at the ground as he rode. If any of the Sioux Indians had come this way bringing Mary Anne, he might, with good luck, catch sight of the trail left by their horses. Wherever there was soft ground near a watercourse, wherever the fresh grass had been newly trampled or the branches of a willow thicket had been recently broken, there were plenty of footprints of animals, large and small. There he drew rein and studied the marks of buffalo and the marks of the small, sharp hoofs of deer and antelope. The bent and broken twigs among the willows showed where a buck deer had slept the night before and—perhaps startled by some unfamiliar sound—had jumped up and gone crashing away through the low, tangled branches. But of the traces of horses' feet he found none.

It was late afternoon when they mounted the first slope that brought them into the hill country. All about them ran little streams in beds so narrow that they seemed like deep cracks cut between the rocky ridges. Eric

stopped his pony and stood
wondering and hesitating on
the crest of the first ridge. It
would take hours to explore
even one of the creeks, and
there were a dozen to choose
from. And in not more than
two hours it would be dark.
Which way should he go?
Sancho settled the question
by half sliding, half canter-
ing down the nearest slope
toward the largest pool that
they had yet seen. He was
thirsty and cool water was near; that was enough. As
Eric sat waiting for him to lift his head from his luxuri-
ous drinking, the boy saw plainly in the soft earth beside
them the trampled print of hoofs. This time they were not
deer or buffalo tracks; they were the marks of the unshod
feet of an Indian pony. He interrupted his horse's gulp-
ing with an abrupt jerk of the reins.

"Go on, Sancho!" he ordered, in fierce excitement.

The creek wound and twisted in and out among the
hills. Eric followed it mile after mile, looking, listening,

getting down now and again as the shadows grew deeper to examine the wet margin of the stream. Once, then again, he found new footprints; he was going in the right direction. At every turn of the crooked way he would think, "Now, I will find them!" But each new stretch of the narrow valley was as empty as the last.

The ravine broadened finally to a green, grassy bowl, wide enough to catch a gleam from the dropping sun. A spur of rocks ran down from the ridge almost to the edge of the water, but all the rest of the hillside was smooth and covered with close-growing sod. The stream wound through the level space at the bottom, its banks covered with fresh, green willows. Eric and Sancho stood still and looked and looked.

Was that a faint curl of smoke going up from beyond the rocks? It was so thin and transparent that he could not be sure. Was that an animal moving up the far slope of the valley? Was it a deer grazing—or a pony with a deer-colored coat? And if it was a pony, if that was the smoke of a burned-out campfire, to whom did both belong? To friendly Sioux Indians, or to hostile Arickarees? How could he know?

A little breeze stirred the willows. Something moved close to the green bank, something showing a glint of red. Then, drifting softly on the wind, there came a thin, wavering sound, a high, shrill piping. No Indian could have cut and fashioned a green whistle that would blow just that note. There was no one who knew how, except the friend and playmate whom he had come so far to seek.

"Mary Anne!" he shouted with all his might, and in answer the sound came again, the clear call of a willow whistle.

222

IT was growing dark and a cold wind blew up from Lake Michigan. Suddenly a crow cawed and all his family joined him. Hester woke from her dozing.

"Oh dear, I'm so cold, Mother," she complained to her mother who was driving the wagon.

Hester- and Timothy were tucked between the bundles of luggage in the wagon and their mother was urging the horse.

"I see Father is stopping now!" shouted Timothy, suddenly awake as he leaned out as far as he could to look ahead.

Mrs. Clark shouted, "Whoa, Flora, whoa!" to the horse.

"Well, family," said Mr. Clark as he tied his Indian pony to a birch tree, "here's a fine grove for our first night's camp."

"Is this Little Fort, James?" asked Mrs. Clark, climbing down from the wagon.

"Yup," answered Mr. Clark.

Hester and Timothy, Pioneers

BY RUTH L. HOLBERG

Illustrated by

Richard A. Holberg

"Oh, Father, I'm so stiff I can't move," lamented Hester. "Come and help me out."

"That's Timothy's job, Hester," he answered. "I'm helping Mother unhitch the horse."

"Here, Hester," said Timothy, "give me your hand."

"Ooooh! my knees won't unbend!" groaned Hester. She unfolded herself and climbed over the wagon wheels.

223

"Stamp your feet the way I'm doing, Hester," said Timothy.

Hester jumped up and down, then she drew off her red mittens and blew on her cold fingers.

"I'm going with Father to get wood for the fire," announced Timothy.

"I want to go, too," said Hester who was beginning to feel warm and tingly.

"Hester," said her mother, "there's work for you right here. Find that crock of butter and the middle-sized kettle."

"Oh, goody!" shouted Hester. "We're going to have butter!"

"Yes, and white bread, too!" smiled her mother. "But I don't know how much white bread we'll have when we get settled in Milwaukee."

Just then Timothy came running. "Hester, this was an Indian camp!"

"How do you know?" she asked, peering all around her.

"Why, I saw a pile of ashes and bones left from meals."

"Ooooh!" gasped Hester. "I wish they were here now."

Soon the fire was burning and supper was hot.

"Ummm, how good the beans taste tonight!" said Timothy, stuffing them in as fast as he could. Then he yawned and announced he was full up to his neck.

"Say, Father, how far do you think we traveled today?" he asked.

"Well, son, I think we have gone about twenty-four

miles since we left the old home in Chicago. But come now, all of you. We must go to sleep because we want a very early start tomorrow."

Soon they were all tucked in the tent snug and warm. Timothy woke once and heard wolves howling in the distance, but he was too sleepy to keep awake.

They were all up at dawn and had their breakfast under a cloudy sky. Mr. Clark gazed at the gray sky and gray waters of Lake Michigan.

"Doesn't look so good," he commented. "But hop in, children, we'll do our best today to reach Hickory Grove."

It was a long day but Hester and Timothy didn't complain. They told each other all the Bible stories they could remember.

"I wish Father would tell us the story of *Pilgrim's Progress*," said Timothy.

"Oh, no," objected Hester. "It isn't a warm story. It doesn't make me feel good inside."

"Pooh!" snorted Timothy. "You're a silly one!"

When darkness came and camp was made at last in Hickory Grove, Mrs. Clark said, "Hester, I'm going to make some horehound tea for you to drink."

"Oh, Mother!" cried Hester.

"Never mind, dear, I'm afraid you got pretty cold today and this will be good for you."

Hester drank the horehound tea while the others put up the tent. She felt very uncomfortable and tired and she didn't like the horehound tea even if it did make her feel warmer.

"Oh, why did we ever leave Chicago?" she complained.

226

"Why, Hester!" said her mother, "you know Father thinks Milwaukee is much more up and coming than Chicago." Her tired eyes looked on the bleak country and she shivered, thinking of the little home she had left for the wilderness of Wisconsin.

Then Mr. Clark joined in, "You see Mahn-a-waukee, as the Indians named it, means 'Beautiful Land.' "

Hester didn't think it was beautiful just then.

But Timothy said eagerly, "I'm going to learn what Indian names mean."

"I want an Indian girl playmate most of all," declared Hester. "Will there be some?"

"There may not be many white children. Perhaps you will play with Indians—if they are nice and clean," her mother said reluctantly.

"Bedtime!" called Mr. Clark.

When they woke the next morning there was a fall of snow over everything.

"The first snow!" called Timothy as he looked out the tent.

Hester put on her coat and hood and mittens and ran out and threw herself on her back in a snow bank. She moved her arms up and down. Then she got up with great care.

"Look, Mother! See the snow angel I made!"

"Oh, that's a nice one with big wings!" admired Timothy.

Her mother said, "Hester! Hester! Brush off that snow at once before your clothes get wet through!"

While they were eating a hearty breakfast, Mr. Clark said, "If we can keep on going in spite of the snow, we'll make Skunk Grove tonight."

227

"Let's hurry and clean up the camp then," urged Timothy as he brushed the last crumb from his mouth.

It was a very windy day and the air was raw with dampness.

"I don't think I will ever love Lake Michigan," mourned Hester and she covered her cold cheeks with her mittened hands.

"Wait until next summer, Hester, perhaps you'll feel different when you want to go wading," laughed her mother encouragingly.

"Oh, Mother, you always say such nice things," said Hester and she began to make plans for next summer. Her mother made it seem so close and soon.

"I wish I could ride ahead with Father," grumbled Timothy. "This wagon bumps so."

"But you wouldn't know the way, Timothy," objected Hester.

"I bet I could follow any old trail," boasted Timothy.

"Father says this trail leads along the bluffs right to Milwaukee. It is an old Indian trail."

"When we get to Milwaukee, maybe we can find some Indian trails of our own, Timothy!" And Hester's eyes began to sparkle.

"Maybe we can be explorers!" added Timothy. "And find new places where white men have never been before!" he cried excitedly.

"And give them names, too!" chirped Hester.

They talked and talked about exploring and names for the new places and forgot all about the bumpy wagon and the cold lake wind.

When they reached Skunk Grove at dark they were surprised to see a log cabin. Their father rode up on his pony, and an old man came out. He was very friendly and

228

invited them to stay there for the night. His cabin was a trading post and the children were excited to see piles of skins brought in by the Indians.

"How many furs there are!" said Timothy.

"Trapping has just begun," said the old trader. "Wait till spring and you'll see some furs. The beavers go to Europe for fine hats," he added, pointing to a very soft skin Timothy was stroking.

"Some are sent back to America. My father wore one," said Mr. Clark. "It was a grand tall hat."

It was fun to sit before the open fire that night and eat the venison stew the trader made. The Indian corn pone that had been baking all day in a corner of the hearth was covered with ashes and coals. The trader brushed off the ashes and gave Hester a hot crusty pone.

"Umm, how good it is," sighed Hester. She broke it in half and began to crunch through the thick soft crust.

Timothy's eyes were ready to shut, it seemed to him. He was only too glad to roll into his blanket and crawl into one of the bunks built along the wall.

The next day traveling was very hard; they had to

cross so many small creeks and swamps. Hester and Timothy thought they would be shaken to pieces before night. All the afternoon Mrs. Clark had to urge the horse.

"I think Flora is tired, Mother," said Hester.

"Well, I hope she gets us over this creek," her mother answered, and called, "Come there, Flora! Pull hard, Flora!"

But Flora was stuck in the mud.

Mr. Clark on his Indian pony had crossed easily.

"I guess there's nothing to do but unload the wagon," he called over the creek. Then he splashed back to them.

Timothy and Hester helped unload the wagon. They took the bundles of household goods and clothing as their father passed them down.

"Come now, Flora! Giddap! Giddap!" shouted Mrs. Clark. She pulled on the reins once more. Flora kicked and pulled but she was very tired. She had done the work of two horses the past few days. Finally Mrs. Clark threw the reins over Flora's head and climbed down from the back of the wagon to a log over the creek. Mr. Clark went into the water and unhitched the horse. She splashed and struggled until she scrambled on dry land.

"Now, Timothy, here's your chance to do some good work," said Mr. Clark with a jolly wink at Timothy.

Timothy waded into the creek and helped his father to move the wagon so that it could be pulled without too much effort.

Hester and Mrs. Clark stood in a dry place. They saw the wagon begin to move.

"Once more, son!" groaned Mr. Clark. And after one more pull the wagon was out of the creek.

While Timothy and his father hitched Flora again,

230

Hester and her mother crossed on the log until they could hop to a hummock. Soon they were all ready and started off on the trail that was now higher and along the bluffs.

"I'm afraid this has delayed us," said Mr. Clark.

"And we won't get to Milwaukee tonight?" asked Timothy.

"We'll see what Father decides to do," Mrs. Clark answered.

They rumbled on and on, and when it was getting late and darker every minute Mr. Clark stopped his pony.

"We should come to Colonel Walker's store very soon, Daisy, and we'll stay there tonight. It's impossible to go further."

The log cabin was reached in an hour. Colonel Walker's storekeeper came out to greet them.

"The colonel is in Fort Dearborn, sir," he said. "But bring your family in and be comfortable."

When Mr. Clark told him that Fort Dearborn was now called Chicago, he said, "Land sakes, how fast times are changing!"

Hester and Timothy were so tired and sleepy that they hardly knew what they were eating. By the time they were wrapped up in blankets and fast asleep Mr. Clark said, "Oh, hum, this business of pioneering makes me sleepy, too."

Mrs. Clark's eyes were half shut. She said sleepily, "The children have decided to be explorers and find new places where white folks have never been."

"Well," said Mr. Clark tucking one of Hester's hands under her blanket, "there's plenty of undiscovered places around Milwaukee."

232

EVERY afternoon Father would break off work.

"Time to go swimming," he'd say to Terry and then shout, "Hi! Swimming!"

The two little girls, who had been playing under an apple tree, would come running down the hillside and catch hold of Daddy's hands, and Mother and Robert, who might have been pitching hay in another part of the field, would leave their work and come, too.

The first day, Terry left Nuisance and Neighbor to wait where they were, but he didn't like having them miss the fun, and after he had learned the way to the little stretch of beach beyond the young alders and popples, he'd drive the pair down with the rest of the family, usually with Eudora on one steer and Cherry Pie on the other.

Then in their slips or shorts —for they had no bathing suits—the family would go swimming. The shore shelved very gently into the water and there were no treacherous holes into which a small child might step. The little girls waded and splashed, and Robert pretended to be swimming, while really he had one foot on the bottom, and Mother kept an eye on everyone, and Father swam out among the cloud reflections.

Terry could swim a little, too, but not very well. He

The Swimming Steers

BY

ELIZABETH COATSWORTH

Illustrated by Grace A. Paull

234

had never had much time to learn. He liked to let the steers wade out to drink, sucking up the water contentedly and then lifting their heads and letting the drops fall from their big muzzles.

One day Robert began shouting orders to the steers.

"Heish! O Heish! Neighbor! Heish! Nuisance!" and the big creatures began to wade out deeper and deeper, while the little girls screeched with excitement.

"Here! You stop that!" Terry shouted, about to order the pair back, when his father said, "Go on, Terry! Let's see if they can swim."

"Well, I'll do the bossing," said Terry, wading out beside Nuisance and calling, "Heish!"

Now the big creatures were up to their throats in the clear pond water. Now up to their chins. Terry, up to his own chin, felt like bringing them back, but he, too, was excitedly wondering what would happen next. Nuisance looked completely placid; Neighbor rolled his eyes toward the shore but continued to obey orders.

Now they were swimming. Only their heads and horns showed above the water. They moved almost silently with no splashing, but Neighbor blew out his breath in uneasy snorts.

"Did you ever see the like?" asked Father. "Better bring them in now, Terry."

So Terry brought them in, and, wet and shining, they began to browse on young popple leaves. After that the steers always went swimming with the rest of the family, and it was clear that Nuisance at least loved it, and would hurry down to the beach, dragging the less willing Neighbor with him.

There was an air of ease that summer because there was a good crop of hay, the corn was coming well, and the garden and orchard had all had a good year. Then with the tractor laid up for nearly a month, while Tom Bigelow waited for new parts, the steers had come in more than handy. His father this summer had never once said anything about selling the steers, but had taken them for granted as he did the cows, and that was a great relief.

One afternoon about swimming time, Father was called to the Hall's house for a telephone message. Mother had stayed home that day to do some early canning. When Father came out he looked bothered.

"Got to go and get those parts and bring Tom over," he said. "Guess you kids had better come along."

There were immediate protests and sad looks. Every-one wanted to go swimming.

Father hesitated.

"Can't see as you can come to any harm. Terry, you keep an eye on them and don't swim the steers today. None of your monkeyshines, Robert. You all just stay in the shallow water and play. I'll be back as soon as I can."

Today, everything seemed more exciting than usual with no grown-ups around. Terry let the steers go only up to their knees in the water, where they stood after drink-ing, looking out across the pond. A thunderstorm was working up from the southwest. Black clouds lay low over the trees behind them, and the children could hear the far-off rumble of distant thunder. But where they played, the hot sunshine lay all about them, and the dragonflies slept on the pads of the water lilies, which grew a little off to one side.

Because they were alone, the children did not go out into the water as far as usual, but waded along the pond in and out of the reeds by the bank. It was Cherry Pie herself who found the old barrel top like a little raft. It was too light to hold any weight but hers, they discov-ered, so, while Terry went over to the steers to slap at some deer flies which were always bad before a storm, Robert and Eudora pulled Cherry Pie about on the bar-rel top in the shallow water. A little storm-wind had come blowing up from the shore. In the shelter of the popples, they did not feel it, but the surface of the pond beyond was beginning to be ruffled, and a few pond lily leaves turned to show their dark red undersides.

The thunder, too, came more steadily and a little louder.

237

"Whack!" went Terry's hand, and a fly ceased his sharp stinging on Neighbor's flank.

Behind him he heard Eudora exclaim, "You quit that, Robert!" She spoke sharply, but Terry paid no attention. Robert was always teasing and Eudora was always protesting. He felt no alarm as he reached carefully to get within striking distance of a fly on Neighbor's neck. Then, just before he struck, he heard Eudora again.

"You're going too deep with her, Robert!" and he turned. There, nearly up to his neck in the water, stood Robert with Cherry Pie sitting on her barrel top held out beyond him. She did not look at all worried, but Eudora was scolding from the shallows.

"You haul her in!" shouted Terry, starting to wade hurriedly toward the scene, but the angry alarm in his face only excited Robert's mischievousness.

"Haul her in yourself!" shouted Robert, and, grinning impishly, he gave the barrel top as big a push as his arms were capable of.

The frail raft with Cherry Pie still sitting on it crosslegged and looking delighted, skimmed out a bare three or four feet, but it was enough to bring it into the region blown upon by the wind. To the horror of everyone except Cherry Pie, she drifted rapidly into the deep water, and there the barrel top began to tip, and, feeling the added weight of little waves, started to sink.

Cherry Pie kept her head and hung onto the unsteady support as best she could, but even in the second it takes to tell, she was drifting still further away from the beach, half on and half off her little raft. Terry had been wading after her as fast as he could, but now the water was up to

238

his mouth, and the distance between them was still widening.

He heard Cherry Pie call, "Terry! Terry!" and just as he started to swim with his weak, uncertain stroke toward her, knowing perfectly well that he could never bring her to the shore, he heard Robert (and all the mischief had gone from his voice) shouting, "The steers, Terry, the steers!"

Instantly, Terry stopped where he was and regained his footing, shouting to Neighbor and Nuisance with the water half choking him.

He heard them moving behind him. "Oh, faster! faster!" He heard his voice, hoarse with shouting. Beyond reach, Cherry Pie was slipping further off the barrel top, her eyes fixed on his. He felt the nightmare closing in upon him, and something deep inside him knew that he could never control the bewildered steers in this way.

He forced himself back a few steps. He kept his eyes on the steers, not on Cherry Pie. He quieted his voice. He forced back the extra, unnecessary orders on his tongue. Eudora was whimpering from the shore. Robert was silent. The thunder rolled almost continuously.

Now the steers were swimming. Cherry Pie was still there.

"All right, Cherry?"

"I'm slipping."

He must not swing them short, nor send them too far out.

He gee-ed them at just the right moment. Steadily they bore down upon the child.

"Whoa! Whoa, there! Nuisance! Whoa! Neighbor!"

Patiently the oxen slowed down their swimming almost to a halt, even in the strange element of water obeying their master's commands. Terry had brought Nuisance's head near Cherry Pie.

"Catch hold, Cherry Pie. Get a hold of Nuisance's horns!"

Cherry Pie grabbed. One wet hand slipped, but her right hand held. Now both wiry little fists were clenched on Nuisance's horns, as Terry gee-ed the steers in. As the pair got their footing, Terry was there to lift Cherry Pie down. His whole body was shaking with relief as he took her, but she turned a radiant face to his.

"That was the most fun!" she cried. "Let's do it again!"

"No, you don't," said Terry. "Once is enough."

240

Yes, once was enough. Enough to save her. In this emergency, Terry had succeeded in keeping his head after the first panic. He had meant to give Robert a licking, but he didn't feel angry any more. The thunder gave a sharp crackle and the first lightning flared.

"We'd better go up to the house and wait for Dad," Terry said, and all together they started up the hill, with Cherry Pie, wet as a mermaid, riding Neighbor, and Terry's guiding hand on Nuisance's shoulder.

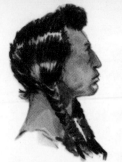

WHEN I was a boy Grandfather told this story to me, and he said he knew the hunter.

Sioux hunters are very brave. They must be as brave as a warrior, but, besides this, they must be wise to the ways of animals and birds.

This hunter whom my Grandfather knew was very wise. He could track any kind of animal whose footprint he saw on the ground. Furthermore, he could see tracks on rain-washed earth or among rocks that other hunters would not see. By these footprints he could tell whether the animal that made them was walking or running, or whether it was jumping and leaping as it sped over the ground. This wise hunter could even tell what sort of enemy was pursuing the fleeing animal. So long had he been out in the solitudes of nature breathing only pure air and drinking only pure water that he could smell the various animals when they came close to him just as the animals could smell him.

When he came to a deer trail the hunter could tell how long since the deer had traveled the path. If the tracks were far apart, the animal had been walking fast and would now be far from him, but if the tracks were close together, the animal had been traveling slowly and was probably not far away.

The Hunter Who Was Saved by Eagles

BY CHIEF LUTHER STANDING BEAR

Illustrated by
Lorence F. Bjorklund

242

Even the tangled chokecherry thickets could not keep things hidden from him. He could tell whether the bears had feasted yesterday or today. He could tell just where they had lain down to rest or sleep and in what direction they had gone. All the secrets of the "forest people" were his. The woods and the plains were like a book that he read each day and that told him of the travels and lives of his brothers and the animals.

One day this hunter was a long way from his village. He had killed a buffalo and had loaded the meat on his pony. While traveling toward home, he noticed two eagles circling high about a cliff. Not being in a hurry to reach home he stopped to watch them. Finally he decided to climb to the top of the cliff, to better observe their flight. There he saw the two eagles were keeping watch over a nest which had been built on a ledge far below the

243

top of the cliff. He tied his pony to a tree, and, lying down, peered over at the nest. In it were two young eagles; they were about half-grown and fully feathered. To a hunter here was temptation. So he took the meat off his horse and got the skin which was wrapped about it. This he cut into strips for a rope. The hide being fresh, he cut it into wide strips to give it the strength of a dried rope. One end he tied to a pine tree that grew not far from the edge of the cliff, and the other end he tied around his waist. Looping the rest of the rope in his hand, he slowly went over the edge of the cliff. This was thrilling sport and delighted this brave hunter. He was thinking how fortunate he was to have noticed the two old eagles flying in the sky. But his pleasant thoughts were interrupted, for the skin, being raw, stretched too thin and it came apart, letting him drop to the ledge. He looked up to see

244

the end of the rope hanging beyond his reach, while be-low him lay the rocky bottom of the cliff to which he could not leap. He expected to see the old eagles swoop down upon him and to see the young ones attempt to fly away. Being a wise hunter, he sat very still, glad that the young eagles did not fly away, for that reassured the old eagles which continued to circle above his head. Nothing happened to him, so he began to think. Up above was his horse, which would stand patiently waiting for him to return. The fine meat lying there would spoil, and he, forced to stay on the ledge, would starve to death. He tried to think of some means of getting away, but no thought came to him. He tried shouting at the top of his voice, but no one heard, and his calls passed away into the air like smoke. The parent eagles continued to circle close, so he knew that no one was near. Every now and then his mind would go back to his pony waiting for him up on the edge of the cliff, and he thought how comfortable it would be were he once more riding on its back.

At last he decided on a plan and made up his mind to carry it out, for to remain on the ledge meant death to him anyway. So carefully and quietly he began to creep toward the young eagles in the nest. They did not take fright, so slow and noiseless was he. He knew that if he snatched at them roughly, they would tussle in his grasp and perhaps he would not capture them. But he knew the ways of eagles, so did not frighten them. When close enough to touch both eagles, he removed the rope from around his waist. This he cut into two pieces. In a moment he had secured both birds by their feet. One of them he tied to his left wrist, the other he tied to his right wrist. He stretched out his arms, and the young eagles, too perplexed to flutter, sat motionless upon his wrists. He walked to the edge of the ledge and for a moment balanced. With a prayer to the Great Mystery he leaped. The eagles spread their strong young wings and, like an eagle himself, he landed at the bottom of the cliff safe and sound.

Reaching his horse, and with his meat loaded, the hunter started happily on his way home. He took the young eagles with him and fed and watered them. Then he painted their heads and necks red, and carried them back to the edge of the cliff. On a nice white deerskin he reverently placed them and left them there in thankfulness to the Great Mystery and Keeper of All Things.

KO-MO-KI is a Hopi Indian boy. His home is in the village called Oraibi. Oraibi village is on high flat ground called a mesa. To get up on this mesa to visit the village you would have to climb the cliffs for there are cliffs on all sides.

Ko-mo-ki's hair is black and straight. His dark eyes are large and kind.

Ko-mo-ki wears earrings made of pretty blue stones tied to pieces of string. The string goes through holes in Ko-mo-ki's ears and holds the pretty stones in place. Ko-mo-ki doesn't remember when the holes were made, for it was done when he was a little baby.

Ko-mo-ki of the Cliffs

BY ISIS HARRINGTON

Illustrated by Ernest Crichlow

Ko-mo-ki's shoes are pretty, soft ones made of deer-skin. His shirt is made of green velvet. His mother made the shirt.

Ko-mo-ki lives with his mother and father. He has a baby sister, too, but she is not big enough to play. Most of the time she sleeps tied tightly in her cradle in a quiet room of the house.

Ko-mo-ki does have a playmate though, and this playmate is his dog Po-o-ko.

Po-o-ko would be with Ko-mo-ki all the time if she could, but sometimes she cannot go with him. Then when he is gone she will sit all day at the edge of the cliff and watch for him to come home.

One morning, after the corn was up and the melons and squashes were planted, Na-ah-tah said to Ko-mo-ki,

247

"We go to the mountains for eagles." Ko-mo-ki was so happy that he swallowed his breakfast as fast as he could.

"Take two sheepskins and plenty of string," Na-ah-tah went on. "I have seen two eagles in the mountains near the sheep camp where they have a nest."

Ko-mo-ki tied two sheepskins about his waist by rounds of sheepskin strings. Na-ah-tah had a large deerskin. He tied this around his waist and was off down the cliff.

You-ah-tah tucked a bag of lunch into Ko-mo-ki's belt and he followed his father.

It was noon when they reached the sheep camp and

saw the eagles sitting on a crag of rocks on top of a mountain. After eating the lunch, Ko-mo-ki and his father started to climb. The eagles watched them until they were quite near. Then they flew away. Na-ah-tah was first to reach the nest. It was a pile of sticks built on a flat ledge. In it were two young eagles.

On the flat ledge Na-ah-tah lay down close to the rock. He put his deerskin over him. Ko-mo-ki covered himself with the sheepskins. They lay there without moving. They looked just like the ledge of the rock on which they lay.

After an hour or two, the eagles came back. High over the nest they flew round and round. Then one lit on the edge of the nest. It was followed by the other. As soon as the second eagle had touched the edge of the nest, Ko-mo-ki grabbed it, covering its claws and head with the sheepskins. Ko-mo-ki was frightened, but as soon as he had his eagle held tight in the skins, he looked for his father. Na-ah-tah sat smiling with the other eagle in his deerskin.

"I shall have plenty of feathers for prayer plumes and ceremonies," he said as he reached into the nest for the two young ones.

When the feet, heads and wings of the old eagles were tied well, Na-ah-tah and Ko-mo-ki looked about them. All around the nest were bones of lambs, rabbits and birds. Bits of wool, thick on the ledge around the rocks, showed how many of Na-ah-tah's lambs it had taken to feed the young eagles.

It was easier coming down than going up the mountain, even with their load, and the two eagle hunters reached the sheep camp in a short time. They did not rest, but started across the valley for home.

It was sundown when at last they climbed into the village.

"We got the eagles," said Ko-mo-ki as he burst into the door ahead of his father. "We shall tie them to our roof!"

Na-ah-tah climbed to the roof where he tied his eagle by one leg to a strip of strong deerskin. Ko-mo-ki's eagle was soon tied in the same way, and the two eagle hunters went into their house for supper.

"Take this to the eagles," said You-ah-tah just as Ko-mo-ki was ready to sit down on the floor by the table. "They will be hungry, too. Keep safe from their sharp claws and hard wings."

Ko-mo-ki took the piece of dried mutton leg to the roof, laid it in reach of the eagles and was at his supper in no time.

The day has been hot, very hot. Now a burning, drying wind is springing up and little flurries of sand and dust begin. Na-ah-tah has been watching them with a troubled look.

"Ko-mo-ki," he called. The boy looked up from the darts he was making in the shade of the wall. "The field. It will be buried by morning. See, the sand begins to scatter along the ground."

Ko-mo-ki gathered his finished darts and the thorns, cobs and feathers with which he was making others, and took them into the house. He laid them in a basket a bit angrily, but was soon with his father half-way down the cliff to the field.

By the time the two reached the corn, the sand was sifting along the ground in places and the drooping stalks, wilting to the ground, seemed to be ready to die.

250

"Bring the rocks, Ko-mo-ki," said Na-ah-tah. "The sand storm is coming fast. Do you see that cloud lying on the earth away to the south?" Ko-mo-ki looked. There was the cloud, not of rain, but of gray dust and sand moving toward their mesa. It seemed to reach from the earth to the sky.

Ko-mo-ki said nothing, but was off as fast as he could go to the place where the rocks at the edge of the field were piled. He carried as many as he could at once and made many trips. He could not run with his arms full of the thin, flat stones, but on dropping them beside his father, he would run for another load.

The wind was getting stronger and the sand flurries more frequent, blinding Ko-mo-ki's eyes for a moment, but he did not stop. In spite of them he smiled once or twice as he thought of a boy from another village on another cliff. He was coming with his darts the next day to play *mu-de-vuh* with Ko-mo-ki. This boy's name was Da-ha.

Da-ha never worked. His brothers did all the work while he played. He had piles and piles of darts that he had taken from other players in games of *mu-de-vuh*. On days that Da-ha visited a neighboring village, many a boy was left without a dart.

As Ko-mo-ki carried rocks the thoughts of Da-ha made him forget his aching arms and his scratched, tired legs, for tomorrow he meant to meet Da-ha with some of the best darts he had.

"I will have his best one if my arm is true tomorrow," he said to himself as he dropped the last load of rocks.

Na-ah-tah looked back over his shoulder. Every hill of corn was covered. He put an extra rock here and there wherever a plant showed too plainly, rose stiffly and started toward the home on the cliff high above. Ko-mo-ki followed.

By the time the two reached the village the cloud had struck the valley and the air all around seemed still and loaded with dust and fine sand. The sun just setting shone dim as a day moon.

Na-ah-tah and Ko-mo-ki hurried into their house where You-ah-tah had supper set for them.

"Come softly," said You-ah-tah as Ko-mo-ki entered, "Ma-nah is asleep in the other room. I must finish my basket after supper." Then the three sat down and helped themselves, dipping their fingers into a bowl of mutton stew in the middle of the table—which was not really a table—but a sheepskin spread upon the mud floor.

Dressing Up BY MARCHETTE CHUTE

Illustrated by Fritz Kredel

I WANTED to have a cowboy suit
And ride all over the plains;
So I made a halter for the horse,
With leather for the reins.

I made a noble
 kind of gun
From a piece
 of iron pipe,
And I cut up bits
 of overcoat
To give my pants
 a stripe.

I sort of borrowed
 daddy's hat,
And I had some rope,
 of course;
And I'm good at swinging
 lariats,
So all I need's
 a horse.

254

BOB Benton sat up, stared around, and blinked his brown eyes. Where was he? Why was he shut in this little place? Then he remembered. He was in a berth on the train, on his way to his Uncle John's cattle ranch in Wyoming to spend the summer. A pleasant sense of excitement came over him.

It was morning, and he must be in Wyoming. He peered out the window. Sure enough, the country looked quite different, yet for some reason he felt a bit disappointed. He didn't know exactly what it was he expected to see, but it wasn't this bleak, barren land. For miles the country stretched without a tree or a house in sight. Nothing but gray sagebrush and telegraph poles rushing by.

At last Bob saw a herd of cattle and he sighed with relief. He strained his eyes trying to catch sight of a galloping cowboy. Where there were cattle there must be cowboys, but there were none in sight. Still, he felt better. It was cowboy land, all right. Somewhere, not too far away, must be his uncle's Circle K Ranch.

Off to Adventure

BY SHANNON GARST

Illustrated by Douglas Gorsline

There was a sound at the heavy curtains that shut his berth off from the aisle, and he heard the porter say, "You all'd better be gettin' up. We're due at Long Horn in half an hour."

Bob began scrambling into his clothes as if he had

255

only five minutes instead of thirty. He took his toothbrush and comb and went swaying down the aisle to the washroom.

He hurried so much that he still had a little time to stand at the corridor window and watch the fence posts and telegraph poles rush by. Every time the train passed a herd of cattle, Bob's heart leaped with excitement. But still he saw no cowboys. The train whistled and began to slow down. He dashed up the aisle after the porter.

When the train stopped, Bob hurried down the steps onto the station platform. He looked about and felt slightly disappointed. Long Horn was just another unexciting looking town, much like the small towns he had passed through in Colorado. There were no cowboys whooping through the sleepy streets. Then he saw his uncle coming up. To Bob's disappointment he wore ordinary clothes, except for the wide hat that did look a bit cowboyish.

"Howdy, partner! Glad to see you." Uncle John gave his nephew's hand a squeeze that made Bob wince. "I was really surprised that your father and mother let you come all the way from Chicago alone, and that they'd trust their only chick to an old bachelor for a whole summer!"

Bob laughed. "It took plenty of talk before they made up their minds," he admitted. "But Dad couldn't get away from the office this summer, and Mother thought it would do me good to be outdoors. Besides," he gave his uncle an eager look, "they know I want to be a cowboy."

"So you want to be a cowboy!" John Benton chuckled. "But right now, I reckon, you want to eat. So do I. Come along and we'll have some 'chuck' before we start out. It's a long trip to the Circle K."

256

John Benton picked up Bob's suitcase and started down the broad street. Bob had to stretch his legs to keep up. They entered a dingy restaurant and sat on high stools at the counter.

As they were waiting for their order, the door opened and in stalked a tall, lean man. Bob caught his breath sharply, for he knew instantly that here was a real cowboy. He wore high-heeled boots with clinking spurs and a green plaid shirt and orange neckerchief. A very wide hat was pushed to the back of his head. He did not wear chaps, but faded blue overalls with, low on his hips, a wide belt of carved and silver-studded leather.

"Howdy, Montana," John Benton called. "We didn't wait, because Bob, our new hand here, was hungry. Bob, this is Montana, the Circle K's foreman."

Bob nearly fell off his stool with excitement. Montana might have stepped squarely out of one of his dreams. He looked just as a cowboy should look. His face was handsome in a rugged, masculine sort of way. And there was something about his bearing that made Bob feel that here was a man always to be trusted and counted on.

"Howdy." Montana's hand reached over to give Bob's a strong grip. "I'm right glad you're going to be with us at the Circle K. Indeed I am."

Then turning to John Benton he said, "I shouldn't be surprised if we had the makings of a top hand here. Freckle-faced, red-headed boys generally make good top hands."

Bob did not know what a top hand was, but coming from Montana the words sounded good to him. His chest

258

swelled, only to be deflated promptly by his uncle's words, "Bob's only twelve—a bit too young to be much help. But he can have plenty of fun on the ranch. That's what he's come here for."

"Oh, no!" Bob cried. "I want to be a real cowboy."

But his uncle and Montana had begun to talk about yearlings and two-year-olds and market conditions and hardly seemed to hear him.

As soon as they finished breakfast, the three of them went out to the car. Its open back was piled high with boxes of groceries.

Bob sat between Uncle John, who drove, and Montana. He looked at the rolling green hills with herds of cattle grazing on them. Every now and then he saw a low, comfortable looking ranch house with barns and other buildings clustered about it.

"Where are all the cowboys?" he asked.

"Oh, you'll see plenty of them when you get to the Circle K," his uncle answered.

The blue hills crept nearer. Finally the car jounced over the iron rails that formed a cattle guard leading into the ranch.

Montana noticed Bob's questioning look. "Livestock won't try to walk over those rails, because their feet would catch in the spaces between them," he explained. "But cars can cross, and no one has to get out and open the gate."

Over the gate Bob saw a big sign—CIRCLE K RANCH—painted in blue letters. Above the letters was a bleached steer skull with long horns.

Bob sat up straight and looked about. On one side of the road was an alfalfa field, purple with blossoms. On the other side were sandstone buttes shaped like ancient castles and battlements. That would be a fine place to play Indian, he thought, and he wondered if real Indians had ever had a battle fortress there.

Soon they drove up to a rambling house, nestled in a grove of cottonwoods. It was made of logs, and a screened porch ran across the front. Behind the house Bob saw barns, the bunkhouse, and outbuildings, and adjoining these a large, circular corral enclosed by upright poles. He heard the gurgle of a stream a short distance away. Then his eye caught sight of a number of saddles thrown over a fence.

"What a wonderful place!" he cried, and his brown eyes sparkled with delight.

A tan-and-white shepherd collie dog came bounding

260

to meet the car. At his heels leaped a young antelope.

"Jumping Jimminy!" Bob exclaimed. "What's that?"

"This is Shep," said Uncle John, patting the collie's head. "I expect you two will be great pals. And this is our pet antelope. He hasn't a name yet. We'll let you give him one."

Bob patted the smooth head of the little animal while it butted him playfully.

"Jumping Jimminy!" he cried again. "This is going to be great. A dog and an antelope for pets! And—and I s'pose I'll have a horse to ride, and everything."

The last words blurted themselves out. Bob felt that it wasn't quite polite to be asking for a horse so soon, but the subject had been at the top of his mind for so long that he could not keep the words back. He could hardly

261

wait to get on one of the horses he saw in the big corral and go galloping across the green plain.

"Whoa now!" his uncle laughed. "Not so fast. Have you ever been on a horse?"

"No-o," Bob admitted. "Not yet. But I know I can ride. Of course I haven't any cowboy boots yet, but I'm sure my dad will send some soon."

He looked again at Montana's handsome, elaborately stitched boots. To him they stood for everything that was cowboyish, and his longing for cowboy boots of his own was so strong that it hurt.

"Well," his uncle said as he led the way into the house, "it takes a lot more than fancy clothes to make a cowboy. A lot more."

Bob remembered that his father had told him that very thing.

John Benton led the way into a large, cool room, cozy with Indian rugs and shabby, comfortable furniture. Both Shep and the playful antelope followed.

"Come with me," Uncle John said, "and I will introduce you to the boss of the Circle K."

This puzzled Bob. He thought that his uncle was the boss. But he said nothing and followed into an oblong room almost filled with a long table and narrow benches.

"This is where we eat," his uncle said. Then he led the way on into a warm and cheerful kitchen. Good smells hung about it so heavily that Bob's mouth watered.

"This is Cookie," Uncle John said. "You'd better be good to him, because he rules the roost around here. If you make him mad he won't feed you, and then you'd starve to death."

Cookie grinned. He looked to Bob as though he

wouldn't get angry very easily. His cheeks were pink and he had a round, fat stomach. In fact, he looked as though he liked his own cooking very much.

"Bob wants to be a real cowboy," Uncle John told Cookie, a twinkle in his eyes.

Cookie put his hands on his hips and stared down at Bob. "That means," he said slowly, "that I'll have a roustabout for a few months. Young man, if you work hard, you and I will get along all right. I like your looks. But mind, I don't stand for any monkey business. When I need wood, I have to have wood, right pronto!"

Bob looked at his uncle questioningly.

"He means," said his uncle in his usual brisk tone, "that you are to be the boy who does odd chores around the ranch. One of your special jobs will be to carry wood for the cooking. All cowboys start by being roustabouts."

Bob gulped. This did not fit at all into his idea of being a cowboy.

"But when do I start being a cowboy?" he asked. "When do I get to ride horses and punch cattle?"

His uncle's lips twitched at the corners. "Oh, that comes later," he said. "Much later. Probably not at all this summer. Riding is dangerous business. I wouldn't want you to get hurt."

"I won't get hurt!" Bob cried. "I'll be careful and I'll help with the cattle and make myself very useful."

"You can start making yourself useful right now then," said Cookie. "Take that iron bar on the bench outside and whack it against the iron triangle hanging near the door. That will bring the men in to chuck."

Bob went outside and jangled the bar against the triangle. From the barn and corrals and beyond, he saw several men start to hurry toward the log house. Bob's heart leaped at the sight of these real cowboys. Each of them wore high-heeled boots and a wide hat pushed to the back of his head. All wore neckerchiefs, and a few wore chaps. Some were tall, some were short, but all were lean and sturdy looking.

They came to the long bench against the porch and washed their hands and faces in the row of washbasins that stood there. Then they slicked their hair and headed for the dining room.

"Fellows, let me introduce you to the new 'ranny' of the Circle K," Montana drawled. "Bob, this long hombre built like a snake on stilts is Crowbait. This guy with a face like a hoss is called Happy because he's always sad. And this would-be cowpuncher that sort of drags the ground when he walks is Shorty. He's had a hoss under him so long his legs are warped."

Bob bowed politely, uncertain how to respond to this manner of introduction. Each of the men grinned and said howdy.

The cowboys went to the long table and threw their legs over the benches. Immediately dishes of food began to move down the table. Each man piled his plate high, passed the dish along, and started eating. It was plain to see that this part of the day's work was a serious business to these men.

Bob sat next to his uncle at the head of the table and almost forgot to eat, he was so busy watching. Never had he seen such interesting men. Shorty, he decided, must be the clown of the ranch for he had a jolly twinkle in his eyes and chuckled whenever he spoke. Crowbait, he didn't like so well, because there was a mean tone to the

264

way he called Montana, "our movie cowboy," when he asked him to pass the spuds. Of course, Bob thought, Montana did look like a moving-picture hero, all right. He guessed Crowbait must be jealous. He decided that Happy must be the strong, silent type. Scarcely a word came from him, and his long face wore such a melancholy expression that Bob wondered if some secret sorrow weighed on his heart.

As they were eating their apple pie, Uncle John said, "The boys are going to break horses tomorrow. You may watch, Bob, if you wish—after your chores are done."

"Chores?" Bob questioned.

"Of course. Carrying in wood and water. Whatever Cookie wants you to do."

"Oh!" came faintly from Bob's throat, but the more exciting part of his uncle's statement swept the slight disappointment over chores from his mind.

"Gee whillikers!" he cried. "Then I start right in learning how to break horses!"

"Yes," said his uncle, "you can start learning how, but don't start putting what you learn into practice. Breaking horses is dangerous business. I want to send you back to your father and mother in one piece."

"You mean that sometimes horses break people?" Bob asked.

"And how!" Shorty spoke up. "I tried to break an outlaw hoss once. But instead, he broke me. My leg, in three places. I've been out of rodeos ever since. And me the best rider in forty-nine states."

At this modest remark a shout went up from the other cowboys.

"Cowboys like to brag about themselves," Bob's uncle explained. "But none of them is as good as he claims to be."

"I'm the only one as can make such a boast truthfully," said Crowbait.

"Ho!" Montana cried. "Crowbait's apt to get calluses from patting himself on the back. He's been bucked off so often he's loosened till he plumb rattles when he walks."

"Is that so?" Crowbait retorted. "Well, the last time I saw you ride, soon as your hoss bogged its head, you grabbed the saddle horn and nearly pulled it out by the roots, trying to hang on. That animal was sure full of bedsprings, all right. I can see it yet—the way it hid its head and kicked the lid off. And when it warped its back-

266

bone you went flying off, your legs kicking like a flying frog with the jerks."

Cowboy talk, Bob decided, must be almost like a foreign language.

"Get your chores done pronto," Montana told him, "and we'll take a little look-see about the place."

Cookie told him what to do—fill the woodbox, the water buckets and carry table scraps to the chickens.

After supper and chores, Bob went with Montana on a short tour of inspection about the ranch buildings. He saw the huge storeroom where supplies were kept. It was like a small, well-stocked store. He stopped to look at the row of saddles thrown across a fence rail. He saw the bunkhouse where the men slept, with its rows of two-tiered bunks built against the walls.

He stared fascinated at the array of branding irons hanging on the blacksmith-shop wall. Montana showed him where the Circle K brand had been burned into the door—a K inside a circle.

"Why!" cried Bob. "That makes an 'O.K.' Why don't you call this the O.K. ranch? That's what it is, all right."

Montana stroked his chin and grinned. "I reckon you're right. This spread is O.K. But brands were used before that term was."

"I'm going to call it the O.K. Ranch just the same," Bob said. "When I write Mother and Dad tonight, I'll draw the brand mark at the top of the page."

DANIEL Boone at twenty-one
Came with his tomahawk, knife and gun
Home from the French and Indian War
To North Carolina and the Yadkin shore.
He married his maid with a golden band,
Builded his house and cleared his land;
But the deep woods claimed their son again
And he turned his face from the homes of men.
Over the Blue Ridge, dark and lone,
The Mountains of Iron, the Hills of Stone,
Braving the Shawnee's jealous wrath,
He made his way
    on the Warrior's Path.
Alone he trod
    the shadowed trails;

Daniel Boone

BY

ARTHUR GUITERMAN

Illustrated by
Alexander Dobkin

But he was the lord
    of a thousand vales
As he roved Kentucky,
    far and near,
Hunting the buffalo,
    elk and deer.

What joy to see, what joy to win
So fair a land for his kith and kin,
Of streams unstained and woods unhewn!
"Elbowroom!" laughed Daniel Boone.

On the Wildnerness Road that his axmen made
The settlers flocked to the first stockade;
The deerskin shirts and the coonskin caps
Filed through the glens and the mountain gaps;
And hearts were high in the fateful spring
When the land said "Nay!" to the stubborn king.

268

While the men of the East of farm and town
Strove with the troops of the British Crown,
Daniel Boone from a surge of hate
Guarded a nation's westward gate.
Down on the fort in a wave of flame
The Shawnee horde and the Mingo came,
And the stout logs shook in a storm of lead;
But Boone stood firm and the savage fled.
Peace! And the settlers flocked anew,
The farm lands spread, the town lands grew;
But Daniel Boone was ill at ease
When he saw the smoke in his forest trees.
"There'll be no game in the country soon.
Elbowroom!" cried Daniel Boone.

Straight as a pine at sixty-five—
Time enough for a man to thrive—
He launched his bateau on Ohio's breast
And his heart was glad as he oared it west;
There were kindly folk and his own true blood
Where great Missouri rolls his flood;
New woods, new streams and room to spare,
And Daniel Boone found comfort there.
Yet far he ranged toward the sunset still,
Where the Kansas runs and the Smoky Hill,
And the prairies toss, by the south wind blown;
And he killed his bear on the Yellowstone.
But ever he dreamed of new domains
With vaster woods and wider plains;
Ever he dreamed of a world-to-be
Where there are no bounds and the soul is free.
At four-score-five, still stout and hale,
He heard a call to a farther trail;
So he turned his face where the stars are strewn:
"Elbowroom!" sighed Daniel Boone.

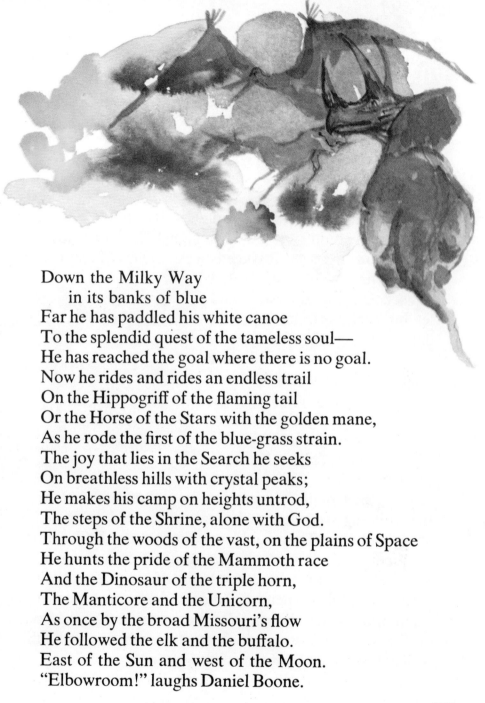

Down the Milky Way
    in its banks of blue
Far he has paddled his white canoe
To the splendid quest of the tameless soul—
He has reached the goal where there is no goal.
Now he rides and rides an endless trail
On the Hippogriff of the flaming tail
Or the Horse of the Stars with the golden mane,
As he rode the first of the blue-grass strain.
The joy that lies in the Search he seeks
On breathless hills with crystal peaks;
He makes his camp on heights untrod,
The steps of the Shrine, alone with God.
Through the woods of the vast, on the plains of Space
He hunts the pride of the Mammoth race
And the Dinosaur of the triple horn,
The Manticore and the Unicorn,
As once by the broad Missouri's flow
He followed the elk and the buffalo.
East of the Sun and west of the Moon.
"Elbowroom!" laughs Daniel Boone.

NOISELESS in their moccasins, and light-footed as foxes, the eight Crees were the first to leap through the door when the teacher's bell sounded for afternoon recess. Out from under a roof they breathed more freely. After them, the smaller fry from the front benches—the whites, the half-breeds, and the Indians—jostled and bustled one another into the autumn sunshine. There would be but few days more when they could play outdoor games, and they lost no time in forming a shrill-voiced circle. Sandy Mackay, oldest of the white boys, seated himself on the doorstep and let his arithmetic fall open at decimals.

Behind Sandy, and last pupil to leave the schoolroom, came wooden-faced Little Beaver, chin slightly forward, elbows close to his body. He was the only Yellow Knife in the school. The Crees, squatting on their haunches in a huddle, a hundred feet from the building, scowled as he passed, turned their heads away and spit. They could not show their dislike more eloquently. They were plotting something to the hurt of Little Beaver, there was no doubt of that. The Yellow Knife, obliged to spend his recess alone, descended the knoll upon which the schoolhouse stood, and walked out on the wooden footway, high on stilts, which carried the trail across a meadow of muskeg swamp.

He was called Little Beaver to distinguish him from his father, Big Beaver, chief of the proud but fast-disap-

Sandy Makes a Friend

BY ROBERT DAVIS

Illustrated by Henry C. P

272

pearing tribe of the Yellow Knives, and from his older brother, Middle Beaver. The boy was thick through the shoulder and chest, his legs were disproportionately long. Across the high cheek-bones his face was broad, and his skin the color of weak coffee. His head and neck inclined forward, for a double reason. As a tracker, by training and by habit, his eyes forever scanned the ground for footprints; and as a porter, carrying bales of fur, fish, or provisions, his forehead was thrust against the pack strap that held the load upon his shoulders. The Indian's most noticeable features were his eyes, within their narrow slits. They were not black, as seemed the case at first sight, but a velvet brown, flecked with copper dust.

Within the vacant schoolroom Mam'selle Duval folded her plump hands across her plump stomach and sighed. At this season of the year the young Indians and their quarrels were so terribly tiresome. Once the warm-weather fishing was over, and the nets and traps were being stored for winter, before the brackish waters of Hudson Bay should be sheathed within their seven-month roof of ice, the ancient feud between the Crees and the Yellow Knives, as to which tribe the fishing rights between the Abitibi and the Hottoway rightfully belonged, was annually revived. And so deep-rooted was the bitterness that it even filtered down to the children at their lessons.

"Heaven be thanked," the thoughts of the little teacher rambled on, "that my boys aren't equally divided in number. They can't stage pitched battles, as they do at Moosenay and Deep Pool. Just the same, my Crees hiss and growl at Little Beaver, bloodthirsty enough for the whole Five Nations."

As her glance wandered to the window, Mam'selle was

pleased to see the ramrod figure of Corporal Donaldson, speckless in black tunic and blue trousers, swinging across the footbridge. He was on his way to pay his weekly visit of duty and sociability. The little teacher hurriedly examined herself in the mirror that was fixed upon the lower side of her desk cover, blew her nose, and fluffed the yellow hair youthfully about her ears. Bell in hand, she then stepped to the doorway. Recess was over.

While the pupils took their seats, the policeman loitered outside. He was one of the four or five men of the settlement upon whom Mam'selle Duval could always count. The straightness of his backbone marked him as an old-school professional soldier, to the last of his tall inches. Although he lived alone in his log cabin, he shaved every day and groomed each hair of his tooth-brush moustache. He had practiced decency, and loved regularity, all his life. A lonely man, he yet found himself good company.

274

The front benches of the schoolroom were for the primary grades. The older boys sat at the rear upon planks, behind board tables. As the pupils came from several sections of the territory within which the Corporal was responsible for maintaining order, his weekly call at the school was a simple means of checking up on what might be going amiss. He could learn who was sick or in need of help, who had been injured, who had seen a suspicious stranger, or any stranger for that matter. Any unfamiliar face, in that thinly peopled district, was the object of Donaldson's curiosity. By reason of his visits to the school every pupil became his scout. Every settler's cabin and Indian lodge, where there were school-age youngsters, was a listening post in his service.

Cap in hand, the policeman stalked into the room, and saluted the teacher, with a smile of mock severity.

"Good afternoon, Miss Duval. Any infraction of good conduct to report today? No monkeyshines or disorder? You have only to say the word, you know, and I'll make all these young rascals toe the line."

The little woman's teeth glistened as she shook her head. The tall officer would never guess what a rock foundation he was to her self-confidence. Without the respect which his visits inspired she could never have disciplined the half-tamed young citizens of the forests and streams.

"Nothing today, thank you, Corporal. Everyone is behaving just as well as he can."

The policeman now wheeled toward the pupils. "Has a boy or girl of the school seen anything queer or unusual? Has anything struck you as odd, or out of place?

276

Either around your home, or coming to, or going from school?"

Curly Bibb waved his hand. "I seen a lynx 'n her two kitten near Egg Rock."

"*Saw,* Curly, *saw* a lynx," corrected Mam'selle patiently.

A bright-eyed girl, in a jacket of quilted flour sacks, raised her arm. "They was a canoe, with a three-corner patch to the front of it, pulled under the bushes where the tree is blowed across. It don't belong around here."

"Thank you, Deb'rah," said Donaldson courteously. "We'll make a note of that stranger canoe."

A little brother and a sister, who trudged in every morning from Broken Bow, were exchanging meaningful glances. It was the sister who spoke. "By the front of the cave where the bear died, they is the track of moccasins toeing-in. Yesterday they was drops of blood on the leaves, but today they is licked off."

"Ah," exclaimed the Corporal, leaning forward, and writing in his book, "That's the kind of news I want. Thank you kindly, Mattie. Don't forget that you and I are after that trapper at White Button, who went looney and set bear-traps on the trails. Any more news today?"

There being none, the policeman smiled behind his moustache again, saluted the teacher, bowed ceremoniously to the school, and clumped to the door.

Thereafter, a class in English recited, another in writing went to the blackboard, Sandy did a problem in advanced arithmetic. During the last period, a Cree boy asked to be excused, to help his father haul the poles of a fish trap.

The afternoon session was finally at an end. Little Beaver cleared the doorway in a single bound, and came to earth running smoothly upon the trail that led north to the Indian Village, two miles down the river. He was expecting trouble on the way home, and wanted to get a good start. One of the Crees was taller than he, but none of them could match the speed of his legs. On the other side of the muskeg swamp, his path left Three-Mile Trail, the main thoroughfare of Porcupine. At the parting of the paths Little Beaver stopped to breathe and listen, and to see whether he could discover any sign of Cree mischief.

278

On his long journeys afoot he often paused in his tracks, as he was standing now, alert but barely breathing, to get the feel of the woods. One must wait many minutes without stirring, before the timid small voices of nature make themselves audible. He was poised on the edge of the alder marsh. No large trees, save the plantation of white spruce which the path to Indian Village traversed, were anywhere near. The waste of alder had a terrifying allurement for the Yellow Knife boy. At the same time it attracted and repelled. A thousand miles it stretched, to the north and northwest, with never a path nor a home, nor yet a firm spot for the traveller's foot.

279

For the alders sprang from a quicksand of rotting vegetation, only inches above sea level, and wet as a sponge. With Indian and white man alike, it stirred deep terror. Little Beaver stood tense, harkening to the whisper of a trillion branches. Once away from the path, drowned in that ocean of caressing boughs, he would count for nothing.

He liked to get far from the habitations of men, to listen to the emptiness. It made him feel the littleness of men. But to be lost in this maze of elastic wands and varnished leaves would be more hopeless than to be adrift upon the farthest ice of the Arctic. This jungle of red stalks and tapering greenery blinded a man, stole away his sense of direction. In the end the carmine shoots, sprouting from the interminable mossy ooze, would drive him to madness. Trapped within the desolation of the alders, unless rescued through the mercy of the Great Spirit, a man must be marked off as dead.

The Yellow Knives disdained fear. Little Beaver, musing at the edge of the bush, did not like to be afraid. Not of anything, out-of-doors or indoors. The terrifying million acres of alder swamp were forever there, but a mile and a half from where he stood on Three-Mile Trail was the door of his father's lodge. The trail to it was clear, and he could run like a caribou. With a sudden deep breath, he turned north on the path through the evergreens, and began to run.

At the schoolhouse Sandy waited in his seat until the younger children had disentangled their caps, mufflers, mittens and lunch boxes. He had a message for Mam'selle Duval from his mother. Both women were of French-Canadian stock, and both from the same parish of Saint

Hyacinthe. His errand was to invite the teacher to eat Sunday dinner with her friends at the Moose Factory, or trading post, of the Hudson's Bay Company, where Sandy's father, John Mackay, was manager. After chatting with Mam'selle, Sandy strapped his books together, and mounted the footway on stilts which would lead him to Three-Mile Trail, to the river, and to his home at the Factory.

At the junction of the paths the boy halted. From behind the screen of spruce, through which the trail to Indian Village cut, could be heard the crack of breaking sticks, the grunts that accompany blows given or received, and panting cries of pain and of triumph.

Sandy tossed his books aside, and guided by the sounds of battle, broke into a run. He had not gone twenty feet before he dived headlong. Between two saplings, four inches from the ground, was stretched a strip of moosehide. Sitting up where he had fallen, ruefully fingering his head for bruises, the white boy took in the situation at a glance. He knew, of course, of the quarrel between the tribes over the fishing. The moosehide thong which had tripped him was a part of that feud, and the person who had tied it there had intended to injure an enemy. Sandy suddenly remembered the Cree who had been excused early.

But more important than his own fall, was the fight which was being waged a few yards farther along the trail. Little Beaver, backed against a tree, was defending himself as best he could, using a broken branch as a club. His other forearm hung limp, evidently hurt by his fall. The eight Crees, stones in their fists, were darting in and out, attempting to stun or pound him.

"Hi there, you quit that!" yelled Sandy. "Eight against one is dirty fighting. You let him alone."

Meanwhile Sandy had cut the moosehide from the trees, tied a slipknot in one end, inserted a stone in the loop, and pulled the knot tight. Whirling the missile in lightning circles, he stepped forward.

"Whoever gets hit, it's his own fault. Eight to one is no fair. Get out of here."

As he advanced, foot by foot, the stone whizzed around menacingly. And step by step, the Crees sourly retreated. It was partly their surprise at Sandy's unlooked-for entry into the fight. It was partly their unwillingness to have their skulls cracked. But even more was their fear of what their fathers would do to them, for fighting with the son of the Factor of the Hudson's Bay Company.

Without a word, they melted from sight among the greens and browns of the October foliage.

Little Beaver's cuts were not deep, and the blood was already beginning to dry. Gingerly he lifted the sprained wrist and tucked the hand into the waistband of his overalls. The expression of his face did not betray any emotion. Nor had he uttered a word since Sandy's fortunate arrival.

"You'll be right enough now, won't you, Beaver?" inquired the white boy. "Here's the strap that Spotty tripped you with. You may want it as a reminder. I suppose I'd better be getting home. So long."

As Sandy finished, Little Beaver, still without a sound, turned abruptly, and vanished in the direction of Indian Village.

The white boy had almost reached the factory and his father's warehouse, when he heard the rhythmic pat-pat-pat that meant hurrying moccasins. The Yellow Knife had returned. He had been running fast but was not out of breath.

"You nice fella. Bimeby I do someding you lak." Like a shadow of the thickening twilight, he was gone.

Sandy had spent his thirteen years among the trading posts of the north. He believed that he understood the Indian character, inside and out. Nothing like this, however, had as yet crossed his experience. It is rare for the Indian to show gratitude, still more rare for him to promise a favor in return.

"Maybe he's not the same as the others," Sandy reflected, coming in sight of the kitchen windows and seeing his mother busy inside. His thoughts reverted pleasantly to what she might be cooking for supper.

I T was a fine spring morning in Lone Tree County, with the prairie beginning to turn green, and the wild chokecherry and plum thickets smelling sweet. Magpies and meadow larks were talking big about the business of starting new nests.

Whitey was headed for Cedar Spring to see if the windmill was working, but along the way he was looking for his two beef steers, which he ran with Uncle Torwal's cattle. He hadn't noticed them around for several days, and was worried.

Old Spot jogged along at his special ambling trot and thought about the days when he'd been a first-class cow horse. Whitey sat up straight and thought about the fine new saddle he'd buy in the fall when he sold those two steers of his.

He didn't really mind wearing a hand-me-down Stetson of Uncle Torwal's, especially

Whitey and the Rustlers

BY GLEN ROUNDS

Illustrated by

Glen Rounds

when it had such a fine rattlesnake hatband, for most cowboys wore battered old hats. And for the same reason he didn't mind the old boots with the run-over heels and the fancy butterfly stitching on the tops, that he'd been given by a puncher with small feet who'd got a new pair of Fort Worths.

But this old saddle was something else again. It was an old Cogshell with a flat Texas horn. It was so old the corners of the skirts were curled up tight, and the strings had long ago been chewed off by calves. Everywhere the

284

stitching was coming undone, leaving great corners of old leather sticking up to give the whole affair the look of a moulting hen. Furthermore, the stirrups were the clumsy iron kind, when the style hereabouts was a neat wooden oxbow pattern. For a long time Whitey had felt that it made him look more like a homesteader than a cowboy.

Of course, when he'd been smaller and first come to live with Uncle Torwal and help him run the Lone Tree Ranch, it hadn't mattered so much. But now that he was practically a top hand he had to think more about the looks of his equipment. People set a lot of store by such things.

So last summer Uncle Torwal had given him two Whiteface calves. Together they'd figured out a brand for him and sent it off to be registered, after they'd put it on the calves with a running iron. It was a fine big squiggle on the ribs with three dots at the end.

The Rattlesnake brand, they called it. Whitey figured it was about as fine a brand as he knew of. He saw no reason it shouldn't some day be as famous as the old "101." And Rattlesnake Ranch sounded good no matter how you said it!

So he rode on for a while, thinking about the time when the Rattlesnake brand would be on thousands of head of good beef cattle instead of only two, and he'd be able to have a new saddle every week if he felt like it.

But just when he had started thinking about how fine a Sunday saddle would look, decorated with silver in the Mexican fashion, he came on a calf bogged in the mud

around an old water hole, so he had to stop thinking about saddles for a while.

The old cow nearby was in a nasty humor, bawling and swinging her tail, so he didn't feel it was safe to get down off Spot. That meant he'd have to rope the calf and drag it out.

As calves will do, that one had gotten out into the middle of the softest patch of gumbo, so that if Whitey missed his first cast, as he usually did, he was bound to get his rope all muddy. That never did a throw rope any good, and was especially bad for a brand-new one like Whitey was carrying. He finally urged old Spot out onto the mud until he could reach down and drop the loop square on the calf.

After that he took a hitch around the saddle horn and in no time at all dragged the calf out onto solid ground. After he'd shaken the loop loose and the cow

286

and calf had gone he found his rope was muddy after all, so he had to get off and find some dry grass to clean it with.

It was then he noticed the fuss a bunch of magpies were making in a little gully not far off, so he decided to go see what it was they were doing.

The rain the day before had washed deeply into a pile of dirt that had caved off the cutbank, exposing some corners of what looked to be green cowhides, fresh enough to attract the magpies.

After some tugging and digging, Whitey uncovered three hides which had been carelessly buried by caving part of the bank onto them. Two hides carried his Rattlesnake brand and the other Uncle Torwal's Lone Tree!

He sat down on the bank, and if he hadn't been almost a man grown he'd have bawled like a kid, for there went his hopes of a new saddle. The two Rattlesnake steers he'd counted on so much were now in some rustler's truck on the road to a butcher shop far off.

He knew how the rustlers operated, going out at night with a truck and butchering two or three steers quickly, destroying the hides to prevent identification, and leaving to sell the meat before anyone knew they were about.

There'd been talk for some time that they must be operating around here, for ranchers all up and down the valley had been missing beef.

When Whitey rode into the ranch and up to the horse trough Torwal saw he looked mighty glum.

"Truck rustlers been getting our cattle," Whitey said, as Spot was drinking.

"There's been talk of such," Torwal said. "But nobody knows for sure."

"I found three fresh hides over by Cedar Spring this morning," Whitey said. "They was buried in a washout."

He brushed dust off his hat and waited for Uncle Torwal to ask him some more. He was trying to talk as any cowboy would instead of being excited like a kid.

Torwal saw there must be more to the story, so he said, casual like, "Was the brands cut out?" For usually the rustlers cut the brand out of the hide and burned it.

"Reckon they must have been careless this time," Whitey said. "One was a Lone Tree steer and the other two were Rattlesnake brand."

Torwal whistled. "That was tough goin', cleanin' out your whole spread."

"Yeah, that's a fact," Whitey said. "Looks like I'll ride this old hull a while longer." He led Spot away so Uncle Torwal wouldn't see how badly he felt.

They didn't say much as they cooked and ate dinner, but afterwards, as they sat on the porch, Torwal spoke up. "Reckon we might as well ride in and see the sheriff. Now that we know for sure that rustlers are workin' around here, maybe we can figure out something."

"I sure hope so," Whitey said. "They did me out of a new saddle and I wish I was old enough to swear!"

288

When they got to town they tied their horses and walked into the sheriff's office. Mr. Hairpants Hagadorn, the sheriff, shook hands with them while Mr. Fort Worth Wilkerson, the deputy sheriff, dragged out chairs.

After some polite talk of this and that, Torwal told the sheriff what Whitey had found.

"Was them hides fresh, son?" the sheriff asked Whitey.

"Yessir, they looked to be only a day or two there."

"This is the first time we've had any proof," the sheriff said, "but there's been a lot of complaints of missin' beef critturs all up and down the valley."

"How you reckon they get in and out of the valley without anyone knowing?" Torwal wondered after a little.

"I been considerin' that myself," the sheriff told him. "They have to come through here or through Hill City to get in or out, and we've been watchin' both places close, yet nobody has seen any strangers or strange trucks."

"I wish we could catch them," Whitey spoke up. "I was going to get a new saddle with the money from the steers they got of mine!"

"Maybe you can figure how to catch them and use your share of the reward money for that saddle," the sheriff said.

At the mention of *reward*, Whitey brightened right

289

up. "You mean there's a reward for those rustlers?" he asked.

"Sure," the sheriff told him.

After some more talk they shook hands with the sheriff, the deputy sheriff, and a man who had just wandered into the office looking for a place to sit down, and rode off towards the ranch.

As they rode along Whitey thought about that reward. It seemed to him that getting a new saddle by trapping rustlers was even better than by selling cattle.

"Uncle Torwal!" he said, suddenly. "A time or two lately I've noticed car tracks up in that little limestone canyon the other side of Cedar Spring. I figured it was somebody building fence, but it might be where those rustlers are getting into the canyon, do you suppose?"

Torwal thought a while. "It could be, maybe," he said. "There used to be an old road through there that went down into the Boxelder road. We might as well drop by and take a look at things."

They found that the old trail, which had for years been overgrown and washed out in places, did now show signs of use. The worst holes had been filled, and it was plain that a truck could travel over it.

"Looks like this might be it, all right," Torwal allowed. "This trail comes out on the Boxelder road where nobody would think of watching for them."

"Why don't we lay for them when they come back?" Whitey asked, thinking of the reward and his new saddle.

"Well," said Torwal, "they might not come back. Those dudes are pretty smart and don't often work the same place twice." After seeing how Whitey's face fell, he went on: "On the other hand, with a trick road like

290

this they might feel safe for a while longer. From all the talk of missing cattle in the valley, they must have made several trips already."

"Tell you what," Torwal said after they'd started home. "We might take turns watchin' that canyon evenings for a while, just in case they did come back."

"Yessir!" Whitey agreed. "We'll catch 'em coming in and collect the reward!"

"We don't want to bother them comin' in," Torwal corrected him. "We jest want to know when they come in so we'll have time to call the sheriff and catch them goin' out with the meat."

Whitey still favored capturing the rustlers without the sheriff, but he said nothing about it. He was bound he'd get that saddle the rustlers had done him out of, and even part of the reward would be enough.

"I'll take my blankets and go out right away to watch for them," he said.

"You won't need any blankets," Torwal told him. "Those fellers usually figure to come in just about sundown so they'll be able to locate the critturs they want before dusk is gone. So if they aren't in sight by full dark they'll probably not come."

After Whitey had eaten an early supper and was leaving to watch the canyon, Uncle Torwal spoke up. "If they don't show up tonight, we'll take turns with the neighbors for a few nights."

"I don't want anyone to take turns," Whitey hollered. "I'm the one they cleaned out, and I'll watch every night!"

So every night for almost a week Whitey rode out to a small butte where he could watch the canyon. Every

291

night he carefully hid Spot in a plum thicket and then crawled Indian fashion to the top of the butte, where he lay hidden in the sage brush like some oldtime scout. But nothing happened, and he was beginning to believe the rustlers had deserted the valley.

On the seventh night, he'd just started down to go home when he thought he heard a truck motor. He hurried back up the hill and the sound was plain there. It was a powerful motor, and working hard. Soon he could see the dimmed lights as they moved to the mouth of the canyon, where they were switched off and the motor stopped.

It was the rustlers, sure enough!

Whitey had been com-
plaining to himself because
Uncle Torwal wouldn't let
him bring his rifle and capture the rustlers single-
handed, but tonight he
thought of nothing but getting back to the ranch as
soon as possible to tell Uncle Torwal and get word to

the sheriff. It seemed to him now that it was the sheriff's
business to deal with such people.

Spot got the surprise of his life when Whitey clapped
spurs and quirt onto him! He couldn't remember the last
time he'd traveled faster than a trot. But as this seemed
to be in the nature of a special occasion he did his best,
and before long Whitey and Torwal were sitting out by
the road waiting for the sheriff and his deputies to come
by and pick them up.

The word had spread, and by the time the sheriff
got there, ranchers and cowboys from up and down the
valley had gathered. Most of them carried rifles on their
saddles, or pistols in their belts. Whitey was looking forward to a right exciting time when they caught up with
the rustlers.

When the sheriff came they all went along to the
little canyon. Whitey had been afraid someone would
tell him to stay behind, but no one did.

The men had all been hidden in the plum thickets
for what seemed a mighty long time to Whitey, when
they heard the truck coming back.

"This is when the bullets start to fly!" Whitey thought,

as the sheriff stepped out into the light of the truck and held up his hand. But the truck stopped without protest.

Deputies and ranch men flashed on flashlights and swarmed all round it. Four weaselly-looking men climbed carefully out and stood with their hands raised while they and the truck were searched.

"There's plenty beef in here!" a deputy hollered.

"All right!" the sheriff answered. "One of you drive the truck along behind me, and we'll haul these gents down to our jail for a spell."

The rustlers didn't say anything, except to sort of mutter to themselves. They didn't look like the tough guys Whitey had been picturing in his mind. They weren't wearing gun belts, and they didn't talk tough to the sheriff. Worst of all, they wore bib overalls, like farmers, and one even had on plow shoes! Whitey was mighty disappointed in them.

Early next morning Whitey and Uncle Torwal went to town, and Mr. Bugeye Beasly, editor of the *Lone Tree Eagle,* interviewed Whitey.

The reward turned out to be only fifty dollars, and that divided six ways, so there was not enough to buy the saddle with. Whitey had built his hopes so high on that reward that he felt mighty bad for a few days. But after reading what Mr. Beasly wrote about him in the paper, how his alertness had helped make Lone Tree County free of rustlers and the like, he sort of got used to the idea of getting along with the old saddle another year.

294

Then one morning Torwal told him, "We gotta go to town this morning, Bub. Sheriff said something about wantin' to see you."

All the way into town Whitey wondered what the sheriff could want. Maybe he wanted to make him a deputy or something. He imagined this and that, but never thought of the real answer. For after some talk the sheriff pointed to a grain sack on the floor and told Whitey, "Feller left that here an' told me to give it to you."

Whitey opened it up and inside was a brand-new saddle. The decorations were hand-tooled, the whangleather tie strings shining bright yellow, the sheepskin lining bright and clean, and the whole thing smelling of neat's foot oil and new leather. It was the most beautiful saddle Whitey had ever seen.

On the back of the cantle was a small silver plate he'd missed at first. It was engraved:

To Whitey for Service in Ridding Lone Tree County of Rustlers from The Lone Tree Stockmen's Ass'n.

Whitey couldn't think of anything to say, so he just grinned and carried the saddle out to try how it looked on Spot.

Magic Lariat

BY GLENN WARD
DRESBACH

We went to a circus
in the town
And saw a cowboy
lasso a clown.
Then, reaching home
through the late sunshine,
We made a lariat
out of a vine
And tried to whirl it
about and cling
To posts, each other,
or anything
That pleased our fancy. . . .
That must be
The reason we
had chanced to see,
At the garden's edge,
a silvery thread,
Like a magic lariat
over the head
Of a marigold
just opened that day,
From a little bare bush
across the way—
A cobweb noose
flung out to hold
A moment that
had turned to gold!

SPRING brought a revival of entertainment. The first troupe to reach Rabbit Creek was the Robinson family, with sweet, golden-haired Sue, "The Fairy Star," as their major attraction. Her father and manager, Joseph Robinson, refused to pay the moderate rental price asked by Taylor for his new theater. Instead, he announced his intention of playing in a nearby dance hall, and letting Taylor keep his log shack till it rotted, or burned down.

Mart Taylor's fighting spirit was aroused. He resolved to put on a show of his own that night to give skinflint Robinson some competition. Tall, friendly, ever-joking Mart was popular in the community, where local talent always drew well. When the public understood the reason for the rivalry, he could be sure of good support. In mid-morning he hurried over to the Crabtree cabin.

Log Cabin Theater

BY PHYLLIS W. JACKSON

Illustrated by Seymour Fleishman

"Can you get up a show on such short notice?" Mary Ann asked doubtfully.

"I think so, by using solo numbers that need little rehearsing. I'll furnish a few turns myself. But what I need most to defeat the Robinsons is a child star. I want Lotta to dance, and sing a song or two. Are you willing?"

Compete against the famous Sue Robinson! This was the little girl from whom Mary Ann had got the idea of

297

teaching Lotta to do a similar performance that dreadful time at the schoolhouse. She told Mart the story.

He laughed. "In a crowded schoolroom, where kids are scared half the time, no wonder! This will be different, a real playhouse, such as it is, but it's a place for fun." He tossed back his black hair and sat on the steps. "I'll risk it with Lotta. I know she's good, and bless her heart, I've got her to know it."

"Thanks, Mart."

"Don't thank me. I'm going to do the thanking. You'll see. Now here's what I have in mind," he said, with a manner of getting down to practical matters that excited Mary Ann. "We've an Irish-ballad singer, and I'd like Lotta to follow him with a jig. If only we had an Irish costume for her. Suppose you could rig up something quick? Say, a tail coat and knee breeches? I have some cardboard for a top hat and can cobble a pair of brogans."

"But I have no material, Mart. And would it be proper to put her in breeches? John wouldn't approve."

"Why not? She's only a little girl. How old? Seven and a half, and so tiny, she looks less than six. But suit yourself. Make something green if you can. I'll get her a little shillelagh. Then let her wear a dress for her song number."

Mart dashed away on his roundup of local talent, leaving Mary Ann in a quandary. She rummaged through her trunk for something to cut over—something green. What could she spare from her scanty wardrobe? Not the good shawl? But it was the only green she had! "Tut!" she said to her qualm. The shawl would have to go into the coat. A dark petticoat could supply enough goods for the breeches. She seized her scissors, and began cut-

298

ting with the swift sure skill she had learned in her mother's shop.

When word spread about camp that Taylor was planning a counter attraction, Robinson was not greatly disturbed. He felt sure Taylor could provide no serious competition against his little Sue. But William, his son, overheard that a child was to appear in Taylor's show.

"She might be pretty good, Father. She was a pupil of Lola Montez in Grass Valley. At least the yokels seem to like her. You'd better try to buy her off."

"That takes money," replied the thrifty manager. But he decided to look into the matter.

When he knocked at the Crabtree door, he was met by Mary Ann, nervously brushing threads from her skirt. He explained politely that he heard she and her daughter were interested in the stage, and had brought them tickets for his performance.

"That's kind of you, I'm sure," said Mary Ann. "But Lotta is—we're otherwise engaged tonight."

Robinson, expecting this, tried another approach. "We heard of your Lotta, in Grass Valley, and my little Susan wants to meet her. Could she come over to the hall with me, so the children could get acquainted?"

"Well," Mary Ann hesitated, "I have no objection, if she doesn't stay too long. I've seen your Sue perform, and I think she's talented and lovely. I'll go call Lotta."

Lotta was shy with Mr. Robinson as they walked along, but not with Sue. The two children made friends at once, although Sue was nearly ten, and a head taller than Lotta. They talked about Grass Valley.

"That's where I was burned, last fall," said Sue. "My skirt caught fire from a candle in the footlights. Oh, it hurt awfully, and I couldn't dance for a month after. Want to see my scars?"

She rolled down her stockings, and proudly displayed her disfigured knees.

Lotta was much impressed. "I wish I'd been there to see you. I wish we still lived in Grass Valley. It was fun to be with Lola. Do you know Lola?"

"No, not really. But in one of our plays I do an imitation of her. It's supposed to be funny, but it isn't, very. What dances do you know?"

Father Robinson came forward with a suggestion. "Lotta, will you show us how Lola dances? Sue would like that, wouldn't you, Sue?"

"Oh, yes! Please do, Lotta. I'll play the hand organ for you."

Suddenly the whole Robinson troupe was there, crowding around the children. Lotta hesitated, wishing they'd give her more room.

"The stage isn't set up yet," said Robinson. "Here, I'll lift you up on this billiard table." He was secretly hoping she might fall off, or sprain an ankle.

Sue, at the organ, ground out a lively tune. Lotta, after listening to catch the beat, did a cracovienne in true Montez style. The Robinsons applauded politely.

"What else do you know?" Sue asked. "Here's hornpipe music."

Lotta danced the hornpipe and the Highland fling as expertly as ever Sue could, and then a fandango and a jig. She liked hand organ music. But the Robinsons soon withdrew for private consultation.

"Maybe Sue can wear her out, if nothing else," Will muttered.

300

They agreed the child was good—too good. Not only had she mastered a number of intricate steps, but she did them with a vivacity that was peculiarly her own. She was so small that Sue looked almost gawky beside her. Audiences liked stage children to be very little. She would be serious competition. The question was, how to get rid of her? Short of actual violence, the surest way would be to buy her mother off.

"The family seems pretty hard up," Robinson mused, "but what if she's too loyal to Taylor?"

"You might offer her a job with us for a short time. No contract, of course," suggested Mrs. Robinson. "She could teach Sue some of her dances—"

"And outshine our Sue?"

"No danger of that," Sue's mother said confidently. "They are such different types. The little redhead might prove to be a drawing card."

"I'll see what I can do," said Robinson. "The main thing is to keep her off the boards tonight."

Mary Ann was deep in her sewing when Robinson came again. Annoyed at this interruption, she forced a smile while standing in the half-open door. Robinson went straight to the point.

"Mrs. Crabtree, we've seen your daughter perform, and we think she has a fine future in the theater—with proper guidance, of course. So I've come to offer her a place in our company, starting tonight."

The astonished Mary Ann was slow to grasp his full meaning. "Tonight?" she echoed. "But she's dancing—"

"For Taylor. I know. But what will this one performance amount to? I can pay her a fair salary for the season, and start her on the road to fame and fortune. Taylor is

only a mediocre song-and-dance man. I can give her real professional training and experience, good connections in San Francisco—"

"But I'm not planning a stage career for Lotta. She's dancing for Mart because he's her teacher."

"You're making a great mistake, Mrs. Crabtree. The child's a dancer. With more training she could go far. Let me take charge of her—"

"Couldn't I think it over and let you know?"

"No, Madam. I take her tonight, or not at all!"

Mary Ann seldom made hasty decisions, but she did not like Robinson's manner. The thought of giving Lotta into his care, letting her go away with a show troupe, was but slightly less absurd than Lola's notion.

"Then I must refuse!" she snapped. "You'll please excuse me, sir. I'm very busy."

By nightfall she had the costume completed, and was pleased with the effect. It was not fine sewing, but it would serve for one performance. The top hat had been covered with scraps of green, pieced together.

Lotta was thrilled with it, her very first costume. She tried it on, and strutted about, tipping the hat, and switching the ludicrous coattails, as she had seen gentlemen do. Mart came, clapping the soles of the brogans he had just finished for her. They were heavy and stiff but made a cheerful clatter.

Anxious that the child should appear once at her ladylike best, Mary Ann had readied the white cambric muslin dress, with puffed sleeves and blue bowknots. It was almost too small now, but it was the best she had.

After a hasty supper, for they were too excited to eat, Lotta and Mary Ann gathered up the costumes and the baby, who had been no trouble this entire busy day, and set out for the theater. There was no one to leave him with, for everyone in camp was going to the show. The streets and saloons were full of men laughing, shouting and laying bets. It was a big night.

If there was one thing all miners loved, it was a contest, whether a gory bull-and-bear fight, or a jumping race between frogs. In this case local pride was involved. Everyone knew and liked Mart Taylor; many were friends of John Crabtree and admirers of his child. Little doubt that Taylor's show would draw the larger crowd.

By curtain time the little log theater was jammed to the doors. Candles shone dimly through a haze of tobacco smoke. The waiting audience stamped and clapped with good-humored impatience. Backstage, Mart was everywhere at once, lining up the acts. In the dressing room where Mary Ann was trying to put baby Jack to sleep in a basket, Mart paused long enough to hand Lotta a small club whittled from an oak limb, and to say, "Here, Lotta, is your shillelagh."

"It's just to carry when you walk on, to make you look real Irish. Throw it down when you start to dance."

Mary Ann was even more nervous than Lotta, but she forced herself to behave as if this were only a dancing lesson.

The Irish tenor warbled "Kathleen Mavourneen," and Mary Ann and Mart stood with Lotta in the wings, waiting.

"Your turn now, Lotta," he whispered cheerfully. "Make your bow, then toss me the shillelagh. See if I can catch it."

The fiddler sawed into the opening bars of "The Irish Washerwoman." Lotta did not move.

"Run!" Mary Ann commanded, and gave the child such a push that she was forced to run or lose her balance. Thus, with a headlong plunge, a stumble and an unintentionally comic bow, Lotta Crabtree made her first appearance on any stage.

But she stood there in a daze, blinking at the footlight candles while the fiddle played on.

"Catch!" Mart called from the wings, holding up his hands.

Lotta's trance was broken. She turned and hurled the stick toward him, so high he had to jump for it. His wild grab tickled her, and she burst into her merry, rippling laugh, to the vast delight of the audience. Then, still smiling, she began to dance. The music wove a spell around her, so that she saw nothing, felt nothing, but the joy of rhythm and motion.

It was amazing that a chubby child could be so light on her feet.

And those flying feet, clad in the grand new brogans, made such a lovely clatter upon the rough boards that she danced as she had never danced before.

A wave of excitement surged through the densely packed hall. To the spectators the dance seemed all too short. "More! More!" they shouted, above the thunder of applause. Those who knew Lotta called her name, and others took up the cry.

"Do it again!" cried Mart, and Lotta willingly repeated. Still the crowd would not let her go.

"What'll we do?" cried Mary Ann, in a panic. "Oh, I wish we had another costume."

"Take her hat off, and let her do a hornpipe," Mart quickly decided.

Before she had finished it, coins began to rain upon the stage about her—silver dollars and half-dollars, two-bit pieces, huge Mexican pesos. Then gold slugs and nuggets! Some coins struck her ankles, hurting and frightening her. She faltered, paused and might have fled from the stage had not Mart and Mary Ann nodded and smiled encouragement. Lotta smiled back, and finished her number in good style. Mart then brought down the curtain.

He stepped out and quieted the noisy audience with the promise that Lotta would soon reappear. While he sang one of his original song-parodies, Mary Ann changed Lotta into her dress and brushed her tousled curls. The miners' gold and silver she gathered up in the top hat. No time for counting it, but to her it looked like a fortune. There was one slug worth fifty dollars.

Lotta returned, sweet and demure in white, to sing the plaintive ballad, "Lilly Dale," with the posturing and ballet movements Lola had taught her. Here was a different Lotta, and the men fell in love with her all over again. More coins came glinting and tinkling through the bright lamplight.

Mary Ann walked home that night with her head in a whirl. She now had more money than she had seen since coming West. And how easily it had been earned!

"That was fun, wasn't it, Mama?" Lotta said, as she skipped along. "Let's do it again sometime."

308

ONE morning in September the grass was white with frost. It was only a light frost that melted as soon as sunshine touched it. It was gone when Laura looked out at the bright morning. But at breakfast Pa said that such an early frost was surprising.

"Will it hurt the hay?" Laura asked him, and he said, "Oh, no. Such a light frost will only make it dry faster when it's cut. But I'd better get a hustle on, for it won't be long now till it's too late to make hay."

He was hustling so fast that afternoon that he hardly stopped to drink when Laura brought him the water-jug. He was mowing in Big Slough.

An Errand to Town

BY
LAURA INGALLS WILDER

Illustrated by Garth Williams

"You cover it up, Half-Pint," he said, handing back the jug. "I'm bound and determined to get this patch mowed before sundown." He chirruped to Sam and David and they started again, drawing the whirring machine. Then suddenly the machine gave a clattering kind of yelp and Pa said, "Whoa!"

Laura hurried to see what had happened. Pa was looking at the cutter-bar. There was a gap in the row of bright steel points. The cutter-bar had lost one of its teeth. Pa picked up the pieces, but they could not be mended.

"There's no help for it," Pa said. "It means buying another section."

309

There was nothing to say to that. Pa thought a minute and said, "Laura, I wish you'd go to town and get it. I don't want to lose the time. I can keep on mowing, after a fashion, while you're gone. Be as quick as you can. Ma will give you the five cents to pay for it. Buy it at Fuller's Hardware."

"Yes, Pa," Laura said. She dreaded going to town because so many people were there. She was not exactly afraid, but strange eyes looking at her made her uncomfortable.

She had a clean calico dress to wear and she had shoes. While she hurried to the house, she thought that Ma might let her wear her Sunday hair-ribbon and perhaps Mary's freshly ironed sunbonnet.

"I have to go to town, Ma," she said, rushing in breathless.

Carrie and Mary listened while she explained and even Grace looked up at her with big, sober blue eyes.

"I will go with you to keep you company," Carrie volunteered.

"Oh, can she, Ma?" Laura asked.

"If she can be ready as soon as you are," Ma gave permission.

Quickly they changed to fresh dresses and put on their stockings and shoes. But Ma saw no reason for hair-ribbons on a week day and she said Laura must wear her own sunbonnet.

"It would be fresher," Ma said, "if you took care to keep it so." Laura's bonnet was limp from hanging down her back and the strings were limp, too. But that was Laura's own fault.

Ma gave her five cents from Pa's pocketbook and with Carrie she hurried away toward town.

They followed the road made by Pa's wagon-wheels, past the well, down the dry, grassy slope into Big Slough, and on between the tall slough-grasses to the slope up on the other side. The whole shimmering prairie seemed strange then. Even the wind blowing the grasses had a wilder sound. Laura liked that and she wished they did not have to go into town where the false fronts of the buildings stood up square-topped to pretend that the stores behind them were bigger than they were.

Neither Laura nor Carrie said a word after they came to Main Street. Some men were on the store porches and two teams with wagons were tied to the hitching posts. Lonely, on the other side of Main Street, stood Pa's store building. It was rented and two men sat inside it talking.

Laura and Carrie went into the hardware store. Two men were sitting on nail kegs and one on a plow. They stopped talking and looked at Laura and Carrie. The wall behind the counter glittered with tin pans and pails and lamps.

Laura said, "Pa wants a mowing-machine section, please."

The man on the plow said, "He's broke one, has he?" and Laura said, "Yes, sir."

She watched him wrap in paper the sharp and shining three-cornered tooth. He must be Mr. Fuller. She gave him the five cents and, taking the package in her hand, she said, "Thank you," and walked out with Carrie.

That was over. But they did not speak until they had walked out of town. Then Carrie said, "You did that beautifully, Laura."

312

"Oh, it was just buying something," Laura replied.

"I feel . . . not scared, exactly . . ." Carrie said.

"There's nothing to be scared of," Laura said. "We mustn't ever be scared." Suddenly she told Carrie, "I feel the same way."

"Do you, really? I didn't know that. You don't act like it. I always feel so safe when you're there," Carrie said.

"You are safe when I'm there," Laura answered. "I'd take care of you. Anyway, I'd try my best."

"I know you would," Carrie said.

It was nice, walking together. To take care of their shoes, they did not walk in the dusty wheel tracks. They walked on the harder strip in the middle where only horses' hooves had discouraged the grass. They were not walking hand in hand, but they felt as if they were.

Ever since Laura could remember, Carrie had been her little sister. First she had been a tiny baby, then she had been Baby Carrie, then she had been a clutcher and tagger, always asking "Why?" Now she was ten years old, old enough to be really a sister. And they were out together, away from even Pa and Ma. Their errand was done and off their minds, and the sun was shining, the wind was blowing, the prairie spread far all around them. They felt free and independent and comfortable together.

"It's a long way around to where Pa is," Carrie said. "Why don't we go this way?" and she pointed toward the part of the slough where they could see Pa and the horses.

Laura answered, "That way's through the slough."

"It isn't wet now, is it?" Carrie asked.

"All right, let's," Laura answered. "Pa didn't say to go by the road, and he did say to hurry."

So they did not follow the road that turned to cross

313

the slough. They went straight on into the tall slough grass.

At first it was fun. It was rather like going into the jungle-picture in Pa's big green book. Laura pushed ahead between the thick clumps of grass-stems that gave way rustling and closed again behind Carrie. The millions of coarse grass stems and their slender long leaves were greeny-gold and golden green in their own shade. The earth was crackled with dryness underfoot, but a faint smell of damp lay under the hot smell of the grass. Just above Laura's head the grass-tops swished in the wind, but down at their roots was a stillness, broken only where Laura and Carrie went wading through it.

"Where's Pa?" Carrie asked suddenly.

Laura looked around at her. Carrie's peaked little face was pale in the shade of the grass. Her eyes were almost frightened.

"Well, we can't see him from here," Laura said. They could see only the leaves of the thick grass waving, and the hot sky overhead. "He's right ahead of us. We'll come to him in a minute."

She said it confidently but how could she know where Pa was? She could not even be sure where she was going, where she was taking Carrie. The smothering heat made sweat trickle down her throat and her backbone, but she felt cold inside. She remembered the children near Brookings, lost in the prairie grass. The slough was worse than the prairie. Ma had always been afraid that Grace would be lost in this slough.

She listened for the whirr of the mowing machine, but the sound of the grasses filled her ears. There was nothing in the flickering shadows of their thin leaves blowing and tossing higher than her eyes, to tell her where the sun was. The grasses' bending and swaying did not even tell the direction of the wind. Those clumps of grass would hold up no weight at all. There was nothing, nothing anywhere that she could climb to look out above them, to see beyond them and know where she was.

"Come along, Carrie," she said cheerfully. She must not frighten Carrie.

Carrie followed trustfully but Laura did not know where she was going. She could not even be sure that she was walking straight. Always a clump of grass was in her way; she must go to right or left. Even if she went to the right of one clump of grass and to the left of the next clump, that did not mean that she was not going in a circle. Lost people go in circles and many of them never find their way home.

The slough went on for a mile or more of bending swaying grasses, too tall to see beyond, too yielding to climb. It was wide. Unless Laura walked straight ahead they might never get out of it.

"We've gone so far, Laura," Carrie panted. "Why don't we come to Pa?"

"He ought to be right around here somewhere," Laura answered. She could not follow their own trail back to the safe road. Their shoes left almost no tracks on the heat-baked mud, and the grasses, the endless swaying grasses with their low leaves hanging dried and broken, were all alike.

Carrie's mouth opened a little. Her big eyes looked up at Laura and they said, "I know. We're lost." Her mouth shut without a word. If they were lost, they were lost. There was nothing to say about it.

"We'd better go on," Laura said.

"I guess so. As long as we can," Carrie agreed.

They went on. They must surely have passed the place where Pa was mowing. But Laura could not be sure of anything. They thought if they turned back, they would really be going farther away. They could only go on. Now and then they stopped and wiped their sweating faces. They were terribly thirsty but there was no water. They were very tired from pushing through the grasses. Not one single push seemed hard, but going on was harder than trampling hay. Carrie's thin little face was gray-white, she was so tired.

Then Laura thought that the grasses ahead were thinner. The shade seemed lighter there and the tops of the grasses against the sky seemed fewer. And suddenly she saw sunshine, yellow beyond the dark grass stems. Perhaps there was a pond there. Oh! Perhaps, perhaps there was Pa's stubble field and the mowing machine and Pa.

She saw the hay stubble in the sunshine, and she saw haycocks dotting it. But she heard a strange voice.

It was a man's voice, loud and hearty. It said, "Get a move on, Manzo. Let's get this load in. It's coming night after awhile."

Another voice drawled lazily, "Aw-aw, Roy!"

Close together, Laura and Carrie looked out from the edge of the standing grass. The hayfield was not Pa's hayfield. A strange wagon stood there and on its rack was an enormous load of hay. On the high top of that

316

load, up against the blinding sky, a boy was lying. He lay on his stomach, his chin on his hands and his feet in the air.

The strange man lifted up a huge forkful of hay and pitched it onto the boy. It buried him and he scrambled up out of it, laughing and shaking hay off his head and his shoulders. He had black hair and blue eyes and his face and his arms were sunburned brown.

He stood up on the high load of hay against the sky and saw Laura. He said, "Hello there!" They both stood watching Laura and Carrie come out of the tall standing grass—like rabbits, Laura thought. She wanted to turn and run back into hiding.

"I thought Pa was here," she said, while Carrie stood small and still behind her.

The man said, "We haven't seen anybody around here. Who is your Pa?" The boy told him, "Mr. Ingalls. Isn't he?" he asked Laura. He was still looking at her.

"Yes," she said, and she looked at the horses hitched to the wagon. She had seen those beautiful brown horses before, their haunches gleaming in the sun and the black manes glossy on their glossy necks. They were the Wilder boys' horses. The man and the boy must be the Wilder brothers.

"I can see him from here. He's just over there," the boy said. Laura looked up and saw him pointing. His blue eyes twinkled down at her as if he had known her a long time.

"Thank you," Laura said primly and she and Carrie walked away, along the road that the Morgan team and the wagon had broken through the slough grass.

318

"Whoa!" Pa said when he saw them. "Whew!" he said, taking off his hat and wiping the sweat from his forehead.

Laura gave him the mowing-machine section, and she and Carrie watched while he opened the tool-box, took the cutter-bar from the machine, and knocked out the broken section. He set the new one in its place and hammered down the rivets to hold it. "There!" he said. "Tell your Ma I'll be late for supper. I'm going to finish cutting this piece."

The mowing machine was humming steadily when Laura and Carrie went on toward the shanty.

"Were you much scared, Laura?" Carrie asked.

"Well, some, but all's well that ends well," Laura said.

"It was my fault. I wanted to go that way," said Carrie.

"It was my fault because I'm older," Laura said. "But we've learned a lesson. I guess we'll stay on the road after this."

"Are you going to tell Ma and Pa?" Carrie timidly asked.

"We have to if they ask us," said Laura.

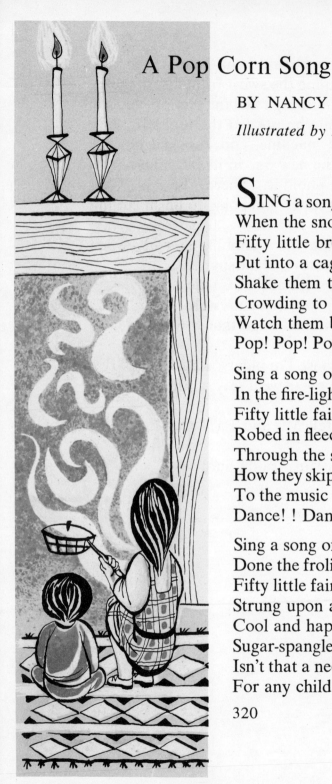

A Pop Corn Song

BY NANCY BYRD TURNER

Illustrated by Nola Langner

SING a song of pop corn
When the snow-storms rage;
Fifty little brown men
Put into a cage.
Shake them till they laugh and leap
Crowding to the top;
Watch them burst their little coats
Pop! Pop! Pop! !

Sing a song of pop corn
In the fire-light;
Fifty little fairies
Robed in fleecy white.
Through the shining wires see
How they skip and prance
To the music of the flames;
Dance! ! Dance! ! Dance! !

Sing a song of pop corn
Done the frolicking;
Fifty little fairies
Strung upon a string.
Cool and happy, hand in hand,
Sugar-spangled, fair;
Isn't that a necklace fit
For any child to wear?

320

P. S.

IN preparing this volume, the editors have selected stories and excerpts from complete books, and in those cases where the text of a book is reprinted in its entirety, only a few of the many delightful illustrations from the original have been used. For the benefit of those who would like to read and enjoy the complete books, the following list is given.

Subject Index

324

325

Illustrators

Index

332

A Bell for Ursli

Foreign Lands

Magic Maps

Roads

The Fairies

Hayride

Adventure

Silver Ships

Elephant-Town

My Airplane

Breakfast with Buffalo Bill

The Swimming Steers

My Father's Dragon

A Boy's Song

Daniel Boone

Pirate Story

A Song of Sherwood

Off to Adventure

The Hippopotamus

Boy with a Harpoon

Jippy and Jimmy

The New Baby Calf

The Wave

Little Lost Lamb

The Camel Who Took a Walk